OSU

A COMING-OF-AGE NOVEL

AN EMPOWERING BOOK OF
SELF-ACCEPTANCE & RESILIENCE

Sensei Sarhn

sarhn.com

 Empowering Books Publishing

© Copyright 2024 by Sensei Sarhn

All rights reserved. No part of this publication may be reproduced or used in any manner without written permission of the copyright owner except for the use of quotations in a book review and other non-commercial uses permitted by copyright law. Permission requests can be made at Sarhn.com

While all attempts have been made to verify the information provided in this publication, the author assumes no responsibility for errors, omissions, or contrary interpretations of the subject matter herein.

This is a work of fiction. Names, characters, places, and incidents are either products of the author's imagination or are used fictitiously. Any resemblance to actual persons, living or dead, is entirely coincidental.

This book deals with some sensitive issues that some readers may struggle with and shares physical martial arts concepts and techniques. This book is not meant to replace real therapy from certified mental and physical health practitioners or in-person martial arts training with an expert instructor.

Edited by Haylee Kerans
Cover Design by Katarina Naskovski

Published by Empowering Books in 2024 (1st edition)
EmpoweringBooks.org

ISBN: 978-1-7636312-1-2 (softcover, paperback)

For Brett, Willow & Carol

Those who achieve great feats, are not carved from a different stone,

nor are they superhuman.

They just know and do things differently.

All of which can be taught and learned if one is open.

Great things are possible for all.

Prologue

They were forever bonded after attending their first international camp as teenagers, instantly connected despite all that separated them. All that attempted to impede their friendship was futile against the solidarity that they had built. Not their culture, their nationality nor geographical distance came between them.

Now, years later, in an unprecedented occurrence, Matthew and Asami were both on Izabela Antov's support team for the Full Contact Karate World Championships. Given that Matthew was Australian and Asami was the current All-Japan Female Champion, standing together beside the mats on Izabela's side – the defending Female Heavyweight World Champion from Bulgaria – raised more than a few eyebrows.

Truthfully their friendship wouldn't have been such a hot topic if it wasn't for Izabela. Both Matthew and Asami were accomplished full contact tournament fighters, both in their own countries and internationally, but Izabela was something completely different, which fuelled the conversations, speculations and even fear.

To date, no one could ever recall any fighter, male or female, like her. Her accuracy, speed and timing were unmatched. There were many male tournament fighters that were secretly grateful that men and women were not allowed to fight each other in full contact tournament competitions, thankful they wouldn't have to fight Izabela.

Standing on the main tournament mats, only three metres from her competitor, Izabela was smiling with absolute confidence.

"*Kumite*", said the centre referee, the Japanese command to fight, but neither competitor moved.

Feeling the need to show that her role as coach could add value, Asami yelled, "Let's go to work Izabela". Hearing Asami's voice rather than her own coach's instructions, Izabela's competitor made the first move, a combination of kicks and punches.

There was much conjecture amongst the crowd as to why Izabela appeared to hold back with her attack at the beginning of the fight. Some said she was warming up by merely blocking her opponent's strikes. Some believed Izabela was luring her opponent into a false sense of security before she retaliated. Others wondered if Izabela was sizing up her opponent's strengths and weaknesses, formulating a strategy there and then.

"High kicks, Izabela." Asami's voice was loud and assertive. Despite the advice, Izabela finally responded by kicking her opponent's right leg just above her knee. "Her head, Izabela. Go for her head."

Even with Izabela's speed and accuracy, the next two kicks to the exact spot on her opponent's right leg appeared to be ineffective. Not even a wince could be detected on her competitor's face.

"Listen to me, Izabela. Go for her head!"

Moving to the left while blocking a front kick, Izabela spun around with a hook kick. Connecting her heel, with absolute precision, to her opponent's right leg once again. Despite the roar of the cheering spectators, the sound of bone breaking was unmistakable to those surrounding the mats.

Izabela's opponent lay flat on her back on the ground, perfectly still and quiet. Eventually, as her brain began to process the trauma of her body, her voice communicated her pain, rising into a scream.

The sound coming from the competitor was primal, becoming more animalistic as she took in her injury. A sharp, jagged bone fragment had penetrated her skin and through her karate pants, the white of the fabric blooming with red from the open wound.

The centre referee looked to Izabela, checking she had ceased her attack, then called for urgent medical assistance. As the first aid responders rushed to the side of the injured, Izabela knelt in the traditional position, head bowed and back turned, in respect.

Izabela's support team stood frozen by the mats, experiencing dramatically different emotions. Matthew, filled with concern for his friend, though she meant so much more to him than that. Asami, on the other hand, felt her anger simmer hotter with every passing second. Some of the spectators may have concluded that the injury was accidental. But even if she couldn't explain it, Asami knew without a doubt that this was no accident. Izabela knew exactly what she was doing.

Izabela's opponent's howls were sickening, causing many of the onlookers to lower their heads out of respect. Heads that soon jerked back up upon hearing another scream of an entirely different pitch. From her kneeling position, Izabela's body convulsed and fell forward towards the mats, as if she was having an elliptic fit. She thrust her leg from side to side while clawing at her right knee.

Izabela's friends ran to her side. Matthew grabbed hold of Izabela, trying desperately to still her, seeing up close the frothing saliva at her mouth. Amongst the chaos, Asami looked deeply into Izabela's darting eyes; seeing past the savage moment to discover the truth. To see the gut wrench of remorse and shame. Izabela finally understood. Strength, knowledge, skill, and power are nothing without respect, wisdom and compassion.

Chapter 1
Moving

Olive looked down at her cyan-blue-stained fingertips momentarily before returning her attention to her creation. She continued to smudge the colour on the textured paper of her sketch book, blending it with the array of blues, greens and purples on the page.

At sixteen, Olive was still experimenting with different artistic media. Pastels were not her usual choice, but they were all she had at hand, and unlike the process of painting, pastel colours are mixed directly on the paper to achieve a wonderfully luscious, velvety texture...and a magnificent mess. Olive picked up a darker blue and ground the chalk-like material harder onto the paper, the crush of the pastel beneath her fingers briefly cathartic. Seeing the contrast of the cobalt against the black leather seats of the family car, a despondent sigh left her lips.

Taking a deep breath into her diaphragm before exhaling with enough force to puff out her cheeks, Olive put her art supplies and paper away. She reached forward slowly to grab her headphones from the back of the front passenger seat, leaving forensic blue handprints on the ear pads as she put them on. She spread the dust across her pants as she pulled her legs tightly to her chest, turning to glare out the window.

Pressing her head gently against the window, the cold of the glass temporarily relieving the tension building in her forehead, until the "Welcome to Buxton" swam into view. The thudding in her head doubled and her stomach tightened in solidarity. They had arrived.

"Honey, we're here!" Olive heard through her headphones. While there were certainly advantages to the family's minivan – like the space, which she was particularly grateful for today – the headset interruption feature was not one of them. Without moving her head from the back seat window, she managed to remove her headphones and place them back on their hook.

"We're here, Olive, look!" Her mum's elation resonated once more as she turned to look at her subdued daughter. "Our new home is just around the corner." Olive took a slow, deep breath and offered a tentative smile. After all, this transition had been thrust upon her mother as well.

While she hadn't seen it on her face, Olive was sure her mum must have felt the same gut churn that she did when they locked up their city house for the final time. How else could she have felt knowing she was leaving their home – and for a place out in the sticks? This morning's images hung heavily in Olive's mind, causing her stomach to clench even tighter.

It had been a whirlwind of movement since her parent's announcement two months ago. Olive's dad had won the new position of Chief Executive Officer of Wollondilly

Council, one of the largest semi-rural councils in Australia and consisting of thirty-four villages. Buxton was one of the smallest and oldest in Wollondilly ("Small but mighty", according to her dad), and therefore the least attractive to Olive.

Her dad's excitement about the new position and the move had been palpable the last few weeks. He'd moved around their old home at pace as he'd taped boxes and bubble wrapped glassware, and he'd taken to shaking his head and smiling to himself at random times. In the short period it took them to sell their house, her dad had told the real estate agent at least three times about the new job.

"It's always been a dream of mine to live in a rural area," he'd said to the agent, who'd tried his best to look interested. "But you know how hard it is to find senior roles out of the city. I'd almost given up on it, then, whaddaya know, I got a call from Wollondilly Council! Apparently, someone had recommended me, and the rest is history!" He'd laughed, and the agent had smiled politely in return.

The whole thing had felt a little off to Olive. When her dad had asked the HR Manager who'd put him forward, she'd said she "wasn't at liberty to say", putting an end to his questions. Though the job offer was a little unorthodox, it was exactly what he'd been looking for, and meant he'd be able to spend more time with her and her mum, no longer having to travel overseas for conferences and meetings. If he'd had any concerns, he'd clearly chosen to overlook them.

There were certainly no signs of hesitation now. Olive's dad turned off the car engine and jumped out with ninja-like reflexes, running around to open his wife's door, then Olive's.

"You going to sit there all day?" he said, leaning in with a gentle smile. He offered his big, warm hand to her, offering to help her out of her car seat fortress. "Come on, Ollie, it's going to be okay. Just give it a chance."

He was the only one who called her Ollie. He usually had a way of putting her at ease and making her feel safe, not just with his words but with his kind and loving eyes. She took no comfort from either today. Accepting his hand reluctantly, Olive placed her feet on Buxton soil for the first time. Not as memorable as the first steps of the moon landing, yet to her they felt just as colossal.

Olive's mother moved next to them, slipping her arm around her daughter's waist and smiled encouragingly at her. The enthusiasm in her mother's face suggested she was already mentally mapping out the upcoming house renovation projects. Olive had been wrong; her mum wasn't sad about the move at all. Watching her gleefully taking in their new surroundings, Olive's shoulders sagged further. *They don't understand*, she thought, biting the inside of her cheek to stop the threat of tears.

Not yet ready to take in the sight of her new home, Olive turned to look at her parents. Her father stood much taller than her, his dark hair and olive-brown skin taking on a more honeyed hue in the afternoon sun. Despite the age shown in the faint wrinkles on his face, he was still strong and well-built, which her mother often told him when she thought her daughter was out of earshot. In contrast, Olive's mother was more than a head shorter than her, but just as fit as her dad. Though only a few years behind her husband, with her perfectly highlighted brunette bob and a tanned, unlined complexion, she appeared many years younger.

To an outsider, they were a close-knit family, though the difference between Olive's appearance compared to her parents was striking. With long blonde hair, fair skin and eyes matching the cyan stains on her fingers, she bore no physical resemblance to them. So, when her mum and dad had gently told her the truth about their family five years ago, she had not been shocked. Olive had already intuited it. Even if she hadn't been consciously aware, her subconscious mind had delivered this revelation years before.

Olive had been an infant when Thomas and Sarah Ullman adopted her. Being unable to have their own children, they couldn't believe it when the adoption agency rang them with the news. They had known that the adoption process could take many years and it was unlikely that they would be able to adopt in Australia, and hence would likely have to look overseas. Yet after only 10 months of registering with an agency, they'd been offered a baby, one whose mother had died during childbirth. There was no father named on the birth certificate, no other family nor next of kin. No information, except for a name – Olive – chosen by the birth mother before her death. It was a blessing to the Ullmans. A blessing they accepted with gratitude. A blessing they did not want to risk losing by asking questions.

The Ullmans had taken their baby girl home, honouring her birth mother's wishes by calling her Olive, a name deeply connected to the symbolism of peace and balance. They added two more, their last name and a middle name inspired by the brilliance of their new baby's eyes – Sapphire. Olive Sapphire Ullman.

Despite the abundance of unconditional love the Ullmans gave to Olive, she had never really felt deserving of their devotion, unable to shake the bone-deep feeling that she did not belong. Having adopted parents who wanted her and loved her could never fill the void created from losing her biological mother and the loss of ancestral knowledge resulting from her death. Though she tried to push those thoughts away, they plagued her at the same time every year. Since the day she had been told the truth, Olive never wanted to celebrate her birthday, as it also marked the passing of her mother.

Olive felt the gentle squeeze of her mum's hand around hers, breaking the sombre silence which filled her thoughts. "Let's go inside," she persuaded.

As the family walked towards the front door, it was clear that this early 20th century farmhouse definitely needed some love to restore it to its former glory. It was just the kind of house Olive's mum loved, and her dad had been delighted to indulge her, knowing she had a designer's eye and the energy to take on the renovation project. Stepping onto the front verandah across numerous cracked decking boards and avoiding the various holes, they finally stood outside the front door, which hung crookedly from rusted hinges.

"Awesome," Olive mumbled sarcastically.

Olive's mum had the honour of placing the key into the front door for the very first time. "Why don't we all turn the key together?" she suggested.

With her arms still tightly crossed against her body and her face blank, Olive made it clear she wouldn't be contributing to this family moment. Looking to her father for moral support, she whispered to him snarkily, "She can add this door to her list of unloved items needing urgent attention." He shot her a look of warning, less than impressed with her tone.

Inside the home, the abundance of boxes proved the removalist had a much earlier start on the journey to Buxton than the Ullmans. They had been and gone before the family had arrived, following Olive's mum's instructions to put each clearly marked box in its correct room. The tremendous number of boxes needing unpacking and sorting was overwhelming, so Olive wandered off to become acquainted with her new environment while her parents went to unpack the most needed items.

Olive walked first into the L-shaped loungeroom, which was cold and dark despite the multiple windows. She surmised the lounge faced south, offering little opportunity for sunlight or warmth to permeate its space. A weathered pot-bellied wood stove occupied the corner where two walls met, a nostalgic nod to the past. Her gaze settled on the stove, fixating on the rusty interior flue, before her attention was abruptly diverted by a series of scratching noises from the ceiling above the stove. *What the hell is that?* A shiver of repulsion traversed her skin, leaving her feeling unsettled.

Pulled by the allure of a brighter space to the north of the lounge, Olive's gaze briefly brushed the minuscule yet functional original kitchen to her left as she passed by. Continuing on, she unlatched two glazed internal doors crafted from rich red cedar, entering a room radiating warmth and light. The sun streamed in through expansive floor-to-ceiling sliding doors, nearly encompassing the entire northern wall.

Peering through the glass panes of the back sliding doors, Olive scrunched her face tight at the sight of the overgrown jungle of the backyard. Vines snaked along the decking boards, and a sapling had taken root in the middle of the deck, prompting a scowl on her face.

Walking back through the cedar doors, Olive screamed as a large brown cockroach scattered across the kitchen floor as she walked past.

"Dad!"

"What? Are you okay?" Olive's dad yelled from another room.

"There's a friggin' huge cockie in the kitchen!"

"Good to know." Olive's scowl deepened.

Following the direction of her father's voice, Olive walked to the west of the loungeroom to what appeared to be a bedroom. Greeted by the smell of mothballs and mouldy furnishings, she watched as her parents attempted to put together their wooden bed frame.

With her parents claiming this room for themselves, Olive walked towards the front door, near the staircase and started climbing, each step groaning under her weight as she ascended. At the top she saw a hallway landing with bedrooms at either side. Following the sunlight, she stepped into the bedroom on the western side which was warm with the afternoon sun. She frowned at the small black wardrobe, then looked up to cathedral ceilings decorated with ancient spider webs where no feather duster could possibly reach.

Crossing her fingers, Olive turned towards the last bedroom. Her heart sank when purple walls and ceiling greeted her.

Despite this room being cooler, which would be better in Summer, Olive could not bring herself to dwell in an all-purple room. The West room may have had a black cupboard but at least the ceiling was white and walls beige. *Looks like beige is my best option.*

Olive marched downstairs to her parents' room, where they were arguing over which end of the wooden bed frame should go up against the wall.

"Can I go for a run?" Olive interrupted. "I won't go far, and I'll start unpacking when I get back."

"Uhhhh…" her mum inhaled slowly, the idea of her daughter running in an unfamiliar neighbourhood making her nervous. "Ah, okay, yes - but only for thirty minutes, and stick to the streets. No bush adventure jogs without Dad." Surprised, Olive grabbed her brand-new smart phone and ear buds and rushed out the door before her dad had a chance to protest. Deciding to not bother warming up, she started jogging, heading south along Buxton Avenue.

Chapter 2
First Sight

Olive's feet pounded the ground in perfect unison with the fast-paced song pumping in her ears, feeling the music pulse throughout her whole body. Her heartbeat rising, she turned left onto Boundary Road, noticing the contrast to the city route she'd often run with her father. There, cars parked in every tiny driveway and lined the street, while here they were tucked away in garages, or back behind houses, out of sight. Back home – *not home, not anymore* – paved walkways were rarely interrupted by greenery. Here, she had the choice of running on the road or the grass verge, yet trees of all sizes were abundant as was the wildlife; especially the Australian native birds. In the space of only a few minutes, Olive had spotted White-Crested Cockatoos flying overhead, their squawking antics cutting through the thumping music in her ears.

Halfway down the road, she saw a large spotted pig behind a fence. As she got closer, it started to run in time with her, like an excitable dog. Stopping once it reached the boundary fence of the next farm, Olive noticed something even stranger in the neighbouring paddock.

Is that a Doctor Who replica Tardis in that garden? she laughed to herself. Where had her parents moved her to?

Until this move, Olive would not have described her inner city living as enjoyable. It wasn't until she'd had to leave her small terrace house and the bustling streets that she realised she liked the noise, liked her home, and liked her lifestyle in Sydney. She'd had the library around the corner, her favourite noodle place down the road and only a short bus ride to museums, art galleries, markets, shopping.... any number of things to keep a loner like herself amused. How was she going to fill her time out here?

Reaching the end of the road, Olive stopped to check her watch. *Four minutes, not bad.* Enjoying the freedom that twenty-six remaining minutes provided, she turned left along West Parade, Buxton's main thoroughfare. Despite the sixty kilometre speed limit, the cars passed by at a much faster speed. Finally, something she was used to.

She picked up her pace, the endorphins started to kick in and her heartbeat quickened. As the wind blew her hair back, she felt her shoulders soften and a smile spread across her face. Running at this pace usually exhausted Olive within a few minutes, but right now she felt alive and energised. She had no intention of stopping now.

Up ahead, she spotted a community hall which looked even older than her 'new' house. Getting closer, the sound of voices united in a scream, stopped her mid-stride. She froze on the spot, listening intently. Curious to find the source of the noise,

Olive walked, puffing, towards the faded red barn-like doors of the hall.

Stepping inside, she saw a group of children positioned in precise lines, their white, loose-fitting clothing a contrast to a black banner which hung upon the wall. Obviously, this was a martial arts school of some kind and a very busy one as well. Not a single person noticed Olive as she entered the hall, and she felt solace in her anonymity. She took a seat at the back of the hall, strategically positioned closest to the main entrance, and picked up a brochure from the seat next to her. *Ah, it's karate,* she thought as she glanced at the cover.

"*Seiza.*" A stern male voice rang out through the hall. All twenty-four children in the middle of the hall followed the foreign command, moving in unison into a seated kneel. These students made perfect vertical and horizontal lines on the mats, which lay on top of the hardwood floor, equal distance apart, like a checkerboard.

"*Mokuso,* eyes closed." Olive followed the voice to the front of the hall, seeing a man with a black belt tied around his waist. He stood, unmoving, watching the equally still children – an impressive feat given the children looked to be no older than seven.

With their hands resting on their hips and heads gently inclined forward, the silence they held sent a ripple through the surroundings. The hall had hushed entirely and everyone within its confines seemed frozen in time. Olive wondered fleetingly if the children's legs were starting to protest their position.

"*Mokuso yame, Sosai ni rei.*" The man's words broke the silence. He moved from his kneeling position, bending his chest to the ground in time with his students, before rising again.

What was that? Olive was unsettled by the entire spectacle, but something about it spoke to her. A desire to comprehend the bond uniting these people compelled her to remain seated, observing the scene with a mix of intrigue, bewilderment, and perhaps a little fear.

As the children individually thanked their teacher, Olive finally glanced again at the brochure in her hand, the design a little amateur in her opinion. *I hope they didn't pay anyone for this layout*, she smirked to herself. Opening the folded paper, she read about the origins of karate in Japan, as well as the various classes at this *dojo* (which, the brochure stated, meant "place of the way"). According to the leaflet, Wollondilly Karate held classes for teenagers, too. *Surely there aren't enough teenagers here to justify all these classes*, she wondered.

"Hello. Can I assist you?" Olive lifted her gaze to see the warm smile of the black-belted teacher. Towering in height and boasting a well-toned physique, he exuded strength, yet his kind blue eyes and gentle aura tempered his imposing presence.

His thick brown hair was cut stylishly, streaks of grey glinting at his hairline, and Olive guessed he was about the same age as her father. He wore a large, loose fitting white uniform, which the brochure identified as being a *dogi* (or *gi* for short), with a Japanese logo on the left side of his chest.

When she didn't respond, the man continued. "Are you interested in trialling one of our classes for free?"

All Olive could manage was a small nod, struck by an odd sense of reverence. Eventually, she summoned what felt like a deranged smile.

"I'm Sensei Matthew – Sensei just means 'teacher'," he said, handing her a sheet of paper. "If you would like to trial any of our teen classes, just get your parents to fill out this form." He gave a gentle nod then walked over to a group of parents waiting to speak with him.

Olive walked out of the hall, red-faced. *Idiot, why didn't you say anything?* Pulling out her phone, her embarrassment was quickly replaced with panic as she noticed an hour had passed.

Crap, she thought, *they're going to be fuming.*

Chapter 3
Boyan

Another round of rhythmic thuds against the solid punching bag stopped abruptly at the chime from the well-used interval timer. Boyan bent down to smash the stop button with his palm for the last time today, leaving another layer of sweat on the device, then stood tall and absolutely still in defiance of what his body pleaded for. Rest would come soon, but for now, with both hands still clenched in a tight fist, Boyan watched the punching bag in front of him swing slowly like an exhausted pendulum. Sweat added to the blurring of his vision, assisting the exhaustion of twenty-one-minute rounds, but he refused to relax. To stand tall, still and strong at the end of every round, though brief, was paramount to his training.

Boyan turned to the right, nodding his head and bowing slightly in acknowledgement of the three photographs sitting on the shelf, each portrait varying in age. An ornate, golden frame surrounded the portrait of his mother. With her flowing blonde hair and youthful appearance, she wouldn't have been much older in the photograph than Boyan was now. A dark mahogany frame enclosed the image of a muscular man with soulful eyes. He was the man Boyan considered his father, yet he never addressed him as such.

The third frame, in painted white pine, was the newest addition to the shelf. The portrait was of a young woman with long, flaming red hair, her locks an outward display of the fire within her. Despite being in the garage, the photographs overlooking his training progress from above were sparkling clean, as he regularly dusted them in a mindful act of care.

Finally, Boyan slumped onto the worn exercise bench, giving his body the rest it was craving. The tattered towel positioned between him and the bench served to soak up his sweat and protect his skin from the bench's cracking vinyl. Picking up a large drink bottle from the floor beside him, Boyan flipped the lid and sipped, before pouring the water over his head, sighing with relief as the refreshing liquid ran over his face and chest. A benefit of training in the garage was the minimal concern Boyan and his adoptive father had about a little water on the floor.

Boyan's home gym wasn't Instagram-worthy, squished into one of the car spaces and shared with tools, garden machinery and storage for sentimental items which his father couldn't bear to part with. Though small, Boyan looked after his gym with pride, each element carefully chosen, from the second-hand exercise machines, punching bags and weightlifting equipment to the old Turkish rugs on the concrete floor.

The wall facing the gym was almost completely covered in large sheets of white paper, filled with training notes and motivational quotes. He'd even added one on the ceiling, directly above Boyan's weightlifting bench, which read "All

Things Are Possible", with a thick black line under "All". As Boyan pushed the barbell from his chest, he focused on this personal affirmation, which held historical significance.

A loud mechanical click followed by the hum of a motor startled Boyan, and he looked up to watch the garage door rattle open. With the *dojo* next door, it was odd for Matthew to be driving home after the day's karate classes, and he rarely parked in the garage. Something was off, and it registered uneasily in his gut.

Matthew eased the four-wheel drive into the garage with care, then turned the engine off. He was momentarily motionless, resting both hands on the steering wheel, then finally got out. The loud beep of the lock echoed throughout the garage.

"Everything okay?" Boyan called out, as Matthew disappeared from sight behind the car.

"All good. There's a storm warning so thought I'd bring the car in."

Unconvinced, Boyan grabbed his towel and water bottle and followed Matthew inside.

Walking through the garage door, Boyan threw his sweaty towel and t-shirt into the laundry, then continued to the open plan, and well-used kitchen. Given the supplies in the pantry and fridge, and the overflowing fruit bowl on the bench, the kitchen looked like it belonged to a large family, not two men and a young female Japanese exchange student. Yet, thanks to the incredible amount of exercise of the home's inhabitants – and Boyan's insatiable appetite – the house was almost bare come shopping day.

Looking left towards the rarely used media room, then into the dining and living rooms, Boyan finally spotted Matthew on the back deck, his favourite cap pulled down over his head. With Matthew's back turned, Boyan could see why people occasionally mistook them for one another at a distance, both six foot two with strong, lean physiques and light olive skin. But while his adoptive father's hair was a slightly greying brown, Boyan was a sandy blonde, and Matthew's face was a little weathered as would be expected for a man approaching fifty.

Boyan slowly opened the glass sliding doors and popped his head through. Upon observing Matthew staring unseeingly into their backyard, he decided to take a gentle approach to initiate the conversation.

"How did the Karate Kids classes go?" The question barely managed to lift Matthew from his trance-like state. Following Matthew's gaze, Boyan took in the alluring expanse of native bushland just beyond the back fence, then the somewhat sadder state of their yard. The prevailing drought wasn't the sole culprit for the garden's current state; it seemed both Boyan and Matthew lacked both the expertise and interest in nurturing plants.

"Any newcomers?" Matthew's head snapped toward Boyan with a sudden intensity.

"Have you picked up on something?" Taking a seat across from Matthew on the well-worn outdoor furniture, Boyan angled his head slightly.

"I feel that something's unsettling you," Boyan said, measuredly.

Watching Matthew carefully, Boyan felt the weight of history between them. "I'm nineteen," he began, his words deliberate and respectful, "you don't have to shield me any longer."

Matthew nodded then shifted his attention to Boyan's reddened knuckles tightly grasping his water bottle. "How did your training go?"

Now it was Boyan's turn to look into the chaotic tangle of plants that constituted their garden, taking a moment to collect his thoughts. "I've never felt stronger or more prepared."

Sensing there was more, Matthew probed gently. "But?"

Boyan moved his hand over his forehead, as if trying to smooth out his thoughts. "What if I end up failing as well? What if I never find balance?"

"She managed to find equilibrium."

"Not on the mats."

A melancholic sigh escaped Matthew as Boyan's gaze bore into him. He had been one of the two dearest companions to Boyan's mother. Side by side, they had honed their skills through years of shared training and numerous tournaments in each other's corner. Now a seasoned Karate instructor in his own right, if the answer eluded Matthew, what hope did Boyan have?

Throughout his life, Boyan yearned for the warm embrace of his mother. Though he was only a toddler when she'd passed, he retained vivid memories of the sanctuary her arms provided and the unreserved love she radiated. The passage of time had scarcely diminished the void left by her departure.

She alone would have understood the wellspring of his incredible strength, his uncanny ability, and the responsibility to balance both.

Since beginning karate training as a boy, he'd been searching for a solution. He looked directly at Matthew. "I have always believed I'd be able to find a way to compete."

"You don't believe that anymore?"

"She would have found a way, if she lived. For me, and for herself," Boyan confessed. "That's what I believe."

Chapter 4

Trial

Warm weather over the weekend had elevated the local bushfire warning level to 'high'. Until now, Olive hadn't truly comprehended the potential hazards of living amidst the Australian bushland, but now, as she surveyed the abundance of vegetation enveloping Wollondilly Karate's *dojo*, it was unmistakably apparent.

Shaking off the thought, she looked down at the karate trial form in her hand, pleased her second last day of school holidays would be spent in the *dojo*, rather than unpacking boxes. However, with two more days until term started, she wasn't sure she'd be able to entirely avoid it.

To Olive's relief, after returning late from her jog on the weekend, her parents had forgotten their anger as soon as she'd showed them the flyer. They'd been genuinely delighted their daughter was showing an interest in joining a local sports group, and had agreed to let her attend the trial class as soon as the question left her lips.

"Just think of all the new friends you'll make!" her mum had said breathlessly, squeezing her shoulder encouragingly.

Olive didn't have any major issues at her last school. People got along with her, she was included, likely made easier by being seen as generally attractive. Mostly, though, Olive suspected she was liked because when others spoke, she listened. Really listened. She watched their eyes and body language with undivided attention. In a world where everyone was fighting to be heard, Olive was happy to do the hearing, and her peers enjoyed the gift she offered, though they rarely returned in kind.

During lunch breaks, she found herself anchored to the same spot, surrounded by the familiar faces of her long-time schoolmates, girls she'd known since the days of finger painting in kindergarten. They'd considered her a friend, but to Olive, they felt more like a daily ritual, a safety net against the solitude threatening to claim her lunch hour.

Olive appreciated their presence, but in the midst of the chatter and laughter, she often felt like an enigma – a puzzle they hadn't quite solved. Gratitude confused her feelings on the matter, as the girls hadn't teased her for the occasional word fumble or her reading abilities, which trailed behind her peers.

Before her parent's announcement of the move to Wollondilly, Olive had spent Friday lunch times in her school's photography room. Cocooned in the dark, she had thrived, surrounded by moments she'd captured in time. After the news, Olive had frequented her dark fortress daily; deliberately and consciously cutting emotional connections with her schoolmates. She'd wondered if they'd cared about her absence in those last few weeks of term, but doubted it, as they'd never come to find her.

She cast a glance downward at the trial form, now bearing the signatures of her parents, then looked at her mother who insisted on coming today to "size up" this karate community. *Not a great look for my first class.*

"We going in?" Her mum nudged her gently towards the front door. Pulling up the safety lock on the hall's side gate, Olive walked through to take the same seat as she had two days ago, her mum close behind. She sat beside her mother. Running a little early, they watched the Karate Kids class as it was coming to its end.

"Great work," Sensei Matthew's encouraging voice resonated. "You've all given it everything you've got today."

Up until then, neither Olive nor her mother had detected his presence amidst the class.

"He's good," Olive's mum said, nodding at the large group of young students. "A teacher who can instil discipline while nurturing a sense of fun is a rare gem." A former primary school educator, she knew what she was talking about.

After hearing "*seiza*" from their Sensei, the children swiftly complied, moving to their knees. Olive's mother leaned slightly forward in her seat, her breath held in response to the pervasive hush now enveloping the space. She maintained her rapt attention as the children, bowed to their Sensei then each other.

"*Sayonara*, goodbye. See you next class," Sensei's encouraging voice echoed.

In unison, the children bid their farewells cheerfully. "*Sayonara*, Sensei!"

"You're back?!" Olive and her mum turned to find the instructor standing in front of them.

"Olive would like to trial today's teenager class, if that's okay?" her mum interceding. "We've filled in the form as best as we can." Olive handed the form to Sensei Matthew, still a tad embarrassed from her tongue-tied display last time she was in the *dojo*.

Hesitantly, Olive's mum continued. "We couldn't answer the question on parental medical history. We adopted Olive when she was a baby. We don't know much about her biological parents..." she trailed off awkwardly.

Glancing at the form and then at the two in front of him, Sensei smiled briefly. "Glad to have you here, Olive. First things first: please take your shoes off and put them on the rack outside the side door. We train barefoot. When you're ready, come onto the mats and do some stretches to warm up if you like. We'll get started in ten minutes."

As mysteriously as he appeared, Sensei Matthew had vanished again by the time Olive had returned from putting her shoes away.

Glancing back at her mother, she stepped for the first time onto the firm karate mats, nowhere near as soft as gymnastic mats. She had trialled that too, many years ago, but it hadn't gone well – much to her parent's disappointment. *This is different*, thought Olive. *Gymnastics was their idea, this is mine.*

Not really knowing where to sit or stand, Olive selected a position to the side of the room but a distance from her mother. Regretting her decision not to warm up before her weekend jog, she attempted to relieve her tight muscles with a calf stretch. Then from the back of the room came a loud, deep "*Osu*". Olive peered through her legs to spot an older boy bowing as he entered the *dojo*. He was tall with broad shoulders, brown hair and olive skin, and he moved with ease, almost with a skip in his stride. Suddenly, Olive didn't feel as confident. She hadn't anticipated older boys would be in the class.

As the clock ticked down, the room began to fill with teenagers, all exclaiming "*Osu*" as they entered. Fidgeting with her fingers, Olive glanced around, then out the hall doors, trying to distract herself from her nerves. From where she was sitting, she could see a smaller building, which appeared to hold the amenities, the driveway and the garden fence. Olive lifted her gaze towards the bush land which, despite its unfamiliarity, had a calming influence. That was until she saw *her*.

Riding upon a glorious black mare, she burst forward from the bush and onto the dirt driveway, confidence personified. With flowing red hair, lithe physique and flawless pale skin, she further challenged Olive's self-esteem. Olive watched as she pulled the reins to slow the horse as she approached the hall, then dismounted like a world-class gymnast. Much to Olive's dread, the girl also appeared older. Tying the horse to the fence, the Amazonian disappeared out of sight as she walked towards the front of the hall. Without turning around, Olive knew it was the redhead who entered the hall from her self-assured "*Osu*". Though Olive felt the urge to cast a glance backward, she restrained herself, hesitant to provoke a reaction. As the hall now hosted a gathering of at least twenty teenagers, Olive wondered just how big the class would get.

Entering the mats from the side near his office, Sensei Matthew called out. "Okay, line up. Leave a space for Boyan, he's doing a job for me."

Students wearing different coloured belts moved into rows, each knowing exactly where to stand. In the front row stood five students, two with brown belts and three with black, worn by the redhead, the brown-haired boy and a smaller girl Olive hadn't seen enter the hall. The second row held six students showcasing a spectrum of belts, spanning from brown to green, while in the third row, the belts transitioned from green to blue. Three additional rows followed, each featuring students adorned with colours of blue, orange and white.

With no belt of her own, Olive couldn't follow the colour coding to work out where to stand.

"Hi, I'm Joy," said a white-belted girl quietly.

She seemed close to Olive's age and had short raven-black hair highlighting her stunning emerald green eyes and pale skin. Smiling warmly, Joy said, "You stand to my left".

She helped Olive to not only her correct position but also to restore a little of her confidence. Joy's karate uniform looked as if it had just been removed from its packaging, and Olive was instantly fascinated by Joy's apparent ease in what appeared to be a new activity for her, too.

Everyone stood tall with their feet shoulder-width apart, hands clenched in fists at belt level. Once again, the room was filled with silence. Unlike many, Olive wasn't bothered by the quiet, but she wondered what they were waiting for.

Then he walked in. From the tiny room at the back left of the hall came a tall young man, with blonde hair and striking facial features. He felt familiar to her, though she was sure they hadn't met before. He walked to the front row to the space that was left for him. He was older than Olive, possibly the oldest student in the room, and he was everything she was not – calm, brave and full of confidence.

"Seiza!" Sensei Matthew commanded, and all of the students kneeled almost simultaneously. Still fixated on the young man, Olive followed awkwardly, instantly feeling the pull in her muscles. *Man, how do they sit like this?*

"Mokuso, eyes closed." Olive turned to look at Joy, noticing she'd shut her eyes, as had the rest of her row. Olive's curiosity stirred about the significance of this tradition, but her pondering was abruptly interrupted by the Sensei's voice.

"Mokuso yame." Suddenly, all eyes snapped open.

"Sosai ni rei." The students bowed in unison toward the front, with Olive following close behind. "*Fudo dachi.*" Copying Joy, Olive too stood tall, fists at her waist, feeling more than a little self-conscious.

Sensei Matthew, who also stood in *fudo dachi*, surveyed the class with what looked like deep contemplation, his eyes narrowing as he looked at her. His prolonged stare was noted by several students, their heads moving to discover the focus of their Sensei's attention.

Just as Olive was becoming uncomfortable with the attention, the young man from the front row broke the silence. "*Osu*, Sensei. Would you like me to start the warm-up?"

"*Osu*, thank you, Boyan," Sensei Matthew said, shaken from his reverie.

"Make it a ten minute warm up." Picking up Olive's form from a nearby table, he disappeared into the room at the back of the hall.

Boyan now stood in Sensei's position at the front, facing the class. *This guy looks like he should be in Hollywood, not Buxton*, Olive thought, as he took the class through a series of stretches and exercises, designed to get everyone's blood pumping. He spoke almost entirely in Japanese, though Olive didn't need to know the language as she continued following those around her.

Signalling ten minutes were up, Sensei once again appeared. Bowing to him, Boyan returned to his position in the line, the two men looking at each other before sharing a slight nod of their heads. It was a private, silent conversation, the kind shared between people who knew each other extremely well.

"Okay, find a partner, grab a kick and punch shield, then form two straight lines down the *dojo*," directed Sensei. Perhaps responding to the earlier strange behaviour from their teacher, no one moved. "*Hajime*, let's begin," he said louder, causing his students to urgently comply.

"Want to be partners?" Joy asked, and Olive smiled gratefully. "Stand in front of me," she said, handing a large pad to Olive and showing her how to hold it correctly.

"Tight fist, straight wrists. Work on *oi tsuki*, front punch. *Hajime!*"

Joy stepped her left leg closer to Olive while punching with her left hand into the pad.

"I'm still not sure what I'm doing," Joy confessed, "but I know for certain *oi tsuki* means punching with the hand that's on the same side as your forward foot."

This routine of stepping forward, punching then moving back became a continuous loop until Sensei announced, "swap sides".

Olive handed the pad to Joy while looking around her, relieved no one was watching. Everyone seemed to be in their own zone, punching with surprising speed and power.

Boyan seemed unmatched though, the thud of Boyan's fist hitting the bag could easily be heard from where Joy and Olive were. *How does he do that?* Olive thought, then quickly turned her attention to the pad in front of her, hoping Boyan and his partner hadn't seen her watching.

With Joy's encouragement, Olive took a step towards the bag and punched. From the moment her fist touched the pad, she was hooked. The movement was exhilarating and peculiarly familiar to Olive. *Love at first punch*.

With excitement and a little pride, Olive looked back at her mother. She was on the edge of her seat, chin in hand, her face strained. *What's her issue?* Olive wondered, grinning at her. In response, her mum forced a small smile.

With the command "y*ame*," the room came to an instant, soundless stop. The class turned to Sensei, who was now holding a roof tile.

"Sakura, would you like to demonstrate?" The smallest, and clearly the youngest, black belt smiled.

"*Osu*," she confidently responded.

Moving towards her teacher, she reached for the roof tile and positioned it slightly higher, and Sensei braced himself. Olive watched the change in Sakura's body and her expression, her attention lasered in on the middle of the tile.

"*Ichi, ni*," Sakura's voice boomed as her body obeyed; slowly practicing an *oi tsuki* punch against the tile with each count. "*San*," she yelled, propelling her fist. The crash of the shattering tile fused with Sakura's scream, creating a surreal cacophony. Olive's mind raced, struggling to process what she had just witnessed. *She just broke the roof tile with her bare fist, and she's smaller than me!*

"In an era where many are addicted to distraction, learning to focus is paramount," Sensei's words broke through Olive's disbelief. "Distraction comes from our desire to escape discomfort." He looked closely at the class. "What do I mean by discomfort?"

"Grief," said Boyan, and Sensei Matthew looked at him knowingly.

"Fear," the redhead said, while Olive scoffed inwardly.

"Loneliness," the brown-haired teen from the front row said, Olive picking up a South American accent.

Raising her hand excitedly, Joy blurted, "Is boredom a discomfort?"

Sensei nodded. "Yes, all these emotions are a discomfort to us. We as human beings have evolved to flee, to avoid these feelings." He paused briefly, looking around the room to make sure they understood. "Distraction begins within. To learn the art of focus, one first must address and heal from the pain deep inside each of us."

Olive crossed her arms tightly over her chest, feeling as if she had intruded on a private family conversation. While intrigued by the trust and vulnerability the students had shown, this was not what she had signed up for. She began picking at a cuticle on her thumb, looking at the floor. For the remainder of the class, while her body moved through various kicks, punches and combinations, her mind was somewhere else entirely.

"*Sayonara*, goodbye." From her seated position, Olive jerked her head up. Was class over already? Standing up with the others, her shoulders sagged imperceptibly. *That went way too fast*, she thought.

While most of the class began to leave, Olive remained, watching Boyan. Her contemplations were interrupted by a cheerful *"Hola"*.

The brown-haired teen from the front row appeared before her, momentarily obstructing her view. *"Hola,"* he repeated, an infectious grin spreading over his face.

Distracted by her nerves, Olive had not noticed how handsome he was when he walked in the *dojo*. Now, she felt a strong pull to his warm brown eyes.

"*Mi nombre es* Sebastian," he said, gesturing towards himself, then pointed towards Olive. "*Y tu nombre es?*"

Olive was just about to confess to her lack of understanding when the redhead interrupted.

"Sebastian, clearly the girl doesn't speak Spanish. She doesn't know what the hell you're saying."

"You mean that she doesn't speak Spanish *now*. She will." Winking at Olive, he left the mats with a grace remarkable for such a strong, tall physique.

The redhead's gorgeous flowing mane swished around as she turned to accompany Sebastian, and Olive's lip curled in response. *Who does she think she is*, she thought, annoyance rising in her chest.

With effort, Olive unfolded her arms and brought them to her sides. "I'm Olive Sapphire Ullman," she called, smirking at the redhead. "Nice meeting you, Sebastian."

Turning around, Sebastian smiled. "*Mucho gusto*. Nice to meet you, too, Olive." He tapped a finger to his forehead and bowed slightly in a chivalrous gesture.

Flutters began in Olive's stomach and up to her chest, her anger forgotten. She was immediately in awe with the young man and his strangely old-fashioned ways. She felt the redhead's eyes on her, then glimpsed a slow smile overtake her face as Olive turned to walk towards her mother.

"Well, how was that?" Olive's mum asked cautiously.

"I want to join."

Chapter 5
Bush

The thump on the metal roof above her head woke Olive instantly from her sleep, but it was the scratching noise in the wall that got her quickly out of bed. The knowledge that critters were living somewhere in this old country home made her skin crawl. *Way to start the last day of school holidays*. Since she was up, Olive grabbed her robe and slippers, then headed downstairs to the kitchen, where her mum was cooking banana pancakes.

"Good morning sweetheart, how did you sleep?"

"There are animals living in the walls and who knows what's jumping on our roof."

Olive's mum laughed at her dramatics. "How many pancakes would you like?"

"Uh...since this is my last free day, can I go for a jog?"

"What, without eating first?" From the tone of her voice, it was clear her mum was disappointed, especially after going to the trouble of making her daughter's favourite breakfast. "Why don't you wait for Dad to get up and you can go together?"

Olive's pained face and rolling eyes was a silent but effective response.

Taking a deep, controlled breath, her mum conceded. "Alright, fine. But remember, keep out of the bush!"

Olive jogged along Buxton Avenue, this time deciding to turn left onto Arden Road, passing properties which were the same size as the Ullman's, but much newer and more attractive. *Why didn't we buy one of these?* she lamented.

Choosing to turn left two more times, Olive found herself at the end of the road. From the top, it appeared this road was a dead end, but as the end drew closer, she could see it extended further via a narrower dirt track.

Remembering her mother's rule, Olive internally debated. *Well, this could be a road... for smaller vehicles.* Stepping onto the track, a sneaky smile creeped across her face. As she ventured further down the track and houses vanished from sight, her smile widened.

For as long as she could remember, she had an affinity with the Australian bush. Though she'd only experienced it on holidays and weekend getaways, it spoke to her. It was raw. An ancient and unrefined beauty, with its perfect imperfections and rusted colour palette. Olive suddenly yearned for her sketch pad and pastels. *No need for cyan blues here*, she thought. Her stride slowed to a dreamlike meander as she feasted on the light, texture and tones of nature's most accomplished composition.

Discovering a large boulder to the left of the track, Olive sat down and leaned back. Looking up to the canopy of gum trees, she watched as the top branches gently danced in the breeze. In her peripheral, a rounded greyish shape caught her attention. Turning her full gaze directly towards the shape, she realised it was moving, albeit very slowly. Then the realisation hit her. *Oh man, it's a koala!*

Olive had heard from her father there was a colony of koalas in the area but to actually see one only metres away was extraordinary. He'd told her the colony was under threat from over-development, loss of habitat and family dogs. With Southwest Sydney at the doorstep of this rural community, the demand for more land from developers could see these koalas vanish forever. With many more colonies around Australia facing similar issues – not to mention bush fires – the threat to the koala was very real, and it filled her with anguish.

In solidarity with the koala's plight, Olive made the decision to leave the animal in peace. Standing from her resting rock, she walked further along the track and away from the road. Now totally immersed within the sights and smells of this slice of Australian heaven, she was filled with the joy of her surroundings. It wasn't long before she became aware that the terrain was starting to change noticeably, sloping downwards into a gorge or valley. Watching her footing, she started descending towards a gentle flowing creek. Fuelled with a sense of adventure, she picked up her pace, eager to reach the water as if she were the first person to have ever done so.

Standing only inches away from the creek, she yearned to feel the freshness of the water against her skin. Taking her shoes and socks off, she was shocked to find the water was more than fresh – it was icy cold. The temperature was at odds with the warm mid-Spring weather. Olive made a mental note to come here when Summer reached its peak, and wondered if the local kids came here to escape the heat. Part of her hoped to make friends down here, while another part of her hoped to keep this small slice of paradise to herself.

Placing her shoes and socks back on, she started to climb up the other side of the gorge. Upon reaching the top, she closed her eyes and tilted her head towards the sky. In that moment, Olive could have been anywhere in the world. The same light now touching her skin also blessed the lands of the khans, powered the rainforests of the Amazon and enlightened the temples of Tibet. With her eyes still closed and music pumping in her ears, the warmth of the sun was her only connection to Earth.

Olive opened her eyes and took in the scene around her anew. Inspired to capture the beauty surrounding her, she grabbed her phone from her pocket, turning slowly to capture different angles. As she was framing her last shot, Olive noticed dark shadows moving in the distance, interrupting the light beams ahead.

Intrigued, she moved closer. Squinting her eyes to focus, she realised the shadows belonged to people. Taking a further step, Olive crouched down behind a tree, watching closely without being discovered.

The swift and agile movements of the people up ahead kicked up dust from the dry, drought-stricken ground. Looking closely, Olive realised she recognised these people. Having swapped their *dogi* uniforms and bare feet for tracksuits and sneakers, Sebastian and Sakura were sparring while the redhead looked on. Olive crouched a little lower and held her breath, the intensity and speed of their fighting intimidating her.

Soon, the fighting pair stopped and bowed to each other, Sebastian moving to the side to allow the redhead to stand in his position. The two girls repeated the bowing custom then the redhead hastily picked up her back leg, kicking sharply in Sakura's direction. Using her right hand to push the attacking leg away, Sakura blocked the advance, spinning her opponent. With the redhead's back now turned, Sakura kicked her rear anchored leg at the ankle, knocking her onto her back, legs in the air.

"Yeaahh! Another brilliant Sakura-sweep," Sabastian hooted. "Girl you might be small but you're mighty. You are the queen of using your opponent's weight and size against them."

The redhead gave Sebastian a death stare as she stood up to brush the dirt and dry leaves from her clothes. "Hey, less talk about my weight and size!" she snarled at Sebastian.

Pulling both hands up towards his face in immediate and apologetic surrender, Sebastian grovelled, "Um, that's not what I meant. I didn't mean to-"

Hysterical laughter interrupted Sebastian's horror.

"Sorry, I was just messing with you," the redhead confessed with delight. Turning her attention towards Sakura, her laughter stopped. "Nice technique but you won't be doing that again today," she vowed.

The two moved towards each other again, using varying attacking, counter and defending techniques. Olive remained frozen in place, looking more termite mound than teenager. Even if an inhabitant of one such mound walked over her hand, she doubted she'd so much as flinch she was so absorbed. Watching the karate display filled her with awe, yet she could not help but feel like she was trespassing, like this sparring scene was sacred. A scene in which she so badly wanted to belong.

Stepping aside for Sebastian, Sakura now watched as he sparred with the redhead. Sebastian didn't move his position as much as his opponent, possibly due to his size. His techniques were fast and extremely sharp in their delivery, yet the redhead seemed unconcerned, matching every attack with an equally impressive counterattack, almost in sync with the music playing in Olive's ears.

As the trio continued to take turns, Olive noticed they all had their own distinctive fighting styles. Styles appearing to match not only their body types but perhaps their personalities, too.

As she watched, Olive became aware of a tightening in her stomach, a sense of unease which grew in intensity. Dismissing the sensation, she continued watching the fights until the hairs on the back of her neck stood up. *Relax Olive*, she told herself, *no one knows you're here*. However, she could not dismiss the large, strong hand grabbing her shoulder from behind.

Her senses were overwhelmed by a deep, immeasurable alarm. Then, in an instant, the assailant's hand slipped under her armpit, yanking her to her feet and turning her to face him. Crippling fear consumed Olive at a cellular level, seizing every ligament, tendon, and cell, paralyzing her completely.

"Do you have any idea how dangerous, how irresponsible, how stupid it is for you to deliberately block one of your senses?" the man said.

Olive said nothing, but her brain reacted instantly, signalling to her nervous system to increase her blood flow and heartbeat, internally responding to the threat.

"You can't even hear me with those things in," he rebuked, while pulling the earbuds from Olive's ear. "Your hearing is a gift. Fear is a gift. Your gut instincts are a gift. But you waste them, misuse them and ignore them."

His face reddened as he continued. "I could've been anyone. I could've been someone with bad intentions."

From behind her, another male voice spoke. "Come on, Boyan, I think you've made your point. You're freaking her out."

Olive turned to see Sebastian's gentle eyes smiling comfortingly at her. Turning back to face the male who was chastising her, Olive was confronted again by Boyan's anger, which was slowly waning as he took a slow, shuddering breath.

"Your body warned you, but you didn't listen to it," he said softly.

Unnerved, Olive thought back to the physical feeling of unease she'd experienced. How could he possibly have known?

Olive watched Boyan's body language shift from anger to what looked like remorse, and perhaps even sadness. Eerily, she also witnessed his beautiful blue eyes change to a dull shade of grey. He lowered his head, turned and walked away. The redhead, who was also standing behind Olive, followed after him. Sebastian smiled encouragingly at her then headed off in Boyan's direction.

"Are you okay?' Sakura asked gently. The meekness of Sakura's voice triggered Olive's tears, her fears giving way to sobs. Guiding Olive to a seated position on a fallen tree trunk, Sakura waited till the intensity of Olive's fright had passed.

Eventually, Olive's sobs subsided. All that remained were red puffy eyes, embarrassment, and a hell of a lot of questions.

Chapter 6
Retreat

Blood pumped hard in Boyan's chest, frustration coursing through his veins. Frustration at Olive, but also with himself. Feet heavy, he trekked out of the bush towards his house.

Ah man, I hope Matthew's home, Boyan thought as he patted his pockets for his keys. Upon reaching the bright yellow door of his family home, Boyan turned the doorknob. *Excellent.* Walking inside, he took off his shoes, placing them neatly in the hall as he has done almost every day of his life.

"Knock, knock." Aednat announced her arrival as she kicked off her shoes.

"What the hell was that about?"

"What was what about?" Boyan said, looking away from her.

"You know what!" She shook her head, walking towards him. "That was so over the top, so intense, so not like you–" Aednat's rant was interrupted by banging at the front door. "Jeez, Sebastian, just come in!"

Popping his head meekly around the hallway, Sebastian inquired, "Everything okay?"

"What are you doing hiding around the corner?" Aednat huffed. "You're a big boy."

"I didn't want to intrude."

"Intrude on what? I've been here less than a minute!" Aednat retorted.

"Which is enough time for a lecture," Boyan shot back.

"Not a lecture," Aednat shook her head again, pointing towards the bushland. "I just want an explanation for whatever that was!"

"I don't know." Boyan slumped into his favourite loungeroom chair and cradled his head with his hands. Sebastian and Aednat sat down, giving him space to answer.

"It was like…" Boyan massaged his temple. "Her eyes were so blue, I could read everything in them. I could *feel* her."

Sebastian looked towards Aednat before returning his attention to his best friend. "You like Olive?"

Boyan jerked his head up and looked at Aednat earnestly. "No, it's not like that!"

Sebastian looked relieved. "Why did you walk away?"

Boyan's gaze flicked between his girlfriend and best friend, seeing only support and concern in their eyes.

"Guilt, maybe. I felt her fear and sadness, because of what I said, what I did. More than I've ever felt anyone else's feelings."

"You've just met – how is that possible?"

"I assume it was my out-of-whack emotions getting a kick up the butt."

"Huh?" Aednat's face scrunched in a portrait of confusion.

"A good dose of my own medicine to bring me back to some kind of balance."

"Ahh, got you. Well, that's good to know," she said, standing and stretching her arms above her head, "we can't have you stealing Olive away from Sebastian."

"Wait, what?" Sebastian choked.

"Confess! I saw how you two looked at each other in the *dojo*!" Sebastian opened his mouth but was not granted the opportunity to speak. "You're the one who likes Olive!"

Boyan leaned back in his chair and smiled at Sebastian. "Is that so?"

Realising he'd been found out, Sebastian got to his feet. "What's not to like?"

"I knew it!" Aednat yelled triumphantly.

"She's beautiful, obviously, but she has kindness about her, and a strength, that's even more attractive."

"Strong enough to give it to you!" Boyan said. "But did she smack you in the face the first time you met?"

"Hey!" Aednat protested. "When are you both going to let that go?"

Boyan and Sebastian shot each other a look. "Never!" they said in unison, as they burst out laughing.

"You came at me from the back in the setting sun! What did you expect?"

"I don't know, maybe a thank you for handing back your wallet?"

"You two really are couple goals."

"Well, I haven't hit him since meeting!"

"What's the joke?" Matthew asked as he came in through the verandah doors.

"We're reliving the joy that was Aednat and Boyan's first encounter," Sebastian sniggered.

"And interrogating Sebastian on his new love interest, Olive," Aednat said slyly.

The smile on Matthew's face fell instantly. "You and Olive, huh?"

"Nothing official...yet."

"I see", Matthew said. "Don't want to intrude, just on my way to the garage."

Boyan registered Matthew's reaction silently. *I guess I'll add that to today's list of weird moments.*

Chapter 7
First Day

The constant monotonous chime from Olive's alarm failed to pull her from her bed. Rolling away from the phone to face her bedroom window, Olive pulled her warm, soft bedcovers closer to her chest as she gazed outside. *Of course it's grey and gloomy*, she sighed. Her self-pity felt as comforting as her doona, her blue internal narrative a toxic yet familiar friend.

Without bothering to turn her head, Olive slapped on the bedside table to locate her phone. Finally, she felt the smooth palm-sized device and brought it to her eyes, turning off the alarm before checking if she'd received any messages. No notifications. Not that she should have expected anything else. Her parents were the only ones who contacted her and, annoyingly, they preferred to ring.

As her brain sluggishly awoke, she remembered the events of yesterday, her shock, tears and embarrassment.

"It's hard to explain to those outside the *dojo*, the bond and respect you share with those you train with." Sakura's words had failed to comfort her after Boyan chastised her in the bushland. Despite Sakura's attempts to explain why Aednat and Sebastian walked off with Boyan, they only added to her feeling of isolation. She didn't belong to the black belt group or understand their strange, secretive antics.

Kicking off the bed covers, Olive stood and stretched, raising her arms towards the ceiling and balancing her weight on the balls of her feet. A small, reluctant smile crept across her face as she realised she'd learned the stretch at her karate trial, but it was quickly extinguished realising she'd see her karate classmates at school. *I just got to get through today*, she thought, trying to reassure herself. *Better to break the ice at school than at karate this afternoon.*

Lowering both heels back towards the ground, Olive gazed towards the antique chair in the corner of her room. Her mum had lovingly restored the wing-backed chair only yesterday, reupholstering it in her daughter's favourite pink and green colour scheme. Though busy with setting up their new home, her mum had found time for the project so she'd "have something beautiful in her new space." Olive's new school uniform was now carefully laid out over it, which she realised her mum must have done while she was sleeping. Unable, or unwilling, to appreciate the gesture, she trudged over to get dressed.

Getting dressed quickly before pausing briefly in front of the full-length mirror, Olive looked reluctantly at her reflection. The single pleated bottle-green skirt went past her knees, though it was an improvement from the mission brown one she'd had to wear at her last school. Olive frowned at the mirror as she took in the grey blouse with its cuffed half-sleeves and wide trim ballooning from her frame. *It's a sack*, she sighed. Though she wasn't a fan of ties, she was grateful that the green and grey-striped addition to her uniform pushed the blouse a little closer to her body. After quickly braiding her hair into a school-acceptable style, she trudged out of her room.

"Morning, Sweetheart." Olive's mum beamed with pride as she saw her daughter in her new school uniform for the first time. "Wow, that fits you perfectly. You look amazing!"

Taking a seat at the kitchen bench, Olive didn't return the smile. "What's for breakfast?"

"Roasted vegetable quiche," she said, removing a dish from the oven and unleashing an incredible aroma, not that Olive would dare admit it.

"Why can't we, just once, have cereal like everyone else?" Olive moaned. "You know most people consider that dinner, right?"

"Why would you want to be like everyone else? Choosing the best option for yourself is what really matters."

Olive rolled her eyes so hard they hurt. "We're talking about quiche, right?"

Responding with a wink, she continued working in the kitchen, humming as she went.

Olive's mum loved to cook because, as she said so often, "cooking is love". Olive suspected she'd been up early to pick fresh spinach, cherry tomatoes and herbs from the garden, the only part of the property the previous owners had looked after. For a woman in her fifties, her mum was in amazing health, and it showed in her age-defying looks, thanks to her wise food choices (though no one believed her when she told them).

Loading her dirty plate into the dishwasher, Olive kissed her mother on the cheek and turned to go. Refusing to settle for a mere peck, her mum wrapped her arms around her, hugging her tightly.

"Go and have an exceptional day," she whispered into her ear, hugging her tighter. "I love you."

With a pained groan, Olive prised herself from her mother's embrace, grabbed her lunch box from the kitchen table and headed out the door. She didn't have far to walk – the school bus stopped right outside the Ullman's home. While convenient, she now realised it meant everyone would know where she lived. *In the ugliest house in Buxton.*

After a matter of minutes, the bus arrived and Olive walked on, her heart beating hard and fast beneath her balloon blouse. Looking down the aisle, she was unsure whether to be relieved or disappointed she recognised none of the faces staring back at her. Or so she thought.

"Hey Olive! You living in Mr Smith's old place?"

Looking around, Olive finally saw Joy looking at her from a few seats back.

"My house? Was that the owner's name?" Olive asked, sitting down next to Joy.

"Yeah, Mr Smith's father built the house in the early 1900's. They both lived there till the day they died."

"Man, don't tell me some old guy died in my house!"

Joy laughed and patted Olive's shoulder in mock pity. "So, what did you think of the karate trial?"

"I really liked it. You'll see me in those white pyjamas this afternoon."

"Awesome! You can be my partner."

Olive stared at Joy, her comment taking Olive back to the Science lab of her old high school. She'd been partnered up with Gloria for the whole of term two last year.

"You read, I'll pour," Gloria had insisted. Olive had scanned the large body of text on the page of their chemistry textbook in vain.

"How much acetic acid do we need?"

"Umm..." Without the aid of diagrams, Olive had stared at the words on the edge of panic.

Gloria had stabbed at the instructions with her finger. "How dumb are you?"

Seeing the lack of enthusiasm on Olive's face, Joy added, "Well, it's just that we're both beginners, so, um, I thought we could partner up?"

Olive's mind returned to the bus, Joy's dejected expression registering. "Yep, sure, okay." Olive forced a smile. After all, Joy was probably the closest thing she had to a friend right now.

"Cool! We're going to be best karate mates!" she whooped, clapping her hands. Olive leaned ever so slightly away from her enthusiasm. *Wow, she gets super pumped about stuff,* Olive thought.

Olive was never very good at, or interested in, small talk, preferring to sit in peace than fill the air. Upon seeing the school gates, she took a deep breath, relieved the ride was over - and attempting to calm her nerves.

"Everyone has to go to the school hall each morning," Joy advised.

Following Joy's lead off the bus, Olive's throat dried as they weaved through hordes of students, walking, talking and laughing together. Taking a step inside the hall, Olive frowned at the sheer number of students.

Seeing Olive's apprehension, Joy explained, "So, Wollondilly High is like, seriously one of the hugest high schools in Australia. And, you know, there's only this one public high school around here, so it's not like we've got a ton of options or anything."

Then, with a hint of spite, "Unless you want to travel long distances or you've got rich parents who can send you to one of those bougie private schools further south."

Olive knew her father made good money in his new job, so she deducted money wasn't a factor in her parents deciding to enrol her here. *Who knows what was.*

Taking a seat next to Joy on the hall's hardwood floors, Olive looked around, happy to see no one was looking at her. With so many students, she hoped it'd be hard to spot a newbie.

A hush suddenly filled the hall, causing Olive's head to lift in interest. Looking around, she spotted Sakura and the redhead enter the hall. *Did everyone seriously stop talking because they arrived?* she wondered.

A lighter, more relaxed energy settled over the room as Sebastian walked in. Olive watched as various boys and girls nodded and smiled as he walked past, and a few juniors called out, "*Hola* Sebastian!" He replied to each and every greeting with a broad smile.

A strong female voice came over the microphone, interrupting Olive's thoughts.

"Wonderful. Now that Sebastian Matias Jara has arrived, we can finally start our morning."

"*Hola* Miss Bunn, sorry I'm late," Sebastian responded with his usual charm.

"*Hola* Sebastian. Please take a seat." In a lighter tone, she continued. "Good morning, students. I trust you all enjoyed the school holidays. For those joining us this term, I'm Miss Bunn, the Principal of Wollondilly High School. I would like to take this opportunity to welcome Adam Chambers, Rob Jones, Melissa Murphy and Olive Ullman to our school."

Olive froze in place, her breath held tight.

"I look forward to a fantastic school term. Thank you everyone, now off to your first class please."

Following the lead of those around her, Olive stood, her legs noticeably wobbly after hearing her name announced. The fear of standing out in front of hundreds of students she had not even yet met, manifested instantly within her body.

"What class are you in?" Joy enquired.

"Um, I'm...I'm in 10G," Olive managed.

"Awesome, we're in the same home room! We can walk together."

This time, Olive's replying smile was genuine.

Olive was aware she was likely to be the oldest student in Year 10 but was glad no one at this school would know why. Being diagnosed as dyslexic in Year 3 hadn't come as a surprise to Olive's parents, as they had known something wasn't right. Being dyslexic herself, Olive's mum had seen the signs. Her parents had pushed the school for early intervention reading initiatives but noticed little improvement. They'd decided she'd need to repeat Year 3 without consulting her, and she still hadn't gotten over it.

Walking to home room, which seemed to be in the furthest building from the hall, Olive wondered where her other karate classmates were. Well, one in particular.

"Is Boyan away today?" Olive asked, unable to keep her queries to herself.

"Boyan? He graduated last year," Joy replied, clueless to Olive's hidden agenda.

"So, Sakura, Sebastian and the redhead are all in Year 12?"

"Sebastian and Aednat are in Year 12," she said, turning to Olive. "Sebastian is the youngest student in the year, even though he's the tallest and most mature..." Flushing a little, Joy returned to the topic. "Sakura is in Year 11."

"So Aednat is the redhead's name," Olive said. Choosing her words carefully she continued, "She isn't very friendly. She's kinda got a cold vibe, like standoffish energy."

"You sound like Boyan, talking about 'vibes' and 'energy'," Joy giggled. "Aednat's alright, once you get to know her a bit. She moved to Wollondilly like three years ago. Since she's older than me, we haven't really hung out much, you know? Even though we're both at karate, she mostly hangs with the other black belts. But she's been nice to me and all, not gonna lie."

Joy looked around to see if anyone was listening, then decided to spill. "Oh, and those black belts? Super tight-knit crew. They're all besties, friendly with everyone, but they kinda keep to themselves, you know?"

As if worried to appear to be whinging, Joy changed the subject. "So, you'll be at karate after school?"

"Oh yeah, it's the only thing getting me through today."

Joy smiled gently in commiseration, "I can imagine you're super nervous about your first day of school."

Olive nodded, "Yeah, I'm not a big fan of school in general."

"Is anyone?"

"Smart kids, probably." Olive surprised herself with her honesty, disarmed by Joy's warmth.

"Yeah, nah, I'm pretty smart, but I'm not a fan of school."

Olive stared at Joy with interest, refreshed by her openness. Joy was certainly growing on her.

"*Hola* Olive," a familiar voice called out, close behind them.

Olive and Joy turned to see Sebastian walking towards them with his signature smile.

"Welcome to Wollondilly High, Olive. First week of karate and a new school – how you feeling?"

The question gave Olive pause. Up until this morning, no one had asked how she was feeling, how it felt to be leaving everything she knew to start again at a new school, in a new area. Now, in the space of five minutes, two people wanted to know how she was doing.

"A little overwhelming to be honest," Olive's words trembled slightly with emotion.

"Yes, I remember the feeling," Sebastian reflected with sadness before his eyes sparkled again. "Hey, I know what will cheer you up. I'm having a *fiesta* on Friday night – why don't you come?"

Noticing Joy crumple a little, Sebastian added, "Of course, you can come, too, umm..."

"Joy. My name is Joy," she said, a small note of frustration in her voice.

"A *fiesta*?"

"A party," Sebastian explained. "There'll be people from school and karate, and my family will be there, of course."

Detecting Olive's indecision, he tore a piece of paper from one of his notebooks and began writing. "I'll give you my address and number. It starts at 6pm – I hope you can make it."

Looking her straight in the eyes, Sebastian handed Olive the paper. She felt her head get light.

Joy cleared her throat. "Alright, we're turning left here."

Sebastian saluted. "*Adiós Señoritas.* Have a great first day, Olive."

"Well, that was awkward!" Joy huffed, once Sebastian was out of ear shot. "You've just arrived and the hottest – I mean THE HOTTEST – guy at school invites you to his party. He doesn't even know my name and I've lived here my whole life!"

"He invited you, too," Olive said, in an effort to ease Joy's hurt.

"He only invited me because he's a nice guy and didn't want me to feel left out," Joy said, laughing dismissively.

"Boys are a mystery to me," Olive soothed. "I'm sorry, Joy."

After taking a moment for Olive's words to heal her wounds, Joy perked up. "Maybe a party would be good for both of us. Do you want to go?"

Olive looked down at the paper, that taunted her from between her fingertips. "Ummm, I don't know. Parties aren't really my thing."

"What do you mean, 'parties aren't your thing'? Who doesn't love a party?"

Olive placed the piece of paper in her top pocket carefully. "Yeahhhh…"

"Look, he only invited me because of you. I can't show up by myself!" Joy grabbed her shoulder, shaking her playfully. "It's going to be fun, you'll see."

Chapter 8

Anniversary

Despite the dry air on his skin, Boyan enjoyed the sun's warmth streaming through the car window. Parked outside the school gates, he looked forward to surprising Aednat and Sebastian after school. *They're not missing me here*, he grinned.

Boyan leant forward to turn up the song which just started playing through the speakers before settling back into the black leather seats of his father's car. Closing his eyes, he breathed in deeply through his nose, focusing on the air reaching his diaphragm and ballooning his stomach.

The final toll of Wollondilly High's school bell echoed in Boyan's ears. Opening his eyes, he couldn't help but smile as he observed the remarkable speed at which students emerged, their eagerness propelling them toward the gates. *Can't blame them*, Boyan mused, witnessing the initial trickle transform into a throng of students, all motivated by the prospect of departing the school grounds.

Boyan's eyes moved through the crowd, picking out faces he recognised. Despite the size of Wollondilly High School's enrolment, Boyan knew the majority of the students and teachers. Since finishing Year 12 last year, he hadn't been back until today. He certainly hasn't missed it.

Despite his best efforts not to be, Boyan was popular at school, and he'd won the male position for School Captain by a landslide – a position he'd ultimately turned down. His Physical Education teacher had tried to convince him to reconsider, telling him what a huge honour it was and how great it would be for his resume, but Boyan had been resolute.

Refusing the position had only made Boyan's fellow students love him even more. To them, Boyan was a rebel, so confident in his own skin that he could say no to the teachers. On the other hand, it made many of the school's faculty turn against him, as they mistook his desire to fly under the radar as arrogance and disrespect.

A face in the crowd jolted Boyan back to the present. Despite being bound in tight braids, the sun highlighted the auburn tones in the girl's blonde hair. He immediately recognised her as the girl who recently joined karate – the girl he'd gone off at in the bush yesterday. She was walking beside Joy, another new student to the *dojo.* Boyan leant forward in his seat again, staring at the girl's face. *Who are you?* he wondered as he searched her face for clues. *You look so familiar.*

"Hey good lookin'!"

The strong, familiar voice startled Boyan, as did the loud bang on the car roof. Boyan jumped in his seat.

"Crap man," Boyan chastised.

"What's got you so distracted?" Sebastian questioned while pointing directly in front of the car, "it's not like I was sneaking up – I was walking right in front of you!"

Boyan looked back to find the blonde-haired girl but she was gone. Sebastian followed his gaze and saw Aednat walking towards the car.

"Aha! I see who has you distracted," Sebastian laughed.

Opening the back door, Aednat flung her school bag in before opening the front passenger seat door.

"And here I was thinking I'd ride shotgun," Sebastian declared.

"This is my chariot," Aednat retorted, "court jesters sit in the back."

"He was my knight in shining armour first," Sebastian smirked, enjoying the banter with the queen of repartee.

Cutting their banter short, Aednat asked, "Where's Sakura?"

Boyan looked towards Aednat before turning around to face Sebastian.

"She has English class," Boyan shared.

"Nice for some," Sebastian replied, a note of jealousy in his voice.

Boyan turned back to smile at his friend. "Yeah, I know of a certain newly-arrived Chilean boy who would have benefitted."

Shaking off his momentary negativity, Sebastian asked, "So, to what do we owe the honour of this car-pooling occasion?"

Boyan chuckled at his friend's penchant for formal English language. While Sebastian may not have had the benefit of extra English lessons in his youth, he had invested copious hours in watching cinematic gems from Hollywood's Golden Era, with "The King and I" ranking as his all-time favourite. After enduring multiple viewings of this film during visits to Sebastian's home, Boyan couldn't help but notice his friend occasionally adopted the distinct accent of the lead actor, Yul Brynner. Boyan had once confessed this observation to his closest friend, much to Sebastian's delight.

"What day is it today?" Boyan asked while driving away towards Aednat's house.

Sebastian looked to Aednat but her face matched his own confusion.

"Wednesday?" Aednat asked, her voice full of curiosity.

"Wednesday the 15th, to be exact," Boyan confirmed.

Slowly, realisation dawned Aednat's face.

"Three years!" she exclaimed.

"Happy 3rd anniversary, beautiful," Boyan said, reaching for Aednat's hand.

"Hang on, you two haven't been dating for three years!" Sebastian blurted out. "Ohhhh wait… three years since you arrived in Wollondilly."

"How did you remember? I didn't even remember!" Aednat said, surprised.

Pulling the car to the side of the road, Boyan turned to her. "I remember the way you looked, the way your hair shone in the late setting sun, and even what you were wearing," Boyan confessed. "I couldn't believe my luck when you dropped your wallet," Boyan said, his voice thickening with the threat of tears, "it was my chance to meet you."

"Wait a minute," Sebastian interjected, "the day you met – the day she hit you – was Aednat's first day in Wollondilly?" Sebastian scratched his head. "How did I not know that?"

On her birth certificate, Aednat's first name was listed as Heidi, the name her father chose. A name to distance her from her mother Áine's Irish ancestry. However, her middle name, Aednat, which meant "little fire", meant far more to her. It belonged to her cherished maternal grandmother, who with Aednat's Grandfather, Cormac, came to Australia from Ireland after they married, and it was in this new land that Áine was born. From the day she started school, Aednat had insisted she be called by her middle name, and her classmates, teachers and family had all complied – all except for her father.

The difference between the sealed bitumen road and the dirt, gravel track leading to Aednat's home was marginal, given the numerous potholes in the sealed roads.

"Yeahhh, it's burn out time!", Sebastian yelled hopefully.

"No friggen way! If you do, I'll vomit," Aednat said, staring Boyan down.

"You have a cast iron stomach, you never vomit," Sebastian challenged.

"Happy to stick two fingers down my throat to make it happen, if either of you two even thinks of driving recklessly."

Boyan reduced his speed, a smile spread across his face. "Perfect way to slow a driver down."

The aged four-bedroom weatherboard cottage stood resolutely on 50 acres of cleared land and untouched Australian bushland. Though modest, the farmhouse had been a place of refuge when Aednat and her family had arrived.

Hearing the car approaching, Áine and Cormac came around from the side of the home to investigate. Other than the few lines on her face and the slight height difference, Áine looked remarkably like her daughter.

"My boys have come to visit me!" Áine's face radiated with affection as Boyan got out of the car.

"*Hola Señora*," Sebastian walked towards her with his arms outstretched.

"Sebastian, when will you call me Áine?"

"Hello, Áine," Sebastian replied with a cheeky smile.

"You boys training hard?" Cormac asked, wrapping an arm around Boyan's shoulder.

Despite his shorter stature and advanced age, Cormac was not one to be trifled with. His background in boxing, wrestling and a multitude of martial arts disciplines made him a formidable force, even in his seventies. Thanks to his guidance, Aednat had already become an exceptional and skilled warrior, long before she joined Wollondilly Karate.

"Yep, as always, maybe a little harder than normal," Boyan responded, before hugging Áine hello.

"Why's that now?" Cormac asked.

Boyan felt Cormac searching for chinks in his armour but held his gaze. "Nationals are around the corner and Sebastian will be competing in the heavy weight open male division."

Turning his fierce attention to Sebastian, Cormac smirked. "You're just lucky that women aren't allowed to fight in the men's divisions, or Aednat would-"

"Stop it, Pa, the boys aren't here to be hassled," Aednat said, frustratedly.

Boyan turned away to look at the brown, dry paddocks and nearly depleted dam, feeling pressure rising within his chest. Spotting the change in Boyan's face, Áine changed the conversation.

"Don't suppose you three have learned how to make rain in those karate classes?"

"There may be an ancient Chilean dance," Sebastian chuckled. "I'll ask my parents."

Boyan looked over the tinder-dry bushland surrounding them before turning back to Cormac.

"You've only one exit out of your property." Boyan tilted his head towards the direction he drove in. "They're saying we're in for a bad fire season this year."

"Boy, we have faced far worse than fire and have come out swinging!" Aednat's Grandfather puffed loudly.

"Yes, you have." Boyan looked at Áine and Aednat's defiant faces and felt the tightening in his chest climb up to his neck. "Please, Áine, you need to be ready."

He turned to his girlfriend to plead his case. "What will you do with the horses? There'll be no time to come up with a plan when a fire comes through."

"You're assuming it's a given we'll have bush fires this season," Aednat replied, her arms crossing tightly over her chest.

"What if it does, Aednat?" Boyan shot back. "I'm just asking you to make a plan."

Boyan looked at Áine and saw water welling in her wide eyes, her fingers worrying at a loose thread on her shirt. Boyan had the upmost respect for this woman, who had protected her family from the clear and ever-present danger they had once faced. He watched as she gazed around her property with fresh eyes. If his warning was not received well by his girlfriend or her grandfather, Boyan knew her mother now understood perfectly.

Chapter 9

Accusation

As if attempting to calm her, light rain fell on Olive's face as she ran, but it could neither quench the dry, thirsty land beneath her feet nor ease her panic. Hating to be rushed but hating being late even more, Olive's pace quickened to a sprint down West Parade. Having collected her new karate sports bag from home, she realised she'd have to come to class straight from school in future. As her sports bag bounced around on her back, Olive was both running to the *dojo* and running from her day.

Her mum had been full of enthusiasm when she'd returned home from school, eager to hear how was her first day at her new school, but Olive had only grunted in response. While she'd had nothing troubling to share, it was all just too much. Too much newness. New uniforms, students, teachers, lockers, classrooms, pathways, toilet blocks, staff rooms, home rooms and playgrounds to navigate and familiarise herself with. And, while nothing stressful had happened today, she knew it would come. *It won't be long until they realise how dumb I am*, Olive thought with dread.

Finally stepping inside the hall, Olive became even more flustered when she saw that class had already started. Shoving her bag under a chair and her shoes on the rack, she stepped onto the mats.

"Hey Olive, down here." Olive looked to the left to see Joy sitting in *seiza*, facing away from the class.

"I'm late, too," Joy whispered. "If you're late, you need to sit in *seiza* until Sensei invites you into the class."

Olive smiled at Joy, grateful for her unquestioning support and growing friendship. Kneeling beside her, Olive thought this an odd requirement and wondered if it was a form of punishment.

As if reading Olive's mind, Joy added, "We're not in trouble, it's just what they do here."

"*Osu*, come join the class girls," Sensei said, his voice light. "I'm glad you're here today, Olive, as I have your new *dogi* and *obi*. Please come to the front of the class."

Olive felt a gigantic lump form in her chest, yet her legs propelled her forward. Standing beside him in front of the whole class, she wondered if everyone could see the shake in her legs.

"It is with great pride that I welcome another member into our karate family." Handing a brand-new uniform to Olive, Sensei continued. "Always wear your *dogi* with pride, Olive. Keep it clean and tidy."

Then, while holding Olive's white belt up high, he addressed the whole class. "A black belt is just a white belt that never gave up. The potential for greatness is given to all of us. You must never forget that talent and natural ability has very little to do with achieving your goals. No, success has more to do with your beliefs, your routine, the people you surround yourself with and your environment."

Turning his eyes again to Olive, Sensei smiled and handed the belt to her. "Never wash your *obi*. You must never wash the days, months and years of training away. *Osu*, Olive." Sensei bowed.

Following her teacher's lead, Olive bowed as she responded, "*Osu*". Shyly, she snuck a glance at the class, surprised to see the students smiling encouragingly at her. Even Aednat looked happy for her. Olive straightened her back, standing taller as her eyes glistened. She walked to the back of the room, her legs feeling stronger, euphoric with the new sense of belonging.

Putting the *dogi* pants and jacket on over her leggings and t-shirt, Olive wondered at the size. *This is massive on me*, she thought, then fumbled with her *obi*. Doing the best she could to tie the belt, she returned to her position beside Joy.

"Looking good," Joy said with a wink.

"Okay, grab a partner and form two straight lines down the *dojo*." Sensei's command prompted a quick response from Joy, who nodded at Olive. They turned to face each other, leaving a two-metre gap between them, in line with the rest of the class.

"Those standing on the South side of the *dojo*, please come and grab a kick shield for your partner."

As Olive reached for the kick pad on the top of the pile, she was interrupted by a voice in her ear.

"Take this one – it's slightly smaller and should be easier for you and Joy to hold."

Turning around, Olive was met with Sebastian's friendly face as he passed the pad to her.

"Thank you," she whispered, with a heart full of butterflies.

Walking back to Joy, Olive held the kick shield awkwardly against her chest. Laughing good naturedly, Joy suggested, "Here, place your left hand on the top left corner and your right hand on the bottom right corner, then pull the pad into your chest tight."

Rearranging her arms, Olive received a nod of approval from her partner.

Addressing the whole class, Sensei directed a question to the beginner belts. "Alright, we're going to work on *mae geri*, which in English means?"

"It's a kick!" Joy answered enthusiastically.

"Excellent, Joy", encouraged Sensei, and she beamed with pride as bright as Aztec gold. Then, signalling to Boyan to demonstrate, he continued. "*Mae geri* is our signature front kick."

Sebastian held the kick pad to his chest, bracing himself. Boyan picked up his right leg which was positioned at the back of his stance. Driving the kick first with his right knee, then thrusting forward his right hip and leg, his foot connected with the pad. The intensity of the kick was heard by the whole room and the force pushed Sebastian back by half a metre. Boyan continued to kick the pad while Sensei explained.

"Make sure you kick the pad with the ball of your foot. Your toes must be pulled back when your foot connects with the pad, unless you want to break them."

It hadn't occurred to Olive that she could hurt herself training in karate, much less break bones. While this knowledge might have discouraged others, it filled her with exhilaration. Bracing the kick pad, Olive readied herself for Joy's first kick.

That wasn't too bad, Olive thought as Joy prepared herself to kick again. After another three kicks, Olive felt confident enough to allow her attention to drift around the room, hoping to learn from more experienced students.

"Okay, swap over." Sensei called.

No longer behind the security of a pad, Olive faced Joy, then took a moment to watch the black belts practice their *mae geris*. Taking a deep breath, Olive whispered to herself, "You've got this."

Landing her first kick, she looked at Joy who nodded encouragingly. Olive looked back at the pad, staring at the spot she wanted to kick, then picked up her right leg and kicked a second time.

"Great kick, Olive," Sensei yelled with a note of surprise.

Olive continued kicking with undivided attention.

"*Yame*," Sensei commanded.

As her classmates ceased their movement, Olive deduced the word was Japanese for "stop".

"Change over. Time to show me your *hiza geris*," he continued, signalling to Boyan again to demonstrate the knee kick.

Once Boyan was finished, Sensei walked over to Olive and Joy.

"Let me hold the pad for you two."

Relieved from partner duty, Olive was free to watch the others. Her focus bordered on obsessive as their knees, hips and legs worked together to create momentum and power against the pad.

"Your turn, Olive."

Olive's attention turned again to the middle of the pad as her teacher braced himself. The thud of Olive's knee against the pad increased with each attempt. As she continued, Olive noticed Sensei Matthew's expression change, his eyebrows drawing together and his mouth hardening with each kick.

"*Yame*," he said, loudly so the class could hear. Stepping back from her, Sensei said, "A last minute addition. I'd like you all to try *ushiro mawashi geri* or the spinning back kick."

Olive had no idea what the name of the kick meant but she liked the sound of it, and liked it even more once she saw Boyan demonstrate.

"This is not a novice's kick," cautioned Sensei, "but it doesn't hurt for everyone to give it a go."

Though she resembled a baby giraffe trying to walk, Joy attempted *ushiro mawashi geri* eagerly, and Sensei encouraged her to keep trying. His demeanour instantly changed, however, when it was Olive's turn. There were no kind words, and her teacher was expressionless.

As she tried to replicate Boyan's movements, Olive noticed her belt swaying the direction she rotated. In her mind, she imagined the colour changing to black as it danced left to right, obeying every command of her hips. Looking down at her feet, Olive readied herself to kick again. *Faster this time*, she told herself.

Turning away quickly from the pad, Olive spun with ease to reveal her left leg from behind, hurtling around her body towards the pad. *Yes!*, she rejoiced internally at the loud thud the impact made. *This feels so good!* Ignoring those around her, Olive spun and kicked repeatedly, increasing her speed, power and accuracy.

"Enough!" Sensei bellowed.

Olive froze immediately, her eyes darting in shock to his face.

"You, young lady, are no white belt."

Olive searched his stern face for answers, blood rushing to her cheeks. Looking away, Olive saw that the entire class was watching her and, judging by their surprised expressions, they'd been watching for some time.

"On your trial form, you stated that you have never trained in any martial arts classes. Was that a lie?" Sensei Matthew's eye bored into her.

Olive shook as her eyes filled with tears.

"In my forty plus years of training, I have only ever seen two people pull off that kick on their first try. So, I ask you again, have you trained before?"

Olive had experienced many occasions where teachers had believed her lazy, disengaged and even stupid due to her dyslexia, but this was the first time a teacher had accused her of deception. Nausea filled her stomach as her throat contracted, yet in her heart she knew she had done no wrong. Whatever this reaction was about, she knew she was not to blame.

Olive raised watery yet defiant eyes to meet her accuser, facing the tall, strong man before her with courage and conviction. Though she uttered not a single word, her bold pose translated that which she could not speak.

Olive watched Sensei's gaze wander across the *dojo* at the faces gaping back at him, before taking a deep breath and sighing. His shoulders sagged and his head lowered as he turned back to face her.

"Olive, I am so sorry," he whispered. "I have made an awful error of judgement and I have wronged you as your Sensei." Dropping his head further, he turned and walked out of the class, leaving his students stunned.

The awkward silence remaining in the class was finally broken with Boyan's comforting voice.

"The best way to change the negative energy we are all feeling right now is to train, and train hard. We're going to do one hundred push-ups, sit-ups, squats, and burpees together – 25 of each."

Breathing deeply, he took a moment to make eye contact with each student individually, a personal gesture of support and encouragement.

"*Hajime*, begin!"

As the class moved into push-up position, Boyan walked over to Olive and placed his right hand on her shoulder.

"I don't believe Sensei's reaction was about you." Lowering his voice, Boyan continued, "I feel your hurt. Your hurt is understandable."

He paused, choosing his words carefully.

"Olive, allow the anger that is deep inside you to rise up and empower you. Anger isn't a bad emotion; it's how we handle it that matters. Suppressed anger is as dangerous, as when it is uncontrolled."

Boyan looked around the class to check the students were moving through the exercises then returned his attention to Olive. "Use your training to channel it into a productive and safe outlet."

Olive looked into Boyan's eyes, listening carefully to the words touching her deeply. From the pit of her stomach, the surge of festering anger was finally allowed free. Placing her two hands straight down onto the mats, she felt the power of her unleashed anger. Bending her elbows to lower her nose to the ground and back up again, Olive felt stronger than she ever had.

"That's it everyone," Boyan said, raising his voice while getting into push-up position. "Keep going, don't quit!"

If Boyan had asked Olive at the beginning of the class if she could do all those push-ups, sit-ups, squats and burpees, she would have told him he was crazy. Yet now, she had no intention of quitting, and it seemed her classmates felt the same.

"*Osu,*" Sakura yelled out spontaneously, a call to her fellow karate students that together they would succeed in the challenge.

"*Osu,*" Aednat called in agreement, followed by Sebastian.

One by one, each student yelled "*Osu*" in a verbal pact, and their voices, energy and solidarity drove Olive on. As sweat ran down her face, she opened her mouth, a very loud, primal sound escaping.

"*Osu,*" she screamed, then even more fiercely, she repeated, "*OSU!*"

As each student completed their last exercise, they waited in *seiza* until the last student had finished.

"*Mokuso,* eyes closed," Boyan commanded as silence filled the room.

Olive felt her blood pumping through her veins. Every muscle ached, yet she was filled with a calm she had never experienced before.

"*Mokuso yame,* eyes open."

Olive didn't want to obey, wishing she could freeze time and sit in this peaceful moment forever. But she opened her eyes and bowed in respect with the class.

As she stood, Sakura came over to her. "*Osu*," she said, and they bowed to each other.

Sebastian walked over next, instantly filling her with warmth. As he was about to take Olive's hand in his, Boyan approached.

"Olive, Sensei wants to see you."

Seeing Sebastian's concern, she smiled at him to put him at ease then followed Boyan into their teacher's office.

Entering the small room at the back of the *dojo*, Olive could tell Sensei Matthew was an organised man. On one wall, floor-to-ceiling shelving was filled with folders, books and small storage boxes, all neatly labelled and categorised. His desk was against the back wall, where Sensei was currently seated with his back turned. As Olive walked closer, she spotted the display of sparkling trophies overwhelming another shelving unit by the desk, too numerous to count.

Turning around, Sensei Matthew saw Olive looking at the trophies.

"They're not all mine. Quite a few are Boyan's, but most are his mother's." He looked at Boyan for permission before he continued. "She was a three-times world karate champion. There had never been a fighter like her, and I have only ever seen one since," he confessed, looking at Boyan in admiration.

Gesturing for Olive to take a seat, Sensei appeared to be holding himself tightly, carefully controlling his emotions.

"Olive, I am so very sorry for how I treated you in class," he said softly, then cleared his throat. "Watching you train brought back memories. Incredibly happy memories that can turn painful when realising they are now in the past."

He looked her deep in the eyes. "Olive, I assure you that, if you wish to continue training under my guidance, I will never again react like I did today," he vowed.

Olive was silent while she considered his words.

"If I wish to continue training?" she asked, a bright smile dawning on her face. "Sensei, I'm not going anywhere!"

Placing his hands together in a prayer-like position, Sensei Matthew straightened. "I am very happy to hear that," he said, his voice suffused with joy and relief.

Olive turned towards Boyan with a smile, but noticed he was looking at the ground, his expression a mix of confusion and concern. *What's that about?* Not wanting to intrude, she stood to leave.

Walking to the door, Olive spotted a large, framed photograph of three young adults in *dogis*, one male and two females. The man was clearly Sensei when he was younger. Next to him was an Asian lady who looked just like Sakura, and on his other side was an Amazonian-like woman, strong and fierce with long blonde hair. Olive couldn't put her finger on it, but this woman felt strangely familiar.

Stepping back into the main hall, the three black belts stood as Boyan and Olive returned.

"Is everything okay?" Sakura was the first to break the silence.

Boyan turned to Olive, and she nodded. Sebastian wasn't convinced.

"Are you sure you're okay?"

Feeling more confident, Olive replied, "I have never felt better." She smiled at Sebastian before turning to Sakura, Boyan and Aednat. "Thank you."

Wishing to break the sombre mood, Sebastian piped up, "I'm glad to hear that, *Señorita*. I guess I can cancel the naked clowns."

Aednat snorted, spurting a mouthful of water down her front. "Were you going to be one of them?"

"Maybe," Sebastian smirked, "you'll have to come to my party to find out!"

Chapter 10
Fiesta

Chuckling laughter emanated from the back seat, causing Olive's dad to glance at the rearview mirror.

"That was a very convincing Drew Barrymore," he said, in response to Joy's impressive celebrity impersonation. "Who else do you have up your sleeve?"

A mischievous smile crept across Joy's face, making the most of her captive audience on this early Friday evening. It was a far cry from the frantic scene in Olive's bedroom an hour ago, when she had tried on almost everything in her wardrobe twice before finally settling on what to wear.

Olive looked down at her outfit. She was pleased with her choice but wondered if she should have done something more with her hair, or if she should have put on more make up. Olive regretted her decision to leave her long, blonde hair loose and rely solely on tinted moisturiser for her party look. She had never been skilled with hairstyling or makeup.

"There is no try, Olive, only do!" Joy hunched over in her seat to appear smaller and older. "Yes, my child, that is the way of the Jedi."

Olive's father laughed loudly at Joy's uncanny Yoda. "You have a gift for comedy."

Joy giggled at his suggestion but flushed with delight. Thanks to Joy's comical distraction, the girls failed to notice they were parked outside of a large farmhouse.

"You girls planning on going to the party tonight?"

Joy spun her head quickly to look out the window, then squealed, "We're here!"

Kissing her father on the cheek, Olive whispered in his ear, "Thank you for driving us."

"You do realise I'm coming in to meet this young man's parents?" her dad said, turning around to face her.

Olive pouted but knew there was no use in protesting.

Stepping out of the car, Olive was glad Joy was accompanying her to Sebastian's party. Joy was fun, effervescent and spontaneous, all qualities she wished she possessed. She was becoming very fond of her new friend.

Walking up the front stairs first, Joy pushed the doorbell. With little delay, the host opened the front door, beaming with happiness to see Olive. Clearly having remembered not to leave Joy out this time, Sebastian greeted them both.

"*Hola señoritas, bienvenidas!* Welcome to my home!"

Olive's dad cleared his throat to draw attention to his presence. "Hello, I'm Olive's father. Are your parents home?"

"*Sí*, Mr Ullman, please come in." Sebastian smiled nervously as Olive's father followed the girls through the door and into the celebration.

The room filled Olive's senses with unfamiliar sounds and smells, yet they excited her instantly. Coming from the kitchen was the most delightful aroma, a fusion of herbs and spices that she could almost taste.

Unable to contain herself, Joy swayed her shoulders and hips in time with the rhythm of the music coming from the next room.

"My family love to play their musical instruments when we're all together," Sebastian shared, delighted by Joy's response.

"This is sick!" Joy shrieked. "I didn't expect a live band!"

"*Mamà, Papà*, there is someone here who would like to meet you," Sebastian called out.

Two tinier and much older versions of Sebastian stepped out of the kitchen. With outstretched arms, Sebastian's parents greeted Joy, Olive, and her father with glee and warmth.

"*Mamà, Papà*, this is Mr Ullman, and this is his daughter, Olive."

Olive was grateful Joy was too distracted by the live band to notice she'd been left out of Sebastian's introduction.

"Ohh welcome, welcome, welcome to our home!" Sebastian's mother gushed in a strong Chilean accent. "My name is Javiera and this is my husband, Matias."

"I'm Thomas," Olive's dad said, instantly at ease. Thank you for inviting my daughter."

"You are most welcome to stay, Thomas. Our home is your home," Javiera insisted.

Olive frowned at her dad, shaking her head.

"Thank you, but I think my daughter would rather I leave," he said, laughing.

"Let's dance!" Joy squealed, grabbing Olive's hand and leading her towards the band.

Worried her father might do something embarrassing, Olive cast a glance over her shoulder while being whisked away. She couldn't help but notice Sebastian's hands nervously fidgeting in front of him as he stood awkwardly beside her father. Her curiosity deepened as his parents retreated to the kitchen, and she saw Sebastian's shoulders gradually soften when Sensei Matthew approached. Though she couldn't hear their conversation, Olive watched as Sebastian respectfully bowed and appeared to mouth the word *"Osu"* before he moved out of sight.

This left her father alone in conversation with Sensei. Despite feeling relieved that Sebastian was no longer ensnared in conversation with her father, Olive couldn't help but feel nervous about what he might say to her teacher. *There's nothing I can do about it*, Olive thought, and she closed her eyes to enjoy the amplified sound vibrating through her body, while the Chilean food aromas tantalised her nose.

Olive opened her eyes to a house bathed in a magical glow, thousands of tiny fairy lights and scattered candles casting a warm, enchanting illumination.

"Isn't this the greatest!" she laughed at Joy's unbridled elation. With her eyes bulging and head bobbing rhythmically back and forth, Joy resembled a chicken exploring their surroundings. Olive stifled a giggle.

"Bamboleeeeoooooo!"

The loud but perfectly in-tune singing made Olive turn to witness Sebastian dancing and singing enthusiastically into a microphone. Anyone left seated got to their feet, dancing in time to the Hispanic music. Cringing inwardly, Olive saw her father draw a little closer to the dance floor.

"*Hola*, Mr Ullman, come join us," Sebastian called over the microphone.

Her dad laughed and shook his head before returning to his conversation with Sensei, who had his arms crossed tightly across his body. *That doesn't look good*, Olive thought, and a small knot of dread began to form in her stomach.

"Olive, Joy, you made it!" Spinning around, Olive was overjoyed to see Sakura. With an East meets West fusion, Sakura wore designer blue jeans, white t-shirt and a royal blue silk robe with a splash of soft pink and silver flowers. Her robe was open, looking more like a modern long-flowing blouse rather than a formal Japanese garment. Olive was immediately in awe of her style, as well as her confidence in pulling off the look.

Above the singing and stamping of dancing feet, Olive heard a voice from across the room.

"*Señorita* come dance with me," Sebastian said.

Having put down the microphone, he was now dancing towards her. Olive shyly looked around the room, glad to see the party guests were too busy dancing to pay him any attention. Lighter than air, Sebastian slid gracefully towards her, timing his arrival perfectly with an outstretched hand.

Olive gazed up at him, struck by Sebastian's size. She wondered how she hadn't noticed just how tall, broad and strong he was. His body dominated the space, yet his gentle eyes reassured her that she was safe. Safe by his side, safe to take his hand and now safe close to his body.

Moving in time with the band, Olive surrendered to Sebastian's lead. Despite her lack of dancing experience, she was twirling and swaying beautifully, with Sebastian directing her movement like a marionette, his hand in the middle of her back. As he swung her outwards, Olive's red and black-checked maxi skirt swirled around her. With her black, long-sleeve blouse, she felt like a South American dancer, and she nodded inwardly at her outfit choice.

"You look beautiful tonight, Olive." His words were like honey flowing through her, joining the sweet aroma of his skin.

"Thank you," she whispered, lifting her eyes to find his.

"*De nada Señorita.*"

The tempo of the band picked up speed and the dancers around them moved with increased energy, but Olive and

Sebastian were content to stay in each other's embrace, savouring a slower, more intimate pace.

A voice over the microphone rang out, "Come on, Sebastian, spin her!"

Olive scanned the room for the source of the sound.

"That was my uncle," Sebastian said, chuckling to himself.

With a mischievous grin, Sebastian spun Olive away from his body to the left. Just when she thought she'd land on the other side of the room, she stopped, his hand holding her firm. He gave her a radiant smile, a smile that could brighten even the darkest of rooms, and a smile that was just for her.

As Sebastian began to twirl Olive back into his waiting arms, she noticed Joy watching her, eyes wide and arms crossed. Olive smiled at her but it did nothing to transform Joy's pouting mouth. Figuring she was feeling left out, Olive thought she should go and spend time with her.

"Come on, Ninja Master, you can do better than that," teased Sebastian's uncle, before being distracted by something behind her.

Olive turned around to investigate, forcing Sebastian to release her from his embrace. She saw Boyan and Aednat enter the room, and judging by their body language, it was clear they were a couple. Following Olive's attention, Sebastian called out to them.

"Dance challenge!"

Boyan turned around and laughed. "No thanks, mate. I have zero chance of winning against your Latin hips." Looking at

Olive, Boyan grinned. "Looks like you're having fun! Have you met Aednat?"

"Not officially," she managed to say.

"Nice to finally meet," Aednat replied sincerely, much to Olive's surprise.

"The whole gang is here! *Dansu*!" Sakura burst into the gathering like a sudden summer storm, electrifying the atmosphere with even more energy and excitement.

"*Dansu?*" Aednat inquired, looking between Sakura and Boyan for a translation.

"She wants us to dance," Boyan explained, looking less than thrilled at the suggestion.

"*Si baile*. Girl, we are going to dance tonight!" Sebastian agreed while looking at Boyan in challenge.

"Hey guys, I'm going to head off," Sensei interrupted from behind the group as he approached. Giving Boyan the car keys, he continued, "I'll walk home, you drive Sakura home when you're both ready."

Olive looked over her shoulder to find her dad. Catching her eye, Olive's dad waved before miming a phone call with his thumb to his ear and pinkie to his mouth. She nodded and waved back, realising he was telling her to call him when she was ready to be picked up.

Looking back to the group, Olive saw Joy talking with a girl from the *dojo*, a brown belt she'd also seen at school. Feeling anxious about her friend's reaction to her dance with Sebastian, she walked over to Joy.

"Want to dance?" Olive ventured, but her enthusiasm waning when Joy looked away.

"Hell yeah!" exclaimed the girl next to Joy. "I'm Kell."

"Hi, I'm Olive."

"I know," Kell admitted, seizing both Olive and Joy's arms and leading them toward the dance floor. Grateful for the loud music drowning out potential conversation, Olive noticed Joy was avoiding looking at her while she danced. Aware she'd upset her friend, she wasn't sure how to address the situation. For now, she simply wanted to lose herself in the rhythm of the music and reflect on the past hour since arriving at Sebastian's *fiesta*. Sakura's words, "the whole gang is here," echoed in her mind, prompting Olive to wonder if she was included. The memory of Sebastian's comforting hand on her back briefly interrupted her thoughts, bringing a sense of warmth to her chest and easing some of the unease in her stomach. Despite the lingering discomfort, Olive acknowledged that it had already been a wonderful party.

Moving directly in front of Joy, Olive took her left hand. "Hey, I'm sorry I left you."

Joy acknowledged she'd been hurt with a nod, then gave a subdued smile. The moment was interrupted as Aednat brushed Olive's shoulder, rushing past.

"Turn the music down!"

Olive, Joy, and Kell turned in unison towards the loud voice coming from the front door. Olive walked towards the sound, seeing Sebastian standing in front of a slightly taller man dressed in tracksuit pants, cotton jumper and thongs. Standing between his parents and the uninvited guest, Sebastian's opened hands were raised in what seemed to be a gesture of surrender. Looking down, though, Olive saw his feet were positioned in a fighting stance. While indicating he didn't want to fight, he was ready to defend himself if the need arose.

"It's only 8pm on a Friday night," Sebastian said, his voice calm but firm. "We're not turning the music down."

Aednat walked up behind him, providing back up for her friend. Her pose was far less peaceful, her feet also in fighting stance and her fists clenched at her waist.

"You're not welcome here!" she snarled, looking him up and down.

"I want the music turned down, Princess", he demanded, smirking on his last word.

Aednat and Sebastian stepped towards the man quickly, but Boyan jumped between them and the man. With one hand placed on Sebastian's chest, Boyan spoke directly to the neighbour.

"The owners of the house have registered the party with the police and, in my experience, they always ensure they obey council rules regarding sound volume." He emphasised the words "police" and "council", making it clear the law was on their side. "This is a fight you don't want to have."

Olive watched the man's anger waiver as he began to look unsure of himself.

Javiera approached with a large bowl. "I am sorry for the noise," she said, her voice soothing. "Please enjoy some of my homemade Chilean food."

Olive could understand how a bowl of lovingly-made food could soothe even the fiercest man, but she was fascinated at how Boyan was able to greatly diffuse the altercation with his sheer presence. She wanted to investigate the source of this power, but she got the feeling it was a taboo subject. Not spoken about but probably understood by the other black belts and Sensei, too.

Another mystery to add to my list. Olive vowed she'd get to the bottom of it, but not right now. Now, she just wanted to dance.

Chapter 11
Discoveries

As Olive strolled across the nearly desolate terrain, the wind playfully whisked the earth into graceful spirals around her. A contented smile curved her lips as she observed these delicate, swirling patterns pirouetting at her feet. Her mind drifted back to the revelry of the previous night, and she couldn't help but relish the memories. *I could've danced forever*, she thought.

Leaving early for Saturday's teenager karate class, Olive wanted to check out Buxton's shops before training. With very little traffic and absolutely no one on the streets as she strolled, Olive was free to ponder not only last night's fun but also the conversation she had with her father before going to bed.

She was still surprised by her dad's admission that he had worked with Sensei Matthew's brother, David Creed, many years ago. Apparently they looked very similar. *What are the odds?* Olive's thoughts echoed aloud, her mind caught in a continuous loop since last night. *So Sensei Matthew's last name is Creed.*

According to her dad, he'd learned from Sensei last night that the family hadn't seen or heard from David in years. Police had him listed as a missing person, but he'd never been found. Her chest had tightened at the news and she'd be compelled to try to find out more about David. But, despite trawling the internet late into the night, she'd failed to unveil any more information.

Even after sleep, the news had a stronghold on her heart, she stopped momentarily to take a few deep breaths to loosen it. It was all so strange.

Apparently, David had been a security contractor, investigating a possible security breach in the USA-based company her father had worked for here. Despite Olive's desire to know more about him, her father said there wasn't much to share.

"David was hard to get to know. He was a mysterious guy, but I guess that goes with the job," he'd said.

Olive remembered watching her father's eyes flick up as his mind searched for a memory, one that must have held little significance at the time.

"David never fulfilled his contract with the company. He left before finishing the job, towards the end of the year."

Olive was certain her father's memory and David going missing were connected somehow. *There is no way this is all a coincidence,* she decided as she continued walking.

Olive crossed the train lines via a small makeshift walkway and climbed onto Buxton's train platform. The station had burnt down years ago and only tourist trains visited the platform now, according to her father's historical account. To the west, she could easily see the *dojo* and to the east were Buxton's small collection of shops. It was only about 200 metres from the *dojo* to the shops, with the train line through the middle.

Continuing her stroll, Olive was unimpressed by the modest offerings of the local establishments. There was a takeout joint, an Australia Post office, and a small convenience store. Olive cast a wistful glance back at the train tracks, yearning for the Sydney-bound trains to stop here. Yet, deep down, she knew the longing was futile. She had no particular destination or anyone she truly wanted to visit in the bustling city.

Looking at her watch, she was surprised to see the shops were open at this early hour. *Well I guess you don't get that in Sydney!* As she approached the shops, Olive could already feel the bite of heat on her skin. The weather report predicted hot weather, and it seemed they were right. With plenty of time before her karate class started, she walked into the convenience shop to buy a lemonade icy pole. *Never too early for an ice block*, she smirked to herself while wiping the sweat beading on her forehead.

Stepping outside, Olive had just unwrapped the cold treat when she heard her name.

"Hey Olive," Sebastian beamed while standing beside Boyan, who was placing a letter into the post box.

"You're eating that before training?" Boyan judged, before turning to Sebastian. "She's a female version of you."

"It's a sometimes food, Dude. You need to embrace a little sugar," Sebastian laughed as he turned to look at the food in question, "but probably not before training."

Olive looked at her ice block and then at both young men, her shoulders dropping.

"You're training today, right?" Sebastian asked.

"Maybe not now," Olive said sulkily.

"Ah, sorry, we can get intense about training and food," soothed Sebastian, glaring at his friend.

"Stuff it," she said, taking a bite of her ice block.

"Alright then, let's get going!" Sebastian said, and he and Boyan began walking to the hall.

Olive stood motionless, unsure if they wanted her to join them.

"Want to walk with us?" Sebastian said over his shoulder.

Hell yeah, I do! she declared to herself. Taking another lick of her ice block, before running to catch up.

Enjoying the lemony tang on her tongue, Olive listened as her companions shared their training progress before the discussion pivoted.

"You are ready," Boyan declared.

"Ready for what?" Olive interrupted, immediately regretting her question. She didn't want to seem like she was prying.

"The National Karate Championships," Boyan clarified, placing a hand on Sebastian's shoulder. "You're looking at Australia's soon-to-be National Heavy Weight champion."

"Oh yeah!" Sebastian celebrated his imminent victory with a series of karate kicks before finishing with an impressive double back flip.

Olive pumped her fist in the air in approval, while Boyan nodded his head gently with endorsement. *How are these two friends?* she wondered. *They couldn't be more different if they tried.*

"Are you fighting at the Championships?" Olive asked facing Boyan.

Sebastian stopped in his tracks. Boyan lowered his head as he began kicking the dirt about under his feet. Olive felt the inertia immediately. Her muscles becoming rigid with the tension of the moment.

"That's a hard question to answer," Boyan muttered, his gaze holding fast to the ground.

"I'm sorry, you don't need to answer," Olive said, feeling awkward. "It's none of my business."

"I just don't know if I can anymore."

Unable to contain her natural curiosity, Olive continued her line of questioning. "But in Sensei's office the other day, he was talking about how gifted you are." She turned to Sebastian for moral support but his focus was solely on his best friend.

"Yeah, but that can be a doubled-edged sword as a tournament fighter."

Olive shook her head in confusion, and Boyan looked up to meet her eyes.

"I feel that those gifts give me an unfair advantage," Boyan paused briefly, "and I struggle with that."

Olive leaned forward slightly, listening intently.

"I won't fight again until I can find peace and balance."

Olive watched the sparkle leave Boyan's eyes, watching their hue dull. *His eyes have turned grey again.*

"Okay," Sebastian interjected, "that's enough grim chat for today." He put an arm around Boyan's shoulder, pulling him towards the *dojo*. "After all, I'm keen to witness Olive bringing that ice block back up in class."

Chapter 12
Registration

Blood rushed through Olive's veins and towards her lowered head. *Argghh, they were right,* she thought, more annoyed at being proven wrong than by her decision to consume the ice block.

With her hands placed shoulder-width apart, holding her body weight, Olive's arms were trembling.

"Again. Another ten. *Ichi, ni, san,*" Boyan's voice boomed with authority across the *dojo*.

Olive's arms were disobeying not only Boyan's command but also her own desire. Considering she'd never even attempted a push-up before joining the *dojo*, she figured twenty-seven was a good effort. Stuck halfway between the bottom and top of her twenty-eighth, Olive doubted she could continue. After all, Joy had stopped at eight. The black belts were still going, and they were showing no signs of exhaustion. Boyan hadn't even broken a sweat. Struggling to breathe, Olive wondered how he was able to keep going while also count aloud.

Despite her best intentions, Olive's arms surrendered, her body collapsing onto the mats below. She lay momentarily, feeling deserving of the rest.

"*Seiza*, Olive." When Olive didn't move, Joy whispered a little louder. "Olive, we need to sit in *seiza* once we stop."

Seriously? I'm expected to sit in that painful position after twenty-seven-and-a-half push-ups? Resentfully, Olive turned onto her side, then pushed her body up into a seated position.

As Boyan's booming count continued, Olive looked around. Only Boyan and Sebastian remained engaged in relentless, seemingly effortless, push-ups, drawing her admiration.

"*Osu*," Joy whispered, nodding her head with approval.

"*Osu*," she responded quickly, wondering internally at its meaning. She knew it represented far more than agreement, acknowledgement or understanding. She knew it meant, "yes," but so much more.

"*Osu*, boys, *yame*." Sensei's approving voice rang out.

Without a word, Boyan and Sebastian shifted seamlessly into *seiza*.

Addressing the entire class, Sensei said, "Our ultimate competition in life is with ourselves." He allowed the weight of his words to settle upon the tired, young minds gathered before him, pausing briefly before continuing.

"In just a few weeks' time, many of you will be participating in the Nationals, in various divisions. Those who are competing have devoted themselves to rigorous physical and mental training in preparation. While you will proudly represent our *dojo*, it's crucial to grasp that the moment you step onto the tournament *tatami*," Sensei accentuated his point by forcefully stomping his foot on the mats, emphasising the significance of the Japanese word, "you're not truly in competition with your opponents."

Sensei paused again, giving his students time to contemplate his wisdom. Amidst the sea of thoughtful expressions, Olive couldn't help but notice Joy's perplexed face. It was one of those moments threatening to unleash inappropriate laughter in Olive, but she managed to stifle it by biting her lower lip hard. She turned away from Joy, determined not to risk further glances at the source of her amusement.

Boyan listened to the words of his adoptive father, words he had heard before but which never failed to touch him.

"For those who are competing, remember Nationals is about learning, experiencing and, above all, feeling proud of yourself. Win or lose, if you come off the *tatami* feeling proud of yourself, you will always win." He looked at each of his students. "For those competing for the first time in full contact fighting, you very well may learn more about yourself in your two-minute tournament fight than in six months of training. Truth you cannot hide from."

Matthew's gaze lingered on Boyan. *Oh, don't start*, he thought, sighing to himself. *I've just had a white belt drill me on the same subject an hour ago.*

"I have tournament forms for all who want to compete – in any division," Matthew said, waving his arm in the air. "There'll be fun divisions, too, like fastest kick but, regardless of what you want to enter, you'll need your parents to sign the form and hand it back to me by next week."

Looking at Olive, he said, "Even if you're not competing, you're welcome to come with us. Support those competing and support our *dojo*. Observers will need a signed permission form, too."

Boyan spotted Olive's face as it radiated with excitement and enthusiasm. As the class finished, he watched her approach his father with a skip in her stride, holding out her hands for a form. Boyan nudged closer, trying to hear their conversation.

"Yes, Olive, we would love for you to join us," he beamed. "After all, you are now a part of our *dojo* family."

"Are you thinking of competing?" Boyan asked incredulously.

"Maybe in the beginner's division," Olive said, looking surprised at her admission.

"You've only just started training," Sebastian said, pushing past Boyan to stand beside her. "Maybe wait a few months?"

Before Olive had a chance to defend herself, Matthew gave Boyan and Sebastian a stern look. Smiling encouragingly at Olive, he said, "That is for me, Olive, and her parents to decide – and us alone."

Boyan saw and understood the look Sebastian shot him. Taking a deep breath, he shook his head at his friend, warning him to keep his concerns to himself. *Yeah I don't know why he's considering it either, mate,* Boyan thought.

Without a word, Boyan watched as Olive folded the tournament form in half, before bowing.

"*Osu*," she said, gratitude colouring her voice.

"*Osu*, Olive. If your parents agree to you competing, return the completed form as soon as possible." Before turning to his office, Matthew caught his eye.

We'll be discussing this later, Boyan silently conveyed, as his father walked off.

Olive's classmates were more relaxed than usual, likely due to it being the weekend. In no rush to leave, they gathered in groups, laughing, and talking. As she walked towards her bag, Sakura rushed towards her in a flurry of energy.

"You have to come horse riding with us," she announced. Noticing Olive's hesitation, Sakura took her hand. "Come on, everyone from the *dojo* has been invited to Aednat's property."

Olive looked around and fiddled with the form in her hands.

"We're all going now, if you want to come with me?"

Another invitation to an activity with the black belts was too good to refuse. "I'll just ring my parents to let them know."

After a quick call, Olive's ears were ringing from the pitch of her mother's excitement. She wasn't surprised her mother said yes, as she'd said several times how happy she was that Olive was starting to make friends. Last night, while discussing the strange serendipity of knowing Sensei's brother, her father had said he felt her new friends were decent people. And, as he'd said for the thousandth time, "it's important to surround yourself with good people."

Pulling her *dogi* off to reveal her cute pink shorts and t-shirt, she was glad she'd taken extra care with her outfit today. Once she had her shoes on, Olive was ready for another hang with the black belts. Looking around for Joy, Olive realised with a pang that she'd already left, and would be upset to have missed out. Shaking it off, she left the hall.

Joining Olive outside the *dojo*, Sakura was radiant, defying the intensity of the hour-and-a-half karate class. She kept walking, gestured for Olive to come with her.

"Are we walking?" Olive inquired, her disappointment palpable.

With a mischievous half-smile, Sakura waved her left hand, signalling for Olive to follow without further explanation.

Passing the children's playground, they moved towards the six-foot-high chain-wire fence. Moving to the fence gate, Sakura whipped out a key from what appeared to be thin air, unlocking the padlock hanging from it.

Do all the black belts have dojo keys, Olive wondered as she stepped through the gate, entering a section of the hall's grounds she hadn't seen before.

In front of her lay a vibrant garden paradise. Neat rows of raised beds brimmed with lush lettuces, spinach, and aromatic herbs. Among them, grand pots boasted flowering fruit trees, interspersed with imposing sculptures. As they strolled on, Olive glanced over her shoulder, catching sight of a tree nestled in the far corner. Adorning the branches were oversized, brightly painted but empty frames, seeming to frame the tree itself.

Sakura caught Olive's gaze. "Isn't it stunning?"

"What is this place?" Olive turned to her, curiosity piqued.

"This is Buxton Community Garden – and one of my favourite places in the world."

Pointing to the framed-covered tree, Sakura continued, "the idea was to recycle old wooden picture frames. I had fun with some local children and a lot of old discarded house paints."

Olive's eyes widened. "You did this?"

"Yes. Me, twenty enthusiastic little painters, and their parents."

Olive stood still, her gaze fixed on Sakura as she spoke. "I've been volunteering here for gardening and art activities since I arrived in Australia."

"How long have you been here?"

"About a year. I've been on a student exchange, staying with Boyan and Sensei." Sakura's tone shifted. "My parents will be here soon, to catch up with them, and take me home."

"To catch up? Did your parents know Sensei and Boyan before you came to Australia?"

Sakura nodded. "My mum has been close friends with Matthew and Boyan's mum since they were our age. They met at an international karate camp and trained and competed together for years."

Olive's jaw fell, her brain so distracted by the revelation to keep her mouth closed. "Where's Boyan's mum?"

Sakura's hands immediately clasped closed, and she slowly rubbed her palms together. "She died a long time ago," Sakura quietly replied.

"I'm sorry." Olive regretted asking the question. She stayed quiet, refusing to fill the silence between them with meaningless conversation. The silence needed to be honoured, even if she yearned to know more.

The sound of heavy hoof beats approaching cut through the quiet, and soon Olive could feel their vibration pulsing through her feet. The girls spun around to locate the source of the sound and saw a beautiful brown horse approaching with Sebastian upon its back.

As the majestic creature stopped beside her, Olive raised her hand to touch its side. The warmth of the animal's body and smell of its soft fur stirred her senses, immediately soothing the sadness she felt.

Following the curve of the creature's neck, Olive's eyes travelled to the rider.

"Your chauffeurs have arrived, *Señoritas.*"

Damn, can this guy get anymore charming? Olive wondered.

"Put your right foot in the stirrup and grab my hand," Sebastian said, reaching out. Olive didn't hesitate. "That's it, now put your weight on the stirrup and swing your left leg up and over the horse."

In an instant, Olive found herself straddling the stallion, close behind Sebastian.

Boyan trotted into the space on a dappled grey horse and stopped beside Sakura.

"Well, are you going to walk, or did you want a lift too?" Boyan teased, offering an outstretched hand.

"We won't go any faster than a trot since you don't have helmets," Sebastian said. "Hold on tight!"

Olive threw her arms around Sebastian's waist willingly. Pulling herself closer to him, she could feel the warmth of his body and the tightness of his build. Despite being only seventeen years old, he had a strong physique with big, broad shoulders, a firm chest, muscular arms – and very defined abs, as Olive was now sensing from her grip around his waist.

Olive watched the Community Garden disappear from behind her as the horses trotted towards the bushland beyond.

"Just behind that clearing is Aednat's property," Boyan called from up ahead.

Riding past the break in the trees, numerous fenced paddocks were revealed, with which a number of horses munched contentedly on hay. Boyan and Sebastian stopped along a fence, close to a farmhouse. Olive dismounted with Sebastian's help, while Sakura and Boyan stood waiting beside their horse.

A horn sounding from behind made Olive jump in fright. She turned around to witness Joy hanging out of the window of her mother's car, waving enthusiastically. Her mother attempted to pull her back inside the car while simultaneously trying to remove her daughter's hand from the horn. Olive smiled and laughed as she watched her friend burst out of the passenger side door, and literally skip along the garden path.

"Awesome, you're here, too!" Joy squealed, throwing her arms around her.

Over Joy's shoulder, Olive saw more cars driving in, as parents dropped off more karate students. Though Olive hadn't met most of them, she had seen them in the *dojo*, all senior and intermediate belts. *Sakura did say everyone was invited*, she thought, then wondered why her and Joy were the only white belts in attendance.

Still focused on the arriving cars, she noticed some of the others beginning to turn in the opposite direction. Intrigued, she followed suit. From the far end of the property, charging toward them in a glorious canter, was a horse and rider commanding attention with their breathtaking beauty. Seeing the rider's flowing red locks, Olive stood frozen in awe of Aednat's ability. *It's like something out of a Hollywood movie*, she thought.

Chapter 13
Fall

Boyan gazed in reverence as Aednat approached him on horseback, her presence evoking a scene from Japanese history. With a deep fascination for all things Japanese, Boyan was captivated by the tales of the Samurai and Shoguns. The legendary figure of Tomoe Gozen, a revered female warrior who defied societal norms by fighting in the 12th Century Genpei War, came to his mind. In silent homage, Boyan subtly inclined his head, paying tribute to Tomoe and the striking elegance of the young woman beside him, atop her black mare.

Reaching up to take the reins, he calmed the horse with the touch of his hand.

"There, there, girl," he whispered, moving in closer. With both hands stroking the animal, Boyan nuzzled closer as the horse lowered its head to rest on his shoulder. He locked eyes with the animal as Boyan repeated, "there, there."

"She loves you," Aednat whispered softly.

Boyan glanced up, his response laced with playful banter. "Nah, she's only got eyes for you."

Leaning up to where Aednat sat mounted on her horse, Boyan's tone shifted. "And I've only got eyes for you."

Aednat dismounted without averting her gaze from Boyan. Their hands briefly brushed as Boyan passed her the reins, but they kept any other displays of affection for a more private moment.

As Boyan pivoted to address the group, Olive's gaze caught his attention. Her expression was solemn as she looked between him and the horse. *I wonder what's on her mind*, Boyan mused, tilting his head to the side and adjusting his stance.

"So, are we going to do this or what?" Sebastian said, interrupting his silent questioning.

"We'll do the south track, the short one," Aednat said.

"What?" Sebastian asked, sounding disappointed. "Why?"

Nodding to the west, Aednat said sternly, "Look! The result of last night's storm."

The group turned towards the distant smoke rising from the bushland.

"My Grandfather saw the lightning strike around midnight and reported it." Boyan noted Aednat's solemn expression as she added, "The RFS is worried because the fire started at Yellow Valley, making it inaccessible by foot or vehicle. They're monitoring it closely for now."

Positioned behind her, Boyan saw Olive lean closer to Joy.

"What is the RFS?" she asked her friend quietly.

"The Rural Fire Service," Boyan cut in. Buxton has its own station not far from the *dojo*. Run by volunteers who are trained to combat fires in our area."

Olive swallowed uneasily as she glanced back at the smoke. "Should we be riding today?"

He shook his head and opened his mouth to reply but Aednat got in first. "That's why we're sticking to the short track."

He drew Aednat closer to him, then said softly, "It's time to start planning."

She shook him off and turned to her guests.

"Raise your hand if you're an inexperienced rider."

Boyan let out a deep exhale as he raked his fingers through his hair. *This is madness.* Surveying the group, he noted Olive and Joy's hands were raised. *And we have beginner riders, too.*

Aednat pressed on. "Alright then, I'll match each rider with a horse suited to their experience." She surveyed the group, then continued. "Boyan and Sebastian will stick with their own horses. Louise, you'll ride Honey. Jake and Kell, you're on Butterfly and Toffy."

She assigned each person a horse, handing over reins with care. "You'll take Sweetie, and you'll ride White Beauty," she continued, pointing to her classmates. "Joy, you'll have Gorgeous."

Heading towards the paddock gate, Aednat moved to a separate enclosure to retrieve a horse separated from the herd. Without hesitation, she declared, "Alright, Olive, you'll be riding Dark Death."

The group's collective gasp was swiftly followed by Sebastian's boisterous laughter. "Dark Death? You want Olive to ride on a horse named Dark Death?" His jovial rebuke elicited laughter from everyone except Boyan.

"It's just a name," Aednat chuckled. "Dark Death is the gentlest horse, perfect for a beginner," she said, helping Olive to mount the horse.

Boyan paced alongside his horse, his eyes shifting from the smoke to Aednat and then to the group. He fidgeted with the reins entwined in his fingers.

"Way to go, Olive. You show Dark Death who's boss." Sebastian's booming voice prompted the group's laughter once more.

Boyan fixed his attention on Olive, noticing her shifting in the saddle uncomfortably as she forced a smile. He had no choice but to join the group. He swung his leg up and over his horse and rode towards Aednat as she set off, leading the group.

"Not a word!" Aednat shot Boyan a warning look as he approached, her eyes flashing with a mix of determination and caution.

Exhaling deeply again, Boyan held her gaze but remained silent. As Aednat returned her attention to the track before her, Boyan's gaze lingered. He watched as her fiery hair danced with each step the horse took, a stark contrast to the sombre atmosphere surrounding them. In that moment, amidst the seriousness of the situation, Boyan couldn't help but marvel at her beauty and resilience. Yet, beneath his admiration lay a fear of the imminent danger she was avoiding.

"You know your mum and grandfather didn't keep you and your brother safe from your father by burying their heads in the sand."

Aednat's head snapped around with lightning speed to confront Boyan once more, eyes widened and nostrils flared.

"I know you don't want to hear it, but you can't disregard the threat of fire now."

Aednat pivoted in her saddle, intensifying her stare.

"Come on Aednat, there is a fire due west of your property – your family, your horses – and here we are going on a leisurely horse ride!"

"What do you want from me?" Aednat shot back, her tone tinged with frustration.

"You're not alone. Let me help you plan for when that fire comes this way," Boyan responded earnestly.

"*If* the fire comes this way!" Aednat challenged.

"No! Not *if, when*!" Boyan insisted, determination evident in his voice. Aednat's bottom lip began to quiver. "Rain isn't coming anytime soon, and the wind is pushing the fire directly this way," he uttered, softening his tone as he gestured in the direction of the fire.

Aednat's gaze slowly drifted downwards as she gently nodded her head in surrender. "Okay, fine. When we get back, we'll sit down and come up with a plan."

Boyan gently tugged on the reins, compassion coursing through him as he guided his horse closer to Aednat. Placing both reins in his right hand, he reached up with his free hand to stroke her shoulder. "Together. we'll do it together," he said.

Boyan felt Aednat's energy reverberate within his own body, like a tidal wave sweeping through his senses. It was not a subtle shift, but a profound transformation from the stormy currents of anger and fear to the serene depths of calm and understanding. As her emotions washed over him, he found himself enveloped in a sense of peace, a soothing balm against the tumult of their surroundings. He watched as her face softened and her eyes glistened as she looked at him.

"I love you, Aednat."

Like the impact of a powerful blow to the solar plexus, Boyan leaned forward, his body instinctively reacting to the overwhelming wave of a new emotion now crashing over him.

"What's wrong?" Aednat asked, concerned.

Boyan leaned forward further, shaking his head. "I don't know," he confessed, looking around his surroundings for clues. "Something's wrong". As if struck by an unseen force, he felt his muscles tense, every fibre of his being attuned to the turmoil within.

Boyan jolted his head backwards and froze. "Something's very wrong," he said, feeling the truth of his words deep in his gut.

"Did you feel something?"

"Yes. Fear. And it's strong." Turning his horse around abruptly, Boyan squeezed the horse's body with his heels, beckoning it to speed up.

Soon, he spotted Sebastian up ahead, kneeling beside what looked to be a body. Drawing closer, Boyan pulled against the reins to slow and stop. It was Olive.

"What happened?" he asked, looking around for signs of danger.

"Her horse reared and she came off," Sebastian replied, without pausing his injury assessment. Olive's face was pale, her eyes open but dazed.

"It was a Red Belly," Joy said, shivering.

One of the most commonly seen snakes in the area, Red-Bellied Black Snake's tended to freeze or retreat when faced with a threat. For its size, it was probably the least venomous snake in Australia, but Boyan knew their bite could cause nausea, vomiting and abdominal pain, amongst other symptoms.

"Was she or the horse bitten?" Boyan asked, worried.

"No signs of a bite on her," Sebastian confirmed.

"It happened quickly, but I don't think the horse was bitten either." Joy added from the top of her horse, clearly too afraid to dismount.

Jumping down from his horse, Boyan joined Sebastian beside Olive. "I'm still checking but I don't think anything is broken."

Boyan closed his eyes and took in several deep breaths. "Nothing is broken," he said, confidently.

"You sure?" Sebastian asked, his eyebrows narrowed.

"Yes. I can feel her fear as if it is my own, but no physical pain." Boyan looked towards Olive. Her eyes were fixed on Sebastian, but she said nothing. "I can't explain it but–" Boyan stopped.

"But what?"

"I have never felt someone else's emotions this strong before."

"What's that mean?" Sebastian asked, and Boyan knew his meaning immediately. Coming from a culture where spirituality, mythology and ancient ways were commonly spoken about and referenced, Boyan's empathic ability neither surprised nor concerned him. It was Boyan's intensity Sebastian wondered at.

"We need to get her back to Aednat's," Boyan said, ending the enquiry, "and we need to make sure Joy and Dark Death get back safely, too. You ride ahead and tell Aednat what's happened and help her find Dark Death. I'll take them back," Boyan commanded. "Help me get Olive onto my horse."

Sebastian hesitated, unwilling to let Olive leave his sight.

"Come on, help me," Boyan insisted.

Holding the reins and saddle with one hand, Boyan used his other hand to secure Olive's hands around his waist. "Hold on, Olive. We'll be back soon."

Passing the clearing, Boyan stopped at the closest paddock to Aednat's house, then leaned over to grab Joy's reins as she passed. Pulling Gorgeous to a stop next to him, he instructed Joy on how to dismount as he jumped to the ground, then supported Olive as she slipped towards him.

"Boyan?" Olive said softly, placing her arm over his shoulders. "What happened?"

Boyan was silent, wanting to settle the horses first. As he tethered them and gave them water, Olive sat on a log with Joy next to her.

With pleading eyes, she turned towards Joy, "What happened?"

"Your horse was scared by a snake. It reared and you came off," Joy answered, scrutinising Olive's face for her reaction. "Do you remember?"

Olive furrowed her brow. "I don't think so," she said, pressing her fingertips into her forehead.

Boyan walked up to her. Upon seeing his face, Olive's hands left her temples. "How you feeling?"

"I don't know," Olive admitted.

"You're in shock. You need to stay seated," Boyan advised. "Joy, knock on Aednat's door and ask her mum for a blanket. We need to keep Olive comfortable."

Olive shook her head, closing her eyes tightly. "Where did you come from? How did you know something happened?" she asked Boyan, her confusion evident.

Boyan braced himself for the questions to come. "I felt something wasn't right, so I turned back to check," he explained, removing his tracksuit top from around his waist and placing it over Olive's shoulders.

Though Olive's face relaxed, her focus was steadfast. "You felt something wasn't right?"

Boyan hesitated. "I can feel others' emotions as if they are my own," he admitted finally.

Olive straightened up, intrigued. "You mean you felt my emotions?"

Boyan smiled, relieved by her interest and lack of judgement. "I felt fear, but I knew the fear belonged to someone else."

"How is that possible? Did you learn that at karate? Can I learn to do that?" Olive asked, captivated.

Returning with Aednat's mum, Joy handed Boyan a thick woollen blanket.

"We'll talk more later. First, we need to get you home."

Chapter 14

Connection

Boyan kicked off his dirt-covered boots and peeled off his socks, arranging them neatly in the hallway before shutting the door on the stress of the day. The accident combined with the relentless stream of parental inquiries he fielded at both Joy's and Olive's weighed heavily on his mind. The cool, smooth tiles provided relief to his feet as he stood, gently massaging his temples with both hands.

Rolling his shoulders to release the tension, Boyan walked to the kitchen and reached for the freezer door. Rifling through the newly stocked frozen food, he grabbed a cold pack and took it back to the couch, slumping down in surrender.

Placing the cold pack on his forehead, Boyan felt his eyes relax and gradually drift closed. Inhaling deeply through his nose, he envisioned dark smoke billowing out from his mouth, releasing tension with each exhale. Then, with another breath, he imagined a radiant golden light entering his crown and spreading throughout his body, bringing a sense of calm and renewal. With each cycle of breath, Boyan's mind slowed, and his body sank further into the couch.

"What happened to you?" Boyan removed the cold pack that had slid to cover his eyes and saw Matthew coming through the back door. Wearing his old wide brimmed hat and gardening gloves, sweat poured down his face to soak his t-shirt.

"What happened to you?" Boyan shot back.

"Trying to tame the jungle that is our garden!" he said, throwing the gloves on the table.

"Why don't you pay someone to do it?"

Reaching for the carafe of cold water inside the fridge, Matthew shook his head, "What and admit defeat?"

"Yeah, I think that ship has sailed," he said snarkily.

Sensei lifted the bottle to his lips and drank a full litre of water, then poured the remaining contents over his head, letting the liquid cascade over him before pooling on the floor.

"I'm not cleaning that up!" Boyan protested, scrunching his face in annoyance.

Grabbing a tea towel from under the sink, Matthew lent down to wipe up the mess. "Why are you in such a foul mood?"

Boyan brought the ice pack to his eyes again and slumped back into the couch. "You don't want to know."

"Yeah, I do want to know. What's going on?"

Boyan removed the ice pack again and exhaled loudly. "I just spent two hours talking to Joy and Olive's parents about what happened to Olive."

His father's eyebrows shot up. "What happened to Olive?"

"Aednat insisted we all go horse riding and—"

"What?" Matthew interrupted, "there's a bush fire just near here."

"I know, I told her, but you know Aednat!" Boyan sat up, trying to shake the frustration from his body. "Olive's horse reared and she came off."

Matthew leaned forward in his seat, his concern evident. "Was she hurt?"

"No, no injuries, just shock and a bunch of very concerned parents."

"I see. What did you tell them?"

With a smirk forming, Boyan answered, "That Aednat was irresponsible, and that the *dojo* is fully and legally responsible for the incident."

Matthew tossed the wet tea towel he'd been holding, hitting Boyan squarely in the face. "That isn't funny," he scolded.

"Well, it's slightly funnier than having to explain to Olive's parents the connection I felt when she came off the horse!"

"You had an empathic connection?"

Boyan straightened up. "Yes, and I had to answer all of their questions after Olive told them how I knew she'd been hurt."

Matthew rubbed his mouth back and forth in thought.

"It's the deepest connection I have ever felt," Boyan offered, hoping his dad could provide some insight. "It felt like some kind of panic attack, it was so strong."

Boyan surveyed Matthew's face and body language, frustrated at his silence. "You know, I have a bone to pick with you about Olive," Boyan rebuked, watching the older man lean back, preparing himself for the onslaught. "Why would you encourage a white belt who has just started training to compete in the Nationals?" Boyan threw his hands up in the air. "I don't get your decision, at all. Or, while we're at it, why you've been acting so weird since she started training."

"I haven't been acting weird."

"Yeah, you have!" Boyan shot back. "You've been sullen, moody and distant."

His father held his gaze. "Well, I guess that makes two of us!"

Boyan's head jagged upwards like it was caught in a fishing line. "What?"

"Let me be direct," he said, breathing more deeply than usual. "Are you fighting in the Nationals or not?"

"What's that got to do with Olive and your weird behaviour?"

"It's related, in a roundabout way. I want you to tell me – are you fighting or not? You've been prickly about fighting for weeks." He placed his palms together and moved his fingers to his lips. "I know your mum wouldn't want her challenges to get in your way of succeeding."

Boyan tossed the cold pack to the ground. "Fighting was never about winning for me! I just wanted to learn more about myself. And, as you said today, nothing can do that better than stepping into a ring with someone who wants nothing more than to knock you out."

Sensei nodded his head but remained silent. "After so many years of fighting, I feel I have learned all I can from it." Boyan leaned back, exhausted by his confession. "It can't teach me what I want to learn now."

"And what is that?"

"Peace." Boyan's shoulders slumped, his eyes resting on his hands gathered at his lap. "I don't want to be constantly consumed with thoughts of balancing my empathic ability and fighting. For now, at least, I feel the constant angst is blocking me from learning more about myself."

A smile moved over Matthew's face. "I think that is a very wise decision."

"Really?" Boyan looked up, surprised at the response. "You're not disappointed?"

"Not in the least," he asserted. "If fighting is hindering you from growth, then having a break is the best thing for you."

"Wow," Boyan said, relief flowing through him. "I've been so worried about what you would say!"

"You know what? I learned even more about myself when I started teaching and coaching karate." Matthew looked at him meaningfully. "Given your success coaching Sebastian, your strong connection with Olive, you'd be a wonderful asset for her, and her goal of Nationals."

Boyan's face froze.

"I know you disagree with my decision to allow her to fight but, if you work with her, I know you'll come to understand."

Chapter 15
Permission

Taking two steps down the aluminium ladder, Olive bent forward to dip her paint brush into the pot. Though unremarkable, she had to concede her mother's colour choice of Antique White would brighten her room considerably. Climbing again to the top of the step ladder, Olive reached up and began "cutting in" above the window frame, a technique only recently, and delightedly, imparted from her mum.

She sat on the top of the ladder and looked out the window. She'd come to love this view. The mature liquid amber tree was surrounded by what looked like early-morning fog. Olive had previously watched as the tree's green leaves whimsically swayed with the breeze. This morning, however, the leaves' colours were subdued, forced into grey submission.

Olive turned her focus back to her room. After returning from her riding misadventure on Saturday, however thrilled her mum was with her daughter's suggestion to renovate her own room, she was resolute that Olive wait until the next day. Though disappointed, Olive could see the wisdom in ensuring she recovered from her shock before launching into a massive endeavour. She'd spent the afternoon comfortably watching TV until the news came on. The reporter spoke in grim tones of the bushfires across Australia, including the one threatening Wollondilly.

Olive had spent all of Sunday trying to erase the fear from her mind, pushing it away with the exhaustive preparation of painting. She'd filled the day packing and moving furniture, laying protective sheets, sanding, filling holes and cracks with putty and adding painter's tape to the areas she needed to protect from the paint.

Cheating the alarm clock of its one task, Olive had arisen just before dawn today, motivated to finally getting some paint on the walls before catching the bus to school. Having finished cutting in, she had now created a crisp, white border, highlighting the whole south wall. Olive couldn't wait to fill it in with the roller. *After school*, she vowed.

Without knowing why, Olive knew this house had been a happy home for its previous owners. She felt their love throughout the space, clearer with every passing day. As she looked at her cathedral ceilings that her mother had insisted on getting a professional to paint, a memory popped into her mind.

"I feel other's emotions as if they are my own," Boyan had said.

After wiping her hands on a paint rag – one of the towel's she'd used as a baby – Olive reached for her phone and tapped Boyan's words into Google.

'What is an empath and how do you know if you are one?' was the top search result. Olive sat down on the drop sheets and scrolled through the listings, then selected one at random.

An empath is highly aware of other people's emotions, the website said. *Their ability to discern what others are feeling goes beyond empathy or understanding the feelings of others. Empathic ability extends to taking those feelings on.*

Olive gazed at the paragraph on her phone. *That's what Boyan was saying!* Her eyes dancing over the words, she was unsure where to read next in the extensively long and detailed article. Despite her heightened interest, it was just too difficult for her to comprehend. *Too many words*. Olive frowned and rubbed her forehead.

Being a visual learner, she searched the article for colour, diagrams or photographs to assist her. A brightly coloured pie chart titled 'Types of Empaths' flagged a possible solution. The largest slice of pie was green and was labelled 'Emotional Empaths', but Olive was drawn to the smaller yellow 'Physical Empath' slice to click on. The link led to a tiny paragraph, encouraging her to read.

'These empaths may be able to pick up on symptoms of illness, sickness and even injury, as though experiencing them firsthand.'

Olive returned to the pie chart, motivated to test her rapidly forming theory.

Choosing the green slice of the pie chart, Olive was keen to compare it, to what she had just read. *'These empaths are the most common and can pick up the emotions of others as if those emotions are their own.'* Olive nodded, clarity.

Hitting the back button for the last time, Olive deliberated over two equally-sized slices, 'Fauna Empaths' and 'Geomantic Empaths'. Feeling confident about what Fauna Empaths abilities would entail, Olive selected the earthy brown slice instead.

'Geomantic Empaths have a strong attachment to physical landscapes and are often sensitive to the history of a place, able to pick up on sadness, fear or joy that have occurred there. Recharging in nature is especially important for Geomantic Empaths.'

Olive froze, her body rigid with the realisation transcending years of self-awareness. *Does that mean...?*

The gentle knock on Olive's bedroom door interrupted her thoughts. Poking his head around the door, Olive's dad inquired, "Are you getting ready?" Olive's eyes glanced at the time on her phone. *Ahh crap!* Jumping up with ninja-like agility, she followed her father downstairs.

"Why aren't you dressed?" Olive's mum stressed as she glared at the paint splats on her daughter's hands, legs and face. "You're going to miss the bus!"

Without pausing to engage, Olive sprinted toward the sunroom, where her possessions were temporarily housed during her room's renovations. Swiftly shedding her painting clothes, she slipped into her school uniform, a foresight she'd had before painting this morning. Snatching her school bag, she turned to face her mother, who had been eagerly awaiting her daughter's transformation.

"You can't go to school like that. You've got paint all over your face!" Olive glanced in the mirror above the sideboard table and chuckled, then grabbed a tissue and vigorously wiped her face clean.

Olive faced her mother again, who frowned in disapproval. "You've still got paint everywhere, and you haven't had anything to eat!"

"I'll be right," Olive dismissed, "I've packed a big lunch." The bus horn sounded outside, interrupting the disagreement. With her bag draped over her shoulder, Olive rushed towards the front door. "Sorry, got to go. Bye!"

While running down her front driveway, she realised the driver had purposely signalled for her. *Jeez, you wouldn't see that in the city!* she thought, grateful for the service. As she approached the bus, the double doors opened to reveal the driver's frowning face. Sheepishly, she climbed the stairs and avoided eye contact, apologising as she passed him.

Searching the bus for a refuge, Olive wasted no time in sitting beside Joy, noticing her amusement immediately.

"Did you have a fight with a paint tin?" she teased.

"I'm painting my room." She shoved Joy playfully.

Leaning in closer to inspect Olive's head, Joy asked sincerely, "How you feeling?"

"I'm okay. I rested when I got home on Saturday, then I was all good to start my room makeover."

"You gave me a fright," Joy confessed.

"I'm sorry, I think I gave everyone a fright. Have you spoken to Sebastian?"

"Why would I have spoken to Sebastian? Have you?"

Olive shook her head. "No, he doesn't have my number."

"Really?" Joy said, turning to look out the window. "I would've thought he'd asked you by now."

Joy was unusually quiet as they walked to the school hall. The girls sat on the wooden floor boards in silence.

"Good morning, students," Miss Bunn's voice was uncharacteristically stern. "I trust you all had a good weekend and are ready for another week of learning." Olive slumped, thinking of what punishment the curriculum might inflict this week. "Due to the westerly change last night, there's a higher level of smoke. For this reason," the Principal raised her voice amongst the nervous chatter of the students, "all outdoor sports and activities are cancelled for today."

So, it's not fog, she realised, feeling silly for not working it out sooner.

Collective groans sounded throughout the hall. "Yes, I understand your disappointment, but the safety of students and teachers is always our highest priority. The community is still at 'Advice Level' yet this can change quickly to 'Watch and Act'. If that happens, the school will close."

As chatter spilled over again, rising to a cacophony, Olive rummaged inside her bag for her water bottle. Awareness of the weather situation making her mouth dry. As she continued searching, getting more frustrated by the second, her fingers felt the edges of a small envelope. Pulling it out, she saw it was addressed to Sensei Matthew in her mother's handwriting.

She must have forgotten to tell me about it when I rushed out this morning.

Desperate to see what was inside, she tore the envelope open and unfolded the paper that was inside. Her eyes flicked around the page at rapid speed, until resting upon the signature at the bottom.

"She signed it!" Olive said aloud, as the students around her got up to go to class.

"Who signed what?" Joy inquired, while looking at the paper in Olive's hands.

"Mum's given me permission to compete in the beginner's tournament!" Olive squealed.

"Oh wow! You're entering?"

"Yes!" She couldn't keep the pride from her voice as they stepped out of the hall. Outside, they were greeted with smoke, heavier now than before assembly. The smoke made her eyes water and rasped at her throat. Using the tournament form as a fan, Olive pulled the top of her blouse over her mouth.

"I hope it rains soon to put the fire out," Joy said, looking upward at the sky. Despite the smoke, it was clear there were no rain clouds in sight.

"How are we going to train in this?" Olive asked while coughing into her school uniform.

"I think we have bigger problems." Joy pointed to the bushland in the distance.

Olive followed her finger to see a black plume billowing above the treetops, both surreal and foreboding. It looked like a distant plane crash, rather than a bush fire.

"Do you understand what being on 'Advice Level' means?" Olive shook her head, both an answer and a gesture of her disbelief.

Chapter 16
Ignorance

Tapping on her bedroom window pulled Olive's attention away from her laptop screen. Looking up, she saw a small, bright blue bird hopping on the window ledge in the soft morning light, apparently attracted to its own reflection. It was her mother's favourite native animal, the Superb Fairy-wren. With its loud, continuous *chicka-chicka-chicka-chicka* call, the clever little birds could lure a fully grown Eastern Brown snake up a tree, allowing the bird's family members to safely find seeds on the ground.

Olive turned her head to look at the neighbour's flagpole and smiled, watching it flapping in an easty breeze. It had been two weeks since the community was put on 'Advice Level', and nearly two weeks since the wind had changed direction. *Another smoke-free day,* she smiled to herself.

Spotting movement in her peripheral vision, Olive shifted her gaze to see her mother filling containers with water and placing them in various spots around the garden. No sooner had she finished than two bright red King parrots dived into an old ice cream container on the roof of the veranda. *How on earth did she get it up there?*

Olive looked at her watch. *Thirty minutes to go*. She wriggled back into a more comfortable position on her beanbag, turning to her laptop once more. She'd been up at dawn again, but it had nothing to do with painting this time. Pumped for the day ahead, her body had woken her early, and she decided to use the time to do some more research.

She revisited the sentence in front of her three times but struggled to comprehend it, and it wasn't just because of her dyslexia. "It is possible that some empaths have multiple empathic abilities," Olive read aloud slowly. "Their eyes can reveal their capabilities. What does that mean?"

After two quick knocks on her bedroom door, her dad stuck his head through the opened door. "Aaaaarrrrre yooouuuu readyyyyyyyyy to rummmmblllle?" He boomed, his voice filling the room and scaring her half to death.

"Dadddd!"

"Well, you doing this or not?"

"Hell yes!" Olive slammed her laptop shut, shot up off the bean bag and grabbed her sports bag. Play-punching her father in the stomach as she pushed passed him and ran downstairs.

"It's a knockout!" he bellowed from behind her. "She wins with a knockout to the stomach!"

"Dad, we've got to go."

"Have a great time, Sweetheart," her mum called from the kitchen. "Do you have enough food packed?"

"Yes, Mum."

"Are you sure you don't want us to come and watch?" she asked hopefully.

"I'm good," Olive called over her shoulder as she ran to the front door and out to the car. Following her out the door, her dad paused at the top of the verandah steps and smiled.

"What are you doing? We've got to go!" Her dad's smile just widened further. Once he'd finally unlocked the car, she threw her bag into the back seat and jumped in the front, watching as her dad took his sweet time to walk to the car. *Why is he taking so long?!*

He climbed into the driver's seat, put on his belt then turned to look at her. "What now?!" she cried, desperate to get moving.

"It's just so good to see you excited. It's what I hoped for when moving here."

She groaned in response, pulling her hands down the side of her face, but he just laughed. "It's a perfect fit," he continued, "like a higher power had something to do with it."

"Dad, that's lovely and all, but can we PLEASE get going?!"

"Alright, alright. Let's roll!"

The mere two-minute drive stretched into an excruciating eternity. When they eventually pulled into the empty lot opposite the *dojo*, Olive took off her seat belt and opened the car door before the engine was off. "Stay put," she instructed, planting a quick kiss on her dad's cheek before grabbing her bag and running to the hall. Behind her, she heard two short beeps of the car horn, in farewell.

Stepping back from the rear of the minibus, Sensei looked around towards the direction of the car horn and saw Olive crossing the road towards him.

"*Osu*, Olive," he said, with a respectful nod of his head.

Thrilled to see her teacher and for their outing, she quickly responded in kind then walked to the front of the bus. As she got on, Boyan gave a quiet "*Osu*" from the front seat, his eyes cast down. *He's not a happy chappy*, she thought, pushing aside further speculation. She didn't want her good mood to be ruined so early in the day.

Several of the karate students called out to her as she walked down the aisle, and she was thrilled at the welcoming reception. Taking a seat next to the person who called her name the loudest, Joy gave Olive a quick squeeze. "First tournament, here we come!"

As they drove out of Buxton and joined the highway, a voice called from the back of the bus, "Alright, who farted?"

"We all know it was you, Sebastian," Aednat accused, sitting behind him at the front of the bus.

Turning his head to Aednat, Sebastian boasted, "I may break wind occasionally, but I assure you, they always smell of roses."

"Occasionally?" Boyan laughed from the front passenger's seat. "Your flatulence smells of no rose I have ever encountered."

The eruption of laughter was infectious, and even Sensei started chuckling as he drove. It was the first time Olive had heard him laugh. Olive was glad for the lighter mood – even if it came from toilet humour – as she began to feel the flutter of nerves twinge in her belly.

Picking up on the happy vibe, Sebastian reached down into his backpack. Pulling out a pair of drumsticks, he proceeded to tap out a rhythm on the back of Boyan's chair. Again, and again, Sebastian tapped the consistent rhythm, seemingly in invitation.

Swivelling in his chair, Boyan stared down Sebastian, but he just kept marking the beat, smirking at him, and Olive wondered what he was up to. He paused his drumming briefly to once again reach into his backpack, this time pulling out a small ukulele. He waved it like a fan in front of Boyan's face.

"You know you want it."

Giving in, Boyan took it from his friend, positioning his left hand on the fretboard. Plucking the strings with his right hand, Boyan began playing a melody.

Sebastian accompanied him, tapping a light rhythm against the window beside him. Amidst the conversations around her, Olive remained focused on the distinct acoustic of the sticks against the glass, and couldn't help but smile at Sebastian's beaming face. She leaned forward, resting her arms on the back of the seat in front, spellbound by the impromptu composition.

Olive watched as Boyan breathed deeply through his nose, then began singing in a rich, soulful tone:

"We were warned against the mud and rain's embrace, But I need to dance in the downpour's grace. They urged us to silence, to bide our time and space, But I declare with courage, set my heart to race.

Be bold, be brave, embrace your destiny, Be quiet, be still, rise above with certainty."

The lyrics swirled around Olive's mind, resonating within her. She had not heard this song before and she wondered which artist's cover it was. The intensity of the rhythm surged and then abruptly halted.

"I reckon you should repeat the second line of the chorus," Sebastian suggested, punctuating his comment with taps from his sticks before singing the line for emphasis.

"Yeah, maybe, but I still think the key of the whole song feels wrong," Boyan replied, eyeing the strings of his instrument.

Wait, he wrote this himself? Olive marvelled. *Was there anything he couldn't do?*

She let out a gentle sigh, feeling her muscles relax as she melted into the seat beneath her. Sebastian began to sing, this time in a different minor key. "We were warned against the mud and rain's embrace...Ooohhh, that's killer!" Sebastian exclaimed.

Boyan nodded. "Again, with me."

Listening to the two young men sing the verse and chorus together, she felt as if her body was starting to float, carried away by the harmonious blend of their voices. Boyan's higher notes added a tantalising layer to Sebastian's velvety melody.

"That's beautiful," Olive sighed, the words slipping out louder than she had intended.

"*Gracias Señorita*," Sebastian grinned. "Want to join us?"

Olive sat up quickly, instinctively retreating to the back of her seat. "Oh no, thanks."

"Come on, I bet you have a beautiful voice, like our *Señor* Boyan here," Sebastian persisted. Boyan chuckled at the comment, and she wondered if he was laughing at the suggestion of his own good voice or hers.

"Alright everyone, we're stopping here to get fuel," Sensei announced, pulling into the petrol station. "We have time for you to grab some snacks if you need to". The mere mention of food was enough to empty the bus in seconds.

Sebastian was the first through the doors of the modest yet sufficient store. As Olive and the others followed, she stopped when she saw him. Rather than searching the aisles, Sebastian and his Latin hips were swaying in time to the music playing through the supermarket speakers, uninhibited.

Spotting the gathering crowd only encouraged Sebastian, and he began accompanying his dance moves by singing along to the song. While some laughed and continued on with their shopping, others were inspired to join in, twirling and swaying. Olive couldn't help but join in, too, though in a more subdued fashion than the rest of the crew.

Having been forced to listen to Steppenwolf hundreds of times when her dad drove, she knew every word of 'Magic Carpet Ride', and she mouthed the words as she looked through the protein bars. Amongst the fruit and vegetables,

Sakura crumped and karate kicked to the beat, to the concern of some of the mature shoppers, who relocated to the next aisle.

Another melody broke out over the top of the song, drawing Olive's interest to the baked goods section behind her.

"Go Joy, go Joy, go, go, go Joy!" A blue belt chanted as he swung a shopping trolley around. Joy stood inside, waving her arms to the beat, her legs bracing against the metal. It was enough to make Olive completely lose it. She started cackling and snorting and had to bend over to avoid wetting her pants.

Eventually the song ended, replaced by more sedate tune. With her laughter having calmed to a giggle, she walked over to Joy to help her out of the trolley.

"C'mon, we better grab some snacks before Sensei leaves us behind."

Having selected and paid for an assortment of delicious items, they walked arm-in-arm through the doors. Outside, Sebastian stood with some of the intermediate belts, his smile sparkling at her.

"Hola Señorita, ahora nosotros vamos!"

Shaking her head but loving the attention, Olive replied, "Ah, sorry Sebastian, I don't know what that means."

As if she was the only one present, Sebastian answered, "It means beautiful lady, we are going now." Answering the hollers of his peers at his display of affection, Sebastian yelled, *"Nosotros vamos!"*

"If ya gunna live here, ya should speak English!" Olive turned to see a weather-beaten face scowling from near the bus, pointing at Sebastian. In response, everyone stopped their conversation and began laughing.

Stabbing a crooked finger in the air repeatedly, the older man's fierce expression intensified. Boyan stepped out of the supermarket and stood beside his friend.

"What did you say?" Sebastian asked, walking towards the man, behind whom a handful of men began assembling, having left their utes and trucks in support.

"Ya heard me, this is Australia, and ya should speak our language."

Sebastian laughed derisively. "I'm sure Australia's Indigenous people would not be the only ones to shake their heads at the ludicrousness of your comment."

"Ya calling me an idiot?"

"I think there are certain gaps in your history education."

As the man's fist clenched and stepped closer yet, Boyan jumped between them, placing a hand on Sebastian's chest. "You're right, we don't live here and don't belong here in this community," Boyan said, looking the man in the eyes. "We only stopped for fuel, and we'll be on our way now."

"Yeah, good onya, run back home!"

Sebastian stepped forward only to be met with Boyan's firm hand, pushing him back. "No," Boyan whispered, "it's not worth it." Olive watched the altercation with her breath trapped in her chest.

Breathing deeply and slowly, Sebastian's eyes narrowed on his target. "There's nothing to gain from this, Sebastian. Only trouble," Boyan continued. After a long moment, Sebastian nodded and rolled his shoulders, then walked to the bus.

"That's right, go back to where ya came from!"

As Olive boarded the bus, she noticed Aednat was already inside, leaning out the window. Her lips were pressed hard into a thin line, eyes fixed on the ignorant man who had yet to move. Once the students had boarded and the bus engine began to rumble, Aednat launched her verbal attack.

"Hey loser, it's called multiculturalism. Look it up!" Her outburst was met with a raised middle finger. "*Adiós!*" she retorted.

Sakura leaned out the window, looking as if she'd smelled something foul. "*Sayonara!*"

As Sensei left the car park and rounded the corner, he pulled the bus to the side of the road. "What the hell was that?" he demanded. No one dared speak, aware that their teacher had witnessed everything.

"We've discussed this countless times in class!" Sensei continued, his gaze piercing each of his students. "We train so we can avoid fights, not rush into them!" Shaking his head in disappointment, Sensei focused his attention on Sebastian. "I know you're all young and feel invincible," he said, "but just because you're invited to a fight doesn't mean you have to accept the invitation. Accepting that fight would have led to injury, even if you had won. It could have endangered our beginner belts and put yourself at risk of legal action if you'd caused that man harm."

Sebastian bowed his head. "*Osu* Sensei, I'm sorry," he uttered contritely.

"*Osu* Sensei," Aednat chimed in, closing her window.

With her head lowered and bowing from her waist, Sakura spoke meekly from the back of the bus. "*Osu* Sensei."

Exhaling forcefully while relaxing his tight grip on the steering wheel, Sensei paused before proceeding. "Alright then, we don't have far till we get there. I think we need some tunes." Reaching for his phone, he asked, "What do you want to listen to?"

"Steppenwolf," Boyan suggested.

Like a dip in the ocean in the height of an Australian summer, 'Born to be Wild' took the heat out of the atmosphere immediately.

Chapter 17

Tournament

It took precisely five repetitions of 'Born to be Wild' before they arrived. Taking in the space around her, Olive allowed the others to disembark first, joining them outside the doors of the auditorium.

The students formed a circle, bringing their arms around each other's waists and shoulders. Standing next to Joy and Sakura, Olive took comfort from their embrace while Boyan began to speak.

"Today, you'll battle your fear, self-doubt and mistaken beliefs on the *tatami*. Trust your training when you step out onto the mats." He looked around the huddle. "If you learn something about yourself today, you're a winner, regardless if you win or not."

Boyan's words were met with a unanimous and enthusiastic "*Osu*". Leading the group while punching the air, Aednat shouted, "Let's do this!" Pushing the double doors open wide, Aednat moved with intimidating confidence towards the tournament mats. As Olive followed, she wished she had such certainty. She felt the tension in the space immediately as she walked through the doors, and she wished for the first time that she was just a spectator.

Lacking spatial awareness, Olive couldn't approximate the size of the building in square metres, only that it was impressively, and dauntingly, massive. It was a sensory overload. The sound of hundreds, possibly thousands, of conversations and the constant announcements over the loudspeaker invaded Olive's ears, while the spectrum of differing team jerseys confused her eyes. Her city upbringing did little to prepare her.

"Alright gang, let's head this way to check in," Sensei said while gesturing for the group to follow. Allowing her classmates to register first, Olive attempted to take the advice he'd given in Thursday's class. She looked at the ground and inhaled deeply through her nose, before exhaling slowly and completely. She repeated the exercise several times and, with each cycle, she felt her anxiety diminish.

She raised her head, straightened her back and softened her shoulders, a lightness replacing her nerves. She felt as if she was in an invisible bubble, protected from the fractious energy and in total control of what she would allow to permeate her shield. She checked-in and grabbed her competitor pack, ready for what was to come.

With new eyes, Olive looked around the space. A young man stood on the corner of the mats close to where her team was gathering. Wearing a black uniform with gold stripes and embroidered logo, he practiced a series of punches, kicks and blocks while looking around the room to see if he had an audience. *What a peacock*. She turned her attention elsewhere, determined not to give the teen what he desired.

As if on cue, Joy appeared, excitedly grasping her tournament merchandise. Jumping up and down with childlike delight, she squealed, "Spectators get tournament t-shirts, too!" Offloading her bounty to the floor beside her feet, Joy pulled the shirt over her head then turned a slow circle in front of Olive.

"Looks good on you," Olive said, smiling approvingly, "but a competitor shirt would look even better!"

"Yeah. Nah. I'm a lover, not a fighter."

Olive found the tournament program in her kit and eagerly began flipping through the pages. Like a honeybee to a bright flower, she spotted her name quickly amongst the list of competitors. The longer her eyes lingered on her name the wider her smile became, proud she'd had the guts to enter.

Searching for her team members' names, she couldn't see Boyan anywhere. That was, until she read the team write-up for Wollondilly Karate. There, underneath Sensei Matthew Creed, Head Coach, Boyan Petar Antov was listed as Assistant Coach. *I guess he's still searching for that balance*, she thought, remembering their conversation at Buxton shops.

Olive closed the program and looked at the back page, which featured photographs of previous karate champions from around the world. One face jumped out at her straight away. With her long blonde hair pulled into a plait, she was unmistakably the same woman in the frame in Sensei's office.

Bringing the booklet closer to her face, Olive read the name under the photograph. *Izabela Antov, Bulgaria. Undefeated three-times world champion.* She quickly flipped back to the page where Team Wollondilly Karate's listing was.

"Boyan Petar Antov," Olive said, louder than intended. Looking up to see if anyone heard, she was relieved to see Joy was proudly modelling her new t-shirt for some of the other team members, and anyone else who cared to give her attention.

Izabela Antov was Boyan's mum, and Sensei's close friend. Looking at the photograph again, the resemblance between Izabela and Boyan was obvious.

"Ladies and Gentlemen, boys and girls welcome to the 27th Australian National Karate Championships." The MC's announcement rang out across the auditorium, stealing her attention. "Today there are over 600 competitors from all over Australia, watched by a crowd of 5284 people. We are kicking off in ten minutes' time. All competitors in the first round of their divisions are to report to the centre judges, who are now waiting beside their tournament mats."

Looking down at the auditorium floor, Olive noted it was filled with numerous groups of mats, separated by contrasting-coloured mats. The arrangement allowed several competitions to be run simultaneously over the course of the day, a necessity with so many competitors.

Looking back towards Team Wollondilly, Olive noticed Sensei talking to his students who were huddled together. She cursed herself for not paying more attention and skittered over. "Nervousness is not your friend today," Sensei warned, "but excitement is." Olive leaned in further. "Your nerves will deplete you of energy, slow your reflexes and cloud your ability to think clearly and strategically."

Olive thought back to her own response when entering the auditorium and how deep breathing through her nose had helped remove her nervousness. As if reading her thoughts, Sensei continued. "Yes, you have the breath technique I shared on Thursday, but there's another way, too. Rather than trying to remove them altogether, you can turn your nerves into a positive feeling."

Finding space between the shoulders of two students standing in front of her, she leaned closer to her teacher. "Nervousness and excitement are similar emotions, but excitement can be used to the advantage of your mind and body."

He paused and looked around the huddle. "Today, instead of falling prey to your nerves, say to yourself I AM EXCITED! Repeat it, again and again. Say it 'til your mind starts to believe it. Once your brain believes you are excited, it will release an array of chemicals helping you remain controlled and focused. Chemicals that will also assist with strength, power, precision and stamina."

Though not a word was spoken, Olive knew her teammates were practicing the mantra, the words permeating their minds and muscles as their heads bobbed and fists pumped to its rhythm. Placing his arms around the shoulders of those closest to him, Boyan inspired others to do the same. From within the tight circle, Boyan said with pure, unapologetic confidence, "Go do what you came here for!"

The unanimous "*Osu*" in response may have been pronounced simultaneously yet Olive knew each teammate's meaning of the word differed. Everyone had come here for different reasons. They may have arrived as a team yet on those mats they would face their own motivations.

Olive's ponderings on her own motivation was disrupted by the high-pitched squeal of Joy in her ear. "I am excited" she yelled out, while jumping up and down like a puppy whose owner had just returned from work. Shaken from her reverie, Olive saw Sakura was already standing in mat section 3 of the tournament *tatami*. "Go Sakura!" Joy called, so loud Olive had to lean her head away.

Signalling for Sakura to commence, the judges watched as she bowed towards them while crossing her hands. Then with the judge's command of "*Hajime*", Sakura's temperament magically changed from a quiet teenage girl to a fierce and vibrant warrior. There was no one else on the mats alongside with Sakura. She was alone, demonstrating her chosen *kata* for the judges.

From her home research, Olive understood *kata* was a combination of karate techniques in a set pattern and direction. A bit like a dance routine, but Olive thought it wise to keep that comparison to herself. From the first time she witnessed students moving through *kata* in the *dojo*, Olive instantly respected the practice, as well as those students who excelled at it.

Sakura was one such student, and it was clear she'd dedicated vast amounts of time to study, practice and perfect her *kata*. Finishing in the exact position as she started, Sakura waited for the judges to reveal their score. Given the numerous combinations of kicks, punches, blocks and jumps – all while moving in different directions – Olive wondered how much practice one would need to end in the exact position they started.

As the judges held up their white score cards, Olive tilted her head to see the results, but she needn't have bothered. The reaction from the crowd told her all she needed to know.

"Sakura Sato from Team Wollondilly Karate has just achieved a 9.8 in the female 16-to-17 age *kata* division. Only ten minutes into today's tournament and a new national record has been set!"

The announcement spread excitement throughout the auditorium, aside from Sakura's competitors. Olive could feel the anxiety rolling off them in waves and she wondered if it was even worth watching the other entrants. Her thoughts were interrupted once she became aware Aednat was now standing on tournament mat number 5, clasping what looked like a three-pointed dagger in both hands.

Aednat was an intimidating figure, with her fierce gaze and radiant confidence, not to mention the two very sharp weapons she held. For those who didn't know her, the intimidation would be increased tenfold.

As Aednat commenced, Olive's jaw dropped. She looked just like 'Tomb Raider's Lara Croft, leaping, pivoting and lunging while twirling and striking her weapons with fierce speed and accuracy. "Faarrrrr ouuuuttttt," Olive whispered, considering the damage Aednat was capable of inflicting.

Wondering why she hadn't seen the weapons before, Olive turned to Kell, who was standing beside her. "I didn't think we learned to use weapons in class?"

"We don't," Kell answered, while keeping her eyes firmly on the mat, "Aednat was training in another style of martial arts before joining our *dojo*". Turning briefly to see the interest in Olive's face, Kell continued. "Sensei only allows Aednat to compete in the weapon *kata* divisions, because of her previous training as well as her dedication – she trains at home every day."

With this new information, Olive's admiration for Aednat grew even deeper, as did her desire to know more about her. There was much more to this story.

Chapter 18
Kumite

Boyan moved closer to the tournament mats, grinning as he watched his girlfriend in all her glory. As Aednat commenced her first *kata* manoeuvre, his eyes fixated on the three judges sitting beside the mats. While scoring each competitor's display from 1 to 10, each was expected to keep their expression neutral, showing no indication of either support or judgement.

As Aednat thrusted a weapon towards the judges and let out a scream befitting a darkest nightmare, the middle judge's eyes widened. *That's one!* Boyan smirked, *can she get all three?*

Aednat jumped into the air as her right leg extended into a sharp and powerful side kick. She landed on the ground with perfect balance, then performed a *tobi ushiro mawashi geri*, a jumping, spinning back-roundhouse kick. The kick was delivered at least a metre from the judges' faces, but the speed and power of the kick caused all three to lean backwards, mouths ajar. *Three out of three!*

Looking down at his watch, Boyan realised he had to find Olive. Spotting her on the other side of the mats, he strode towards her. "Hey Olive, it's time to get ready," he said, placing a hand on her shoulder to break her trance as she watched his redheaded warrior.

She turned and looked him straight in the eyes. "Okay. I'm excited," she said, then walked into the female change rooms.

After a few moments, Olive emerged. Her blonde plait stuck out from under her head guard, her *dogi* pants shoved into her shin pads and black mouth guard in place. She'd crammed her gloves under her arm pits and attempted to walk towards him.

"You okay?"

"Yeah! I'm excited."

"No, I mean, you're walking strangely?"

"It's these shin pads," Olive responded, while trying to move them into a more comfortable position.

He pointed to her legs. "May I?" She nodded, and he crouched down to pull her pant legs out from under the pads. "This should make it easier to move." He smiled up at her, trying to mask his concerns.

"You'll be fighting on the other side of the auditorium. Let's go."

As she followed him, she moved like she was wearing an inflatable Sumo suit. *Matthew's made a bad call on this one.*

"Can we get the coach from Wollondilly Karate to mat 8?" The announcement prompted Olive to look up at the large dark green flag above them, bearing the number 8 in bold white type.

"This can't be good," she said, frowning.

He scanned the other side of the mats, finding the judges in discussion with Matthew. Boyan grinned triumphantly as his father walked towards them, understanding the situation immediately.

"Unfortunately, the two others in your division have not turned up," Matthew said. "This happens from time to time."

Olive shook her head as she scanned her teacher's face. "So I don't get to fight?"

One of the judges interrupted, thrusting a large shiny object towards Olive's face. "Congratulations on winning first place," said the man.

"Thank you," she replied quietly while she inspected the trophy. She tapped on the plastic of the gold-coloured kicking figure on the top of her award.

"You're disappointed?" Matthew asked, seeming pleased.

Her shoulders slumped. "I wanted a trophy but not like this." She looked up at her teacher. "I wanted to fight."

"The officials have offered you the chance to fight in the next division. But if you want to fight, you have to decide now."

"Yes!" Boyan could feel the visceral power of the word, sounding deep from her gut. He moved towards her while staring intensely at Matthew, who raised the palm of his hand.

"It's in the intermediate division, meaning that your competitors will have been training for at least 18 months."

"I'm in!"

"Alright then, I'll tell the officials," Matthew said, wearing a proud smile, irking Boyan even more.

Boyan moved in front of Olive to interrupt her view of Sensei walking away. "You don't need to do this!"

"But I want to!"

Boyan scanned her indomitable expression and staunch posture. He knew talking her out of fighting was futile. He needed to prepare her – and quickly. His brain raced to identify the best strategy as his eyes searched the mats for the other fighters.

"These girls are going to see your white belt and think they're in for an easy fight." Olive frowned at his pep talk. "They'll come at you like a bull out of a gate. Just defend everything coming your way."

"Why not attack?"

"They won't give a white belt a chance to attack in the beginning; it will be a flurry of intense action." Boyan took a breath and continued more slowly. "They will tire, but Olive, I have noted in training you are fit. Really fit. When they tire you will still have energy and that is when you attack."

"Attack with what?" Olive asked, her head and shoulders rising.

"With whatever you've got! Don't hold back!"

"Good news," Sensei returned to advise, "there are only five in your division, Olive, and you are up first."

How's that good news? Boyan thought as he rubbed his chin harder.

The announcement blared, "From the red corner, Edith Sonners from Liverpool Fight Karate *Dojo* and, from the white corner, Olive Ullman from Wollondilly Karate *Dojo*."

Boyan watched from the sides as Olive followed the directions from the centre referee. She bowed as she stepped onto the mats and walked towards the two red contrasting-coloured mats amidst the sea of blue mats.

With his chin resting in the palm of his hand, Boyan observed as Olive bowed to the centre referee and her competitor. He spotted the confident smirk of the yellow belt's face and then saw Olive's focus shift to her competitor's belt.

In most martial arts styles, a yellow belt signified a beginner, but in this karate style, it was an intermediate rank – the 5th belt in the progression towards black. "Don't look at the belt," he yelled from the side. "The belt means nothing in a tournament."

With both his hands now clasped near his face, Boyan leaned towards the mats, waiting for the centre referee's command: "*Kumite!*"

As he predicted, Olive's competitor rushed towards her in a burst of rapid attacks. Just like being in the eye of a tornado, Boyan watched as Olive remained calm and in control, blocking every kick and punch as best as she knew how.

"Way to go Olive, just keep blocking!"

Boyan spotted Olive's competitors right leg coming around from the side as she raised her hands to her head in expectation of a high kick. Boyan closed his eyes momentarily as the kick to Olive's ribs resonated with a heavy thud. Her opponent had tricked her with a middle body kick instead. Rubbing his own side, Boyan whispered to himself, "Don't show your pain, Olive."

"Keep blocking!" Boyan yelled supportively. In the storm of the tournament, he wanted his voice to be a lighthouse beam. Boyan felt Olive's confidence waiver and fear rise as her opponent's combinations of punches and kicks kept coming.

Then Boyan spotted it. He saw the yellow belt step back briefly to catch her breath.

"Now, Olive!" Boyan's voice boomed. "She's tired! Give it back to her!"

He watched Olive nod her head in understanding as she stepped forward with her left leg. In doing so, she hid the movement of her right leg now hurtling forward towards her competitor.

"Yes!" Boyan yelled as Olive's perfectly timed *mae geri* front kick hit her competitor's sternum as she attempted to move forward to attack. The kick not only shocking her opponent but pushed her backwards by half a metre off the mats.

As the yellow belt shook her head in pain and disbelief, the judges raised their white flags to shoulder height. Their short loud whistle blasts alerted all those watching to their verdict. Olive turned to him questioningly.

"Well done, Olive, that point was yours!" he explained. "Keep going, she is tired."

"*Kumite!*" This time, the command spurred Olive to rush towards her competitor with the same strategy as before, much to Boyan's surprise. Stepping forward with her left leg and kicking with her right leg, Olive again struck hard upon the girl's sternum. But this time, she followed up with a *hiza geri* knee kick with her left leg, traumatising her opponent's breastbone. As the yellow belt stepped back, the judges' white flags raised again at shoulder height. Three seconds later, they blew their whistles once more and raised their flags high above their heads.

Boyan's jaw dropped in equal parts shock and awe as he clapped, catching Matthew's look. *How the hell did you know she was capable of that?*

Though strong and sturdy on the mats, Olive's legs turned to jelly as soon as she was off the *tatami*. Boyan rushed to her side, placing his right arm around her waist.

"Here, Olive, sit down." Boyan supported her weight as she lowered herself into the stadium seating close by. "Hell, girl, we're going to have to find another strategy now!"

Olive looked at Boyan with concern. "But it worked?"

Looking at the competitors surrounding the mats, Boyan laughed in amazement. "Because no one will be underestimating you now!"

Boyan handed Olive a water bottle and towel for her face then sat next to her. He looked at his hands, shaking ever so slightly. "That was friggin' amazing!" Boyan confessed as he turned to

Olive. "I felt like I was on the mats with you, experiencing my first fight all over again!"

Olive's face was glowing in victory, not just from the win but from overcoming her own fears. "That was so fun!" she exclaimed.

Boyan laughed but tears threatened. "Yeah, I'd forgotten how much fun my earlier tournament fights were." With glistening eyes and open heart, he smiled at her. "Thank you for the reminder."

Chapter 19
Medics

"In less than an hour, the men's heavyweight division will kick off on centre stage," the announcement rang out, pulling Olive's eyes towards the stage at the rear of the auditorium.

Despite its distance from the entrance, the stage undoubtedly held the spotlight for today's tournament. Elevated one and a half metres above the ground and above the other designated mats, there the prestigious number 1 mat area stood atop the stage, adorned in black and red mats. The striking resemblance to the female Red Back spider, with its distinctive red stripe against a black body, crossed Olive's mind, making her wonder if the arachnid had inspired the colour scheme.

"You listening?" Olive's head whipped back, her attention hijacked. "Your next fight is against the girl who had a bye in the first round." Olive stared blankly at Boyan.

"The girl you are fighting next hasn't fought yet," he said slowly for emphasis.

"That's good, right?" Olive hoped.

"Nah, not really. It means she's fresh. You? Not so much."

"What should I do then?"

Boyan scrutinised Olive's competitors before taking a deep breath. "I sense the others are now far less likely to rush you in the beginning of the fight. I think they'll hold back and let you attack first."

"So, I should rush in and attack first?" Olive was uncertain.

"No!" Boyan shook his head strongly. "Stick with the same strategy. Block everything coming your way and attack with whatever you've got."

"In the red corner, Olive Ullman from Wollondilly Karate, and in the white corner, Anne-Marie Garney from Penrith Panthers *Dojo*." Olive looked down at the red ribbon that one of the judges tied to the front of her belt before stepping onto the *tatami*.

Just keep looking at her belt, Olive told herself. *Far less intimidating.*

"*Kumite!*" The Japanese fight command failed to produce any movement from either competitor.

She's wary of me, Olive thought, her confidence bolstered.

Without taking her eyes off her competitor, Olive stepped to the left as her competitor stepped to the right, looking more like dancers than fighters.

"*Kumite!*" the centre referee yelled more firmly. Olive wondered who would win if neither she nor her competitor initiated any attacks. Stepping diagonally to the left, then again diagonally to the right, Olive's competitor quickly closed the space between them.

Seeing the advance, Boyan yelled, "*Hiza geris*, Olive, use your knee kicks!"

Responding to Boyan's advice, Olive picked up her right leg and angled her knee towards her opponent, but she was too slow. Her opponent punched Olive in the ribs from the side while Olive's leg was in the air. With all her weight balanced on one leg, the punch's impact was magnified. Olive cried out in shock and pain.

All judges' white flags were raised at shoulder length, this time signifying her opponent's advantage. Olive realised, with the red ribbon on her belt, any points she scored would be signalled with red flags. "It's alright, Olive. Keep moving to the sides and use your knee kicks."

"*Kumite!*" Olive watched her opponent advance and anticipated she would attack the same way as before, just as Olive would have. As her opponent moved right on a diagonal, Olive was already raising her knee to thrust into the girl's ribs. The timing was perfect, but the girl showed no pain.

"Again, Olive, again! That would've hurt. Keep using those knees!" Boyan bellowed.

Olive stepped around to the side and pushed off the ground with her back foot, increasing the momentum of her knee which she drove into her opponent's solar plexus. Bringing her knee and leg back to starting position, Olive turned her body around to face away from her opponent, her back kicking foot becoming her front foot. With continuous turning momentum, she then picked up that front foot while her body spun, connecting her foot with her opponent's head – a signature *ushiro mawashi geri* kick.

As her opponent bent forward and her knees buckled, sinking her to the mats, the judges' red flags were raised high in the air. "Winner, Olive Ullman!" the centre referee announced.

Olive moved into the centre of the mats to meet her opponent, as was custom. They bowed and shook hands, courtesy and respect being at the heart of karate teaching and training. This time, as Olive bowed and left the mats, her wobbly legs were the least of her concerns. She clutched her left side with both arms, becoming aware her breathing was laboured, and she moved gingerly to the stadium seating.

"Move aside," Boyan demanded as Team Wollondilly members, who had gathered to watch Olive, quickly jumped up from their seats.

With one arm firmly under Olive's armpit and the other arm behind her back, Boyan supported her as she sat down.

"Is she hurt?" Sensei asked, drawing closer to the group.

"She's having trouble breathing," Boyan confirmed.

Sensei lowered himself onto his knees in front of her. "Can you take a deep breath and tell me what happens?"

She nodded and inhaled as much air as she could but was restricted by a stabbing in her side.

"What's happening?" Sensei asked.

"It feels as if my breath is getting stuck where I got punched."

"Can you show me the area?" Sensei remained calm yet attentive. She turned her body slightly to the right, exposing her left side to him. She loosened her belt to allow freer access to her *dogi* top.

Looking down, she saw the skin on the left of her torso was an abstract composition of bright red and dark blue blotches. "May I touch your skin?" Sensei asked. Olive nodded again, gripping both hands under her seat with trepidation.

"It's okay, Olive," Sensei said, changing his mind. "Call the medics, Boyan."

Olive had no doubt that Sensei's call to pull her from the finals was the right one. Though she told her team she was disappointed, she was secretly grateful the decision was made for her. Looking down at the two dramatically different items in her hands, a gentle smile swept across Olive's face.

There was nothing remotely exciting about the piece of paper in her left hand, except it concluded the medics assessment of her injury. A possible broken rib. *Mum is going to freak*. Olive's smile widened. Looking at the object in her right hand, it was as remarkable as the medical report was unassuming. Though not as large as the first trophy awarded to her previously, it was just as bright and sparkly and, to her, far more noteworthy. *This one I earned*. Pride filled Olive's heart as she squeezed her second-place trophy a little harder.

"Hey, Ass-Kicker!" Olive turned to see Aednat walking towards her. "I hear you had the hardest draw in your division, but you still came runner-up."

"You should've seen her last fight!" Sakura chimed in from behind Olive. She turned around and smiled with surprise to see not only Sakura but nearly the whole team seated around her.

"Did you all see my fights?" Olive asked meekly.

"Hell yes!" everyone but Aednat replied, hooting and pumping their fists in the air.

"Thank you," Olive said, trying to hide the tender tears starting to flow.

Distracted by the noise and commotion behind them, the group turned their heads towards the stage at the back of the auditorium.

"Sebastian!" Aednat exclaimed, turning abruptly. Olive narrowed her gaze and saw Sebastian standing on the stage, but he wasn't alone.

"Let's go," Aednat called as she began walking towards the stage.

"Are you okay to walk?" Sakura asked Olive as others rushed after Aednat.

"I'm not sure I can even stand," Olive joked, gingerly pushing herself up from the seat. Sakura grabbed under her left armpit. "Arrhhh, not that side," Olive groaned, prompting Sakura to support her right side instead.

"Is that better?" Sakura asked with concern.

"Yep, thank you."

"Injuries are always more painful once the adrenaline wears off," Sakura laughed, sharing a knowing look.

As the girls walked closer to the stage, Olive could see Sebastian's competitor more clearly. Olive had never met a teenager bigger than Sebastian, but the boy standing beside him now matched his size. From where she stood, the boys on the stage looked more like adults, two seventeen-year-olds prepared to do what many full-grown men would not even consider doing. Aside from their legally-required head guards, the two wore little padding for their upcoming full contact fight.

Sakura carefully led Olive through the crowd until they found themselves standing directly beside the stage. Luckily for the girls, there was a higher step in this part of the stage area, allowing them a clearer view of the fight that was about to commence.

Olive felt conflicted watching. With her left hand on her heart, she watched Sebastian lightly jumping and moving next to Boyan as he kept his eyes fixed on his opponent. She moved her right hand to her temples. As Sebastian bowed to enter the *tatami*, she pressed her fingers into her head, lowering her gaze slightly. *Would he have found it hard to watch me fight too?* As she looked upon his fierce face, she mouthed "I am excited" to herself, hoping this worked when nervous for other people too.

"Sebastian, keep moving. Water, Sebastian, you're water. Let him chase you." Olive jerked her head up towards the direction of the booming voice. Standing with total focus beside the mats as Sebastian's coach, Boyan watched and directed. Boyan's experience and knowledge was unmatched for his age. Olive knew it instinctively, as did the crowd, whose attention split between the two fighters and Boyan. Even the opponent's coach was distracted by Boyan's presence beside the mats, trying to gauge his direction of the fight.

Olive felt the weight of heavy energy amongst the crowd. With no disrespect for the other divisions, she understood the reverence the crowd gave this division. Reverence that those who have never trained could not fully understand. However, like a cool summer breeze on a hot summer's night, Olive now felt a more lighter energy emerging. Curious, Olive turned her attention back to the competitors on the mats. She instantly recognised Sebastian's expression, a wide, cheeky grin spreading across his face. He was up to something.

Halfway through the first round, Sebastian's *dogi* top was forced opened by the punches of his opponent's fists, revealing his sweaty, red chest, but it was the shiny, brightly coloured material showing above Sebastian's *dogi* pants grabbing Olive's attention. She smirked, knowing Sebastian wouldn't be the least bit concerned with what would likely happen next. With each kick, Sebastian's *dogi* pants slipped further down his legs, revealing more and more of his flamboyant boxer shorts.

The crowd erupted into full-bellied laughter which only encouraged Sebastian to take advantage of the situation. Stopping the fight momentarily to allow Sebastian to pull his pants up, the centre referee appeared to appreciate the unusual occurrence, smiling and chuckling to himself.

With both competitors again appropriately dressed, the centre referee signalled for the competitors to continue.

It was clear Sebastian's competitor was annoyed at the distraction and delay in the fight, which only strengthened Sebastian's confidence and speed. Forcing his opponent to constantly move was to Sebastian's advantage. It was unusual for a heavyweight fighter in any age division to move as quickly as Sebastian could. Olive thought back to the first time she saw Sebastian fight, in the bushland. He didn't move much then, but now it was obvious he could move very swiftly when needed. *Move like water.* The meaning of Boyan's words now made more sense.

While having to chase Sebastian's constantly changing position, the competitor's annoyance quickly turned to anger. And it was his anger Sebastian was seeking, understanding that many fighters make careless errors in an enraged state. Making his opponent angry was Sebastian and Boyan's plan all along. With each step taken towards Sebastian, his opponent leaned further forward, leaving his head exposed. With precision timing, unexpected speed and uninhibited power, Sebastian raised his right leg off the floor, aiming his knee at his opponent's head. The head guard saved his opponent from an unconscious knockout but, to the judges, his opponent's staggering movements backward were enough for the unanimous decision.

Red flags were raised high by all corner judges. Olive quickly looked towards Sebastian's back to be sure of his victory. Seeing the bright red ribbon hanging down from his belt was the best sight she had seen at this tournament.

Forgetting her injuries, Olive jumped upwards as she flung her arms into the air. "Way to go, Sebastian!" she cheered before instantly clutching her side again.

"Take it easy," Sakura warned. "Let's find a seat before you fall over." With one arm around Olive's back for support, Sakura led her towards their team's spot, claimed with their bags, equipment and conglomerate of sparkling trophies.

Olive cast her eyes over the table of trophies and smiled when she saw her second-place trophy amongst the sea of bling. Then she spotted Aednat's name on the trophy that read *Open Ladies Weapons Kata Division – First Place. Ladies?* Olive was surprised. *Aednat had competed against older women?*

The delight she felt at Aednat's win surprised Olive, until she thought back to how her view of the redhead had changed since first meeting her. Where Aednat's strength and confidence had once intimidated Olive, these same traits now inspired her.

Aednat's name adorned several of the trophies on the table, having won several first, second and third places. By Olive's calculation, every one of her teammates that had chosen to compete was going home with at least one trophy. Given the large number of entrants across the divisions, she marvelled at the improbability of everyone from Wollondilly having taken out a place.

"Quick! The kickboxing demonstration fight is about to start," Sakura said excitedly, "let's grab front row seats." Taking Olive's right arm, Sakura led her through the crowd towards the front of the auditorium where a large professional boxing ring was positioned. Olive wondered how she could have missed it when she first came in.

"Let's sit here." Sakura sat down, not giving Olive the chance to object. She noted the limited space between the front row and the side of the boxing ring. *What if the fighters fall out of the ring?* Olive worried to herself as she sat next to her friend.

Loud music blasted from the speakers, vibrating through her body. Over the top of the song, the announcement came, "Ladies and gentlemen, boys, and girls; from the red corner, weighing in at 98 kilograms, with seventeen wins from seventeen fights under his belt, is Gary 'Mad Dog' Simmons." Together with the crowd, Olive and Sakura turned their heads to witness Gary proceed towards the ring, his entourage close behind.

"Ohhhhh, I love this song." Sakura clapped louder and faster to the quicker tempo of the new song.

"And from the white corner, weighing in at 97.5 kilograms, Levi 'Take Your Head Off' Jones in his kickboxing debut."

To Olive's surprise, the crowd exploded into spontaneous cheers at Levi's name. She watched as Sakura and many others rose to stand on their seats, pumping their fists as Levi and his much smaller entourage walked towards the ring.

As the two fighters met in the centre of the ring, their eyes locking intensely, the referee checked their gloves while reminding them of the rules. At least, that is what Olive assumed, as the referee's words could not be heard over the noise of the spectators.

A bell sounded, signalling the start of the fight. While she didn't know much about kickboxing, the similarities with karate were obvious, and she found herself wondering if Levi also trained in karate. It would explain why Sakura and the crowd were more supportive of him.

With her own limited training, Olive tried to appraise the fight and the fighters. She watched how they moved, how they reacted, attacked and defended. Yet she wasn't confident in predicting an outcome or a winner. She hoped Levi would win but, as Gary was bigger and, quite frankly, scarier, she assumed he was more likely. While her mum had often schooled her not to judge a book by its cover, Gary personified a raged bull with his flaring nostrils and a bulging, muscular torso.

Olive rubbed her stomach as she watched Gary continuously advance towards Levi. She glanced down at her hands as she remembered Boyan's message about the importance to paying attention to how she felt. *I don't feel good about him*, Olive admitted to herself as she slowly raised her eyes to the ring.

Olive became aware of a man yelling obscenities to her right. By the look of Sakura's disapproving face, he'd been yelling for longer than she'd realised. Becoming lost in her thoughts was a habit for Olive, even in the most tumultuous settings, but she found it ironic that while pondering her feelings regarding Gary, she'd been oblivious to the gross behaviour beside her.

"Ya hopeless, Gary," the man shouted even louder, causing Olive to move closer to Sakura, away from the man who was drawing more and more attention of the crowd.

She tried to ignore the man seated beside her, reasoning it wasn't her that he was interested in. *Not the smartest idea to yell at a guy the size of Gary.*

"Come on, Gary, with all the juice you must be taking, you should be stronger than that boy." Gary glared in her direction, following the jeering to lock eyes with Olive. Eventually, he looked back at Levi and continued the fight, which lasted another five rounds.

Cheers rang out through the crowd as the referee stood in the middle of the ring, holding Levi's hand high in the air. Gary stared at his feet, disappointment evident on his face. Olive turned her gaze to the right and let out a faint sigh of relief. The obnoxious spectator had left.

"I'm a bit lost here. How did Levi manage to win?" Olive inquired, genuinely intrigued.

Embracing her with joyful enthusiasm, Sakura exclaimed, "TKO, baby!"

"Um, what does TKO mean?"

Undeterred, Sakura shouted even louder with excitement, "Technical knockout!" Seeing Olive's puzzled expression, she elaborated. "Levi's uppercut to Gary's nose didn't physically knock him out, but the referee determined that Gary couldn't continue after the injury."

Olive had missed the blow, and most of the fight, distracted by the tension swirling in her belly from the spectator and the vibe from Gary. Watching Sakura twirl, dance and clap her hands with uninhibited revelry, she smiled at last.

"Oi, you, where's your friend?"

Sakura's interpretative dance stopped abruptly. Olive's body became rigid as she saw Sakura's focus fix on something behind her.

A strong hand gripped Olive's shoulder, awakening her frozen limbs. "Your friend implied I take steroids – he needs to answer for that!"

Forgetting her injury, Olive jumped up from her seat and turned to meet the angry face. The man she had been watching (at least for the first round) was now facing her. Gary was even bigger up close.

"Girl, where's your big-mouthed friend?" Olive's senses heightened as she became aware of the danger she was in. Time stopped as she took in his crimson, sweaty face.

Holding her hands up in a gesture of surrender, she said, "I don't know that guy." Sliding one foot backwards away, she moved subconsciously into a fighting stance. "He was just sitting next to me. I don't know him at all."

"Well, where did he go?" he yelled, spit forming at the corner of his mouth.

Olive brought her raised palms closer to her head, ready to defend herself, while fixing him with her own glare. "I don't know!" she said back, raising her voice slightly. There was nothing she could say or do to calm the enraged beast of a man, who had decided she would be the outlet of his fury.

All of a sudden, Gary's angry gaze shifted to somewhere behind her. His wild demeanour morphed into what looked like trepidation and he lowered his head. Olive turned around to see she and Sakura were not alone. Standing right behind her, exuding a fiercely protective aura, was the cavalry, with Sebastian leading the charge. Behind Sebastian, with equal ferocity, stood Boyan and Aednat. Though still teenagers, each was individually intimidating. Together, they were a force of nature. Immediately, a sense of reassurance and safety washed over Olive.

Backing down and vacating the area was the only sensible move for Gary. As he moved further away, one by one they turned their attention to her. Without uttering a word, Olive knew her gratitude was clear as she looked at each of the black belts. There was no doubt in her mind now. She belonged.

"Well, that was intense!" Sakura laughed shakily.

"Girl, that was impressive. You really held your own," Sebastian said as Olive's legs started to wobble. "Take it easy," he soothed, "come take a seat."

"Man, you wouldn't even know you've got a dodgy rib," Boyan chimed in. While his voice was light, Olive saw the concern in his eyes.

"Absolutely!" Aednat agreed, winking at her while patting her lightly on the back. "An Ass-Kicker on and off the mats!"

Chapter 20
Memories

A bump in the road stirred Olive from her nap, which had been induced by the gentle rocking of the bus and the warmth of the sun.

Becoming aware of the chatter around her, she looked about the bus to see Joy standing with her tracksuit pants down around her ankles, revealing her shorts. As Joy attempted to punch and kick with the restriction of the tracksuit, the bus roared with laughter.

"Alright, alright," Boyan boomed, while trying to hold back his own amusement. "Yes that may have been the funniest fight in the history of tournaments, but," Boyan looked at Sebastian and smiled with pride, "there's nothing funny about him snagging the title of Male Heavyweight Champion!"

"Yeeeaaaahhh, Sebastian!" Joy yelled from her seat, her tracksuit still around her ankles.

"Congratulations!" Olive said as she rubbed the sleep from her eyes.

"You're awake! How do you feel?"

Touching her left side, Olive confirmed, "Still sore, but okay." He smiled at her gently, then put his arm around her.

From the driver's seat Sensei entered the conversation. "How's your rib, Olive? Do you feel cold at all?"

Gesturing towards Sebastian's embrace, she replied, "I'm certainly not cold." Laughter again filled the bus, but Olive saw Joy's shrinking smile.

As the attention drifted away from the two of them, Sebastian looked down at Olive. "I'm sorry I missed your fights. From what everyone has said, you were remarkable!"

"I saw your fight. You were amazing." Sebastian's shoulders hunched at her admission. "Congratulations on becoming the Australian Champion. I know how hard you've trained." When he didn't respond straight away, Olive wished she hadn't said anything.

Olive felt the weight of the silence.

"Thank you, Olive," Sebastian whispered, turning to look out the bus window at the sky. His hands gripped each other, his thumbs rubbing over the backs of them. She placed her hand over his. Without shifting his focus, Sebastian unclasped his hands and gently squeezed hers. Determined to give Sebastian the space to think, she stayed silent, observing his distant, pensive expression. Eventually, he cleared his throat quietly and turned his eyes to her.

"It's a great feeling to be number one, but I just wanted to win for Boyan," he confessed. A flood of questions surged into

Olive's mind, but she pushed them aside, focusing on listening to whatever he needed to share.

"I was very young when my family and I moved here from Chile." Olive watched quietly as his eyes started to glisten. "I didn't speak much English when I started primary school. I looked different to the other kids, and they certainly couldn't communicate with me." He nodded his head with the perspective that comes with time. "Perhaps they resented the extra attention the teacher had to give me. I was just trying to survive each day in a strange world. Perhaps that's why I didn't witness their growing resentment until it turned physical."

Olive's eyes began to well as she squeezed Sebastian's hand. "It started with bumping me, which they claimed were accidental. It wasn't long before I was trying to avoid their attacks at lunch time and while walking home…every day. Most days it was four against one."

Smiling darkly, Sebastian continued, "I never knew what they were saying when they were laying into me. Their words were redundant anyway. The bruising was a language I became very familiar with."

With every inch of determination, Olive held back her tears and anger, allowing Sebastian to go on, "I am not sure how many months had passed before I had the idea of taking the long way home through the school oval. I figured I would ditch them, but they followed me from the moment I left the classroom. The beating started off like every other, until I heard his voice. I'll never forget it."

Hope crept into Sebastian's tone. "It was like a ghost had grabbed the boy holding me down, and hurled him backwards." This wasn't where Olive had thought the story was going. "Dazed, I got up and saw a boy from the year above me, taking on the four of them by himself. I must have stood staring for a while as the kid yelled at me – which, of course, I didn't understand, until he started gesturing for me to help him." He looked at Olive and announced, "Well, that's the story."

She looked intently at him, waiting for further explanation. "What happened then?"

"Let's just say that was my first, unofficial, bare-knuckle fighting lesson."

Grinning at the memory, Sebastian added, "Being suspended for two weeks was well worth it." He nodded his head towards Boyan. "We have been best friends ever since, even if we didn't really understand each other in the beginning."

Taking a moment to reflect upon the injustice, Olive asked, "Were you the only one who got suspended?"

"No, all six of us got suspended," he clarified, "but those four boys never returned to school afterwards."

With a while to go till they returned to Wollondilly, Sensei pulled over to a rest area. "Anyone need a toilet break or to stretch their legs?" he asked.

While most vacated the bus, Sensei turned to look at the two remaining in the back seat, eyeballing Sebastian. Sebastian nodded his understanding at what Olive assumed was a reminder to be a gentleman.

Though thrilled to be left alone with him for the first time, a flutter of nerves crept into her stomach as she observed the others through the bus window. Feeling Sebastian's hand touch her cheek, she turned her head slowly towards him, meeting his gaze with a mix of anticipation and affection. In the quiet intimacy of the bus and with the gentle hum of the laughter outside, Sebastian leaned in slowly, his eyes searching hers for permission.

"May I?" he asked softly, his voice barely above a whisper, his breath warm against her face.

With a smile playing on her lips and a nod of her head, Olive gave her consent, her heart pounding in her chest. Sebastian's touch was gentle as he moved his right hand to cup her cheek, his fingers tracing the curve of her jaw with a tender caress. Closing the distance between them, Sebastian's lips met hers in a soft, sweet kiss, sending a rush of warmth through her body. Time stood still for Olive in that moment, lost in the sensation of their connection. It was her first kiss. A kiss she would never forget.

Coming out of the toilets, Boyan caught sight of his best mate sitting at the back of the bus closely with Olive. A wide, genuine smile lit up his face, brimming with happiness for his friend. Turning his head to the left, he saw Matthew on top of a wooden picnic table by himself. He watched as his teacher and adopted father reached into his back pocket and pull out his wallet.

Boyan took a step towards him but stopped. Even from this distance he could see that, behind the clear plastic window in Sensei's wallet, was not his driver's licence but a small photograph. Boyan lowered his gaze and sighed. Turning his head towards the laughter coming from the swings in the playground, Boyan sighed deeper before turning his gaze back towards the only father he had ever known.

"Hey," Boyan called as he approached.

Matthew stopped caressing the side of the photograph and looked up. "Hey."

As Boyan suspected, the small photograph was a reduced copy of the image hanging in the office at the *dojo*. "May I?" Boyan asked, extending his hand.

Looking at Matthew's face first, Boyan remarked, "You haven't changed much," then looked at the two beautiful young women beside him. "If I didn't know better, I would swear this is Sakura. When was this taken again?"

"A few years before that infamous international tournament." Boyan nodded but remained quiet, sensing there was more to come. "Long before I opened my own *dojo*, before Asami married and..." he stopped.

Without taking his eyes off the beautiful blonde-haired woman in the photo, Boyan spoke the words that Matthew could not, even after all these years. "Before my mum died."

"...and before you were born."

A tightness gripped Boyan's throat as he struggled to clear the constriction. "You loved her, didn't you?" Boyan looked up from the photo. "More than a friend would."

"Your eyes turn grey just like hers," he whispered, exhaling. "I had never met any woman like her nor have I since." A smile crept on Sensei's face betraying his melancholy heart. "You remind me so much of her. She was the most remarkable fighter I have ever seen."

Boyan frowned. "You're changing the subject."

"Yeah, I guess I am," he laughed. Looking back at the photograph, he said, "I still remember this time," Boyan saw his eyes moisten, "when I still believed she could love me, too. That we could be more than friends and training partners, but..." he paused and looked into the distance, his eyes glazed. "I wonder if she had already met your father when this photograph was taken. I have searched this photo and my memories for years, but I just don't know for sure who your father is or when she started to fall for him." He took a deep breath and looked at Boyan. "But, yes, I loved her and love her still."

Ignoring the mention of his possible biological father, Boyan remained silent, feeling Matthew's deep love and his loss.

"Not long after this photograph was taken, Asami and I lost contact with her. She became very secretive and aloof. The next time I heard from your mum was years later–" he shook his head. "Ahh, you've heard this story before."

"When she rang you and Asami to be on her coaching support team for the tournament?" Boyan asked, knowing it was true but wanting to hear the details once again.

"You were so small, bundled up in her arms with a blanket around you." He rustled Boyan's hair affectionately. "Your mum certainly didn't need our help to win that tournament. I think she asked as a way of introducing you to us."

"That must have been hard for you."

"I think she was trying to set me free of the chains of unrequited love."

"By ripping off the band-aid?" Boyan sided with Matthew, thinking his mother had been insensitive.

"You know, I may never have got the chance to love your mother, but I was blessed with loving and raising her only child." Matthew gripped his shoulder and looked at him earnestly. "I love you, Boyan."

Chapter 21
Celebration

Casting a warm glow across the room, the sun peeked through Olive's bedroom curtains. The gentle hum of birds chirping outside her window added to the peaceful ambiance of her room, and a smile spread across Olive's face as she stretched her legs downwards in the bed and sighed. *Ahh, Sundays.*

She rolled to the side to reach for her phone, then stopped abruptly, remembering what Aednat had shared about her morning routine. No screen time until she'd meditated and had some water, sunlight and exercise.

With a sense of anticipation, Olive swung her legs over the side of the bed, relishing the feeling of the cool wooden floorboards beneath her feet. Drawing the curtains open to allow the sunlight full access to her face, arms and legs, she savoured the moment before attempting some of the mildly challenging stretches and yoga poses she'd seen Aednat do before and after class. Feeling her left side start to protest, she stopped, deciding she should probably rest it after yesterday's battering.

Becoming aware of the dryness in her mouth, she made a mental note to hydrate before moving her body in the morning. *Tomorrow*, she thought as she reached for her water bottle and took a sip, humming a tune softly as she headed towards the kitchen.

"Good morning!" Olive chirped as she entered.

Her mother, caught in a flurry of cooking, turned to her in surprise. "You're awfully cheerful this morning!"

"Let me do breakfast for you and Dad," Olive suggested, grabbing a chopping board. She began slicing an assortment of fruits as her mother watched with a mix of curiosity and encouragement.

"Thank you, sweetheart, that would be lovely, but remember what the doctor said yesterday."

At the mention of the doctor, Olive's father entered the kitchen. "Is your rib feeling any better today?" he inquired.

"I've never felt better!" She smiled, noticing her parents exchanging puzzled glances at her sudden enthusiasm.

"I'm just relieved we could get you in for an X-ray at a decent hour. We were lucky Bowral wasn't too busy last night."

"Remember what the doctor said. Even though nothing is broken, you need to take it easy for the next few days," her father added, concern evident in his tone.

As Olive placed a large pile of freshly cooked pancakes and a bowl of fruit salad on the dining table, her dad looked at her quizzically. "This is a first!"

"Thought I'd treat you and Mum." Without another word, she moved the pancakes closer to her parents, along with clean plates, cutlery and maple syrup. Gesturing towards the pancakes, Olive stood with a grinning smile, encouraging her parents to eat.

"So, what do you think? I added a third of a cup of almond flour to boost the protein."

Olive's mum's eyes opened wide. "These are really good!" she said, before taking a second bite.

As testament to the success of Olive's cooking experiment, silence descended as the three sat eating. Once they'd had their fill, her dad spoke up.

"Still feeling proud of your achievement yesterday?"

"It was the best day ever," Olive exclaimed. Like unblocking an obstructed water pipe, she gushed with the details of the day's events all over again, even sharing her special connection with Sebastian. She smiled to herself as she remembered the tender kiss in the bus but decided to omit this part of the story for her parents.

Standing to collect the breakfast plates, her dad intervened. "Let me do that, Ollie." As if on cue, Olive's phone beeped, announcing an incoming text message.

Forgetting her father's suggestion to take it easy, Olive ran to the kitchen bench to grab her phone. *Buenos días, Preciosa*, the text read. She hadn't needed to read who the sender was, or look up a translation, knowing it was a declaration of affection. When the bus had pulled up at the *dojo* yesterday afternoon, Sebastian had finally asked for her number. Forgetting her parents were observing, Olive didn't attempt to hide her excitement as she read through his text.

Savouring every word, Olive read slowly, then jumped with excitement as she read his final words. She turned quickly to her parents. "The team are getting together to celebrate our tournament achievements." Without waiting for the questions she knew would come, she said, "It's at Sensei's house and, yes, he'll be chaperoning." Surveying her parent's faces for a hint of their response, she asked desperately, "can I go?"

Without hesitation, they replied in unison, "Of course."

"Make sure you take your phone in case you need us," her mum added.

"Maybe I should drive you?" her dad recommended.

"Why?" Olive said, repulsion in her voice. "I can walk."

"Well, at least you're not suggesting running with your injury," he conceded.

She kissed them both on the top of the head, before turning quickly to get ready. After changing into a casual but cute outfit, she returned to the dining room with rapid speed to grab her jacket and phone, deliberately leaving the ear plugs behind. When she reached the door, she spun back around to face them. "I love you both," she said, then walked out of the house.

Olive was greeted with throat-clogging smoke and she could barely see to the other side of the road. She'd been too wrapped up in making breakfast, and her own happy thoughts, to notice the wind had changed direction since she woke up. With such poor visibility, she decided to stick to the road rather than take the short cut through the bushland to Sensei's house.

Though Olive's heart raced with excitement, her meandering pace honoured the weather conditions and her throbbing injury. She cradled her side as she walked. *I wouldn't want to know what a break feels like.*

Obeying the sign on the front door that said *just come in*, Olive turned the handle and entered, smiling as she noted multiple pair of shoes lined up along the hallway. *Just like the dojo*, Olive thought as she scanned the shoes to work out who'd arrived.

Like a shoe guard of honour, she walked down the hallway, enjoying the cool of the tiles through her socks.

"Ass-Kicker!" Olive looked up, seeing various team members dotting the space ahead. "Ass-Kicker! Ass-Kicker! Ass-Kicker!" the chanting continued. Smiling, Olive moved behind the kitchen counter, looking shyly at the ground.

"No, girl, you are no wallflower!" Aednat said, grabbing Olive's hand to lead her into the centre of the living room.

"I've seen the video of Olive's fights – thanks to Kell," Aednat announced, nodding to the brown belt, who waved her phone in the air. "Astonishing, absolutely astonishing!" She raised Olive's arm in the air. "In all my years of training, I've never seen a beginner fight like Olive. She is one fighter to watch!"

Olive fiddled with her fingers and shuffled her feet, but held Aednat's meaningful gaze. "I just did what Boyan told me to do." Olive turned to see Boyan shaking his head.

"Boyan is a remarkable coach, far beyond his years, but what I witnessed wasn't just Boyan's doing," Sensei said, stepping into the room. "Olive, you are an impressive fighter." A smile crept across his usually serious face. "I think Ass-Kicker is an appropriate title for you."

Olive nodded her head in appreciation. "*Osu*, thank you." She enjoyed this playful side of him, though it wasn't for long. While still smiling, she saw the shadows return to his eyes.

"Enjoy the party, Team Wollondilly. You all deserve it." Sensei said, then left the room. "May I offer you a *hors d'oeuvre*, Madam?" Olive turned to see Sebastian holding an array of small finger foods on a wooden platter. With a tea towel hanging over his left arm, he nudged the platter closer to her.

"Damn, could you be anymore charming?" she said aloud. Her face grew hot as she realised her thoughts had escaped the confinements of her mouth.

"Madam, that is music to my ears."

"You shall refer to her as Ass-Kicker," Aednat interjected.

"She does kick ass, but I shall refer to her as *Preciosa;* simply lovely." Aednat rolled her eyes as she pretended to stick her finger in her throat. She walked away in mock revulsion.

"*Hors d'oeuvre*?" Sebastian asked again.

"I'd actually like to sit down", Olive confessed. "The smoke on the walk over was a bit much."

"Sebastian rushed to put the platter down. "Let me help you," he said, offering his hand.

"Thank you, but I'm good," Olive laughed as she sat down on the leather couch, then reconsidered. "Actually, a glass of water would be good."

"On it!" Sebastian confirmed as he raced away.

Now that she was out of the spotlight, she took a moment to look at her surroundings. Sakura was busy in the kitchen with others, filling up the drink containers with what appeared to be mocktails, while Aednat sat with Kell at the dining table. Looking through the glass sliding doors onto the back deck, Olive spotted Joy amongst the gathering crowd. She had a bright red stocking tied around her waist, with something small and round in the end of it. Some of the karate students had gathered around her, yelling encouragingly as she thrust her hips forward and around, attempting to hit the ball on the ground in front of her. Olive laughed out loud. *She's so random. And so awesome.*

"Hey, how you feeling?" Boyan came to sit beside her.

"Sore but okay. According to the x-ray, my ribs aren't broken, just bruised."

"Stoked to hear that!" Boyan replied with a genuinely relieved smile.

"Thanks for yesterday. Your advice really helped." He nodded in acknowledgement, but said nothing. "Can I ask you a question?" Olive asked, breaking the silence.

"Anything."

"Why didn't you fight yesterday? Was it something to do with that balance thing you mentioned? What did you mean by that?" Having finally gotten the courage to ask the question she'd been thinking about for weeks, the words rushed out from her.

He looked surprised at the question. After a long moment, he took a deep breath and exhaled slowly. "Having strength, skill and smarts is all well and good, but without compassion, respect and control, they're worth bugger all."

"But you have all those things!"

"Thanks mate." He looked at his hands, clasped in his lap. "It has to be next level for me, because of my skills. My mum had similar skills, too, you know."

"Izabela Antov," she said. Boyan looked at her, startled. Olive was quick to explain. "I saw her name and photograph in the tournament program. I recognised her face from the photograph in Sensei's office."

Boyan was motionless for what felt to Olive like an eternity. Finally nodding his head, he replied, "To me, Mum was all about warmth, love and safety, you know? But to everyone else, she was this legendary fighter, like one of the best they'd ever seen."

He reached forward to grab his water bottle from the coffee table and took a sip. "Her final bout at Internationals has become the stuff of legend." Desperate for more information, Olive nearly bit her tongue off in her resolve to remain quiet. "She never lost a match to anyone, but she was always striving to balance her fighting skills with compassion." Olive sat frozen. "Ah, my bad. This is all pretty intense, huh?"

"No, I'd like to hear more," she said. "My biological mum died a long time ago, too. I think it's lovely you talk about her."

"Thank you," Boyan said, his voice husky, "I'm sorry about your mum."

"Thanks, but it's okay. I never knew her. Can I ask you one more question?"

"Sure."

"By 'abilities', I assume you mean more than karate skills?"

"You're right. You remember when I mentioned how I can feel other people's emotions like they're mine?" Olive nodded as she leaned in. "My mum experienced the same thing."

"You're talking about empathic ability, aren't you?"

For the second time in the conversation, Boyan looked at her in shock. "You- you know about empaths?" he stuttered.

Olive pushed herself up to sit straighter. "Um...I've been doing some research. Ever since the horse riding accident, when you told me about your ability."

"And what did you find out?"

Thrilled to finally share that what had been tumbling around her brain for days, the words spilled from her. "I know there are different empathic abilities. Like physical empaths, geomantic empaths and fauna empaths, and lots more." Olive paused, noticing Boyan's eyes turning an iridescent blue. "What I found really fascinating is that physical empaths not only can feel other's emotions but also can feel their physical pain!"

Boyan stared intently at Olive as she continued. "I also read empathic ability often runs in families."

Olive watched the brightness fade from his eyes.

"Yes, I'm an empath and my mum was one also, but I actually believe everyone probably has this ability but have no idea about it or how to strengthen it." Boyan took a deep breath. "Apparently my mum was a very strong physical empath. She could, as you found in your research, physically feel other's pain." Now it was Olive's turn to gawk. "Loads of physical empaths end up in medical jobs but, for Mum, it gave her a leg up in fights. No matter how tough or sly her opponents were, she'd feel their injuries and use them to her advantage."

Olive nodded her understanding while remaining silent. "I was just a kid when Mum had her last fight. She messed up her opponent's leg badly." Boyan's eye's rose towards the kitchen to where Sakura was. "Sensei Sato, Sakura's mum, was there and she reckons Mum was remorseful. Matthew thinks she found peace and balance after that fight." Boyan rubbed his forehead before returning them to his lap. "They were my mother's best friends. No one knew her better."

"I can understand what a weight that must be for you. No wonder you don't want to fight," Olive said.

"My mum chose to name me Boyan because it means warrior or fighter in Bulgarian. I often wonder what she would've called me if I was born after her last tournament."

"Humphrey!" Sebastian panted from behind them.

"What?" Boyan asked as he turned to face the interruption.

"Humphrey. It means peaceful warrior," Sebastian said, while handing Olive a cold bottle of water. "Here you are, *Señorita.*"

Olive and Boyan burst out laughing.

"Humphrey? I'm not sure you could pull that off, Boyan," Olive said, wincing as her laughter caused her injured rib to shoot with pain. As her giggling subsided, she saw that Sebastian was dripping in sweat, his cheeks were as red as a full day's sunburn.

"What happened to you?" Boyan asked.

"Olive wanted some water, but you didn't have any filtered water left in the fridge, so I jogged across to the shop to get some."

"But the shop is just across the road?"

"Have you been outside? It's stinking hot and the smoke has gotten worse."

Boyan and Olive turned to look through the glass of the back doors. Olive could barely see past the steps of the back verandah. *That's not a good sign*, she thought.

Chapter 22

Hamlet

The smoke continued to hold Wollondilly in its suffocating embrace. Resting her head against the window, Olive groaned internally while squinting at the obscured outline of Block C, now lost to the thick, choking haze.

"Happy Monday, Students!" Mrs Smith called as she burst through the classroom doors. Tight brown curls and thin gold glasses framed her sunny disposition, and today she wore a bright floral shirt.

A reluctant smile crossed Olive's face. Out of all her new teachers, Mrs Smith was by far her favourite, ironic given English was Olive's most dreaded subject. *If only I could travel back to yesterday*, she thought. The party had been a blast.

Olive glanced at the fire safety leaflet that had been handed out at this morning's assembly. She saw the three triangles on the front of the small booklet, explaining the three alert levels for bush fires. The yellow triangle was titled 'Advice', which meant a bush fire had started, yet there was no immediate danger. Olive thought back to Joy's incredulous question a few weeks' ago. According to the pamphlet, it was important to stay up to date in case the situation changed. *The threat level may not have increased, but this smoke is catastrophic*, Olive moaned to herself.

She read the words under the orange triangle, titled 'Watch and Act'. This meant the bush fire threat had heightened and to begin taking action to protect yourself. The red triangle, titled 'Emergency Warning', gave Olive shivers. *You may be in danger and need to take action immediately. Any delay will put your life at risk*, it read.

Olive hastily turned the booklet over and rubbed her forehead. *Think of something else.* She distracted herself with memories of yesterday, at Joy's glee when she pulled a glass bottle from her backpack.

Olive had heard about spin the bottle but had never actually played it until yesterday afternoon. A grin broke across her face as she remembered how her tension had mounted as the spinning bottle slowed, each rotation ratcheting up the suspense.

She recalled the mix of excitement and anxiety gripping her when the bottle finally came to a halt, pointing at Sebastian. Joy had tweaked the game's rules: Sebastian could choose anyone from the circle to kiss. The prospect of kissing Sebastian had thrilled Olive, yet, the idea of such an intimate moment on display caused her stomach to knot.

Everyone knew who Sebastian would kiss, would have been an anticlimax had it not been for Sebastian's showman-like performance quality. Pacing around the circle, he'd peered into each person's eyes, repeating, "Hmmmm, who shall I kiss?"

As he stopped in front of Olive, the chorus of "kiss her, kiss her, kiss her" rang out. A big grin spread across his face, and Olive had known immediately that she was not his choice, relief and concern filling her simultaneously. He winked at her, letting her know he was up to mischief, and she was put at ease. She should have known he wouldn't want to make her uncomfortable.

Finally, Sebastian announced, "I choose you", rushing towards Boyan and planting a big, wet kiss on his lips. The group had yelled, laughed and clapped in delight.

Using Sebastian's weight as leverage, Boyan easily rolled his friend off him. Wiping his face with his sleeve, Boyan struggled to say anything through his own laughter.

The memory caused a giggle to escape from Olive's mouth as she sat at her desk, inadvertently gaining the attention of her English teacher.

"Olive, maybe you could explain why Ophelia descended into a state of madness?" Mrs Smith asked.

"Umm," Olive grabbed her copy of 'Hamlet' from under the fire safety booklet.

"In Act Four, Scene Five, reports reach Gertrude that Ophelia is mad." Olive's fingers shook as she flicked through the pages, looking for the correct section. "Perhaps if you read from the start of scene five?"

Every part of Olive, aside from her trembling hands, froze. "Olive?"

Some of her classmates began whispering and giggling. Finally, Olive looked up to meet her teacher's gaze. "I would rather not read out loud."

The laughter and jeers escalated, cut mercifully short by the school bell. As the class began to shuffle towards the door, Mrs Smith called out, "Olive, can you stay behind please?"

"Looks like the new girl's in trouble!" a broad-shouldered boy wearing the school's football uniform chuckled as he walked past.

Olive lowered her head, waiting for the inevitable tongue-lashing. "Don't bother," she muttered, "I've heard it all before."

"I'm sorry I put you in that situation, Olive." She looked up in surprise. "I should never have asked you to read in front of everyone."

Opening her briefcase, Mrs Smith rifled through the papers inside. Upon finding Olive's assignment from last week, she placed the papers in front of her. Licking her index finger, she flicked through the pages of Olive's work. "Olive, I suspect you might be dyslexic."

"I am," she stuttered softly.

"I should have seen it earlier." Olive lowered her head at her teacher's admission. "You have all the earmarks in your writing and your reluctance to read aloud is further proof," she continued gently. "I know not only because I'm a teacher, but because I'm dyslexic, too."

"What?" Olive blurted out, falling back in her chair.

"Yeah I get it. A dyslexic English teacher is pretty funny. Well, that is, until you understand what dyslexia is and is not." Olive stared in rapt attention. "Dyslexia is not the handicap many people believe it to be. Sure, it is a challenge, especially at school where our method of learning is rarely taken into consideration."

"But how...?" Olive started to ask, then reconsidered.

"How did I get to be an English teacher?" Mrs Smith smiled. "The same way I got through high school and then university."

"And how did you manage that?"

"By being kind to myself and trying to remain calm, which helps my brain work better. By choosing different methods of learning that were more suited to how I absorb information, like audio books and videos. And, ultimately, by learning how my brain works."

"How your brain works?" She didn't understand.

"Yes! Your brilliant brain is a finely-tuned engine that works differently, but just as well, as others. The more you understand its strengths, the more you can use them to your advantage. Focusing on your strengths is key, Olive, and I don't doubt you have many!"

Olive sat up in her chair, her eyes wet from finally feeling understood.

"I was proud of you telling me you'd rather not read out aloud. You were polite, but firm, and you knew your boundaries. You are already on your way towards using your strengths."

Olive smiled. "Thank you."

"We can talk more if you like, but for now you better hustle to your next class, which is...?

"Art!" Olive exclaimed with excitement.

"I bet creativity is another one of your strengths!"

Olive grabbed her bag and hastily put the Fire Safety booklet and her copy of Hamlet inside, before racing towards the door. She turned around to look at Mrs Smith once more. "Thank you," she said.

Chapter 23
Arrival

Pushing the large red button to cut the engine, Boyan moved his hand back to the steering wheel. He tightened his grip on the black leather while he gazed out the car window.

"You okay?" Sakura asked.

"I'm not sure why Matthew had to borrow this seven-seater four-wheel drive for today." Boyan huffed, sitting back in his seat. "We're only picking up two people! His car would have been fine."

"Three people," Sakura corrected.

"Oh yeah, sorry, three people, but our 5-seater has enough space."

Sakura smiled gently and nodded her head. "Sorry to be a grump, it's just this darn smoke makes it hard enough to drive, let alone in an unfamiliar vehicle."

"You don't need to apologise; I'm grateful you're picking my parents up."

"I offered", he said, loosening his grip on the steering wheel. "You know what your mum means to me." He turned to face Sakura. "She's the closest I have to a mum."

"You know, this last year I've come to think of you as a brother."

"I think of you as my sister now, too. I'm going to miss you when you return to Japan."

Sakura wiped the tears from her eyes then reached out to touch his arm. Boyan nodded and cleared his throat. "So, we're going to get them or what?" he grabbed his wallet and phone from the centre console, then began walking with Sakura to the International Arrivals terminal.

"Do you think the smoke will delay their flight?" Sakura asked nervously.

"Matthew and I checked before leaving; there were no flight delays then."

As they entered the airport, Boyan took a deep breath then exhaled, visualising the number three and repeating it in his mind. Breathing in again, he did the same, this time for the number two, and then a final time with the number one. After the last repetition, Boyan felt calmer, his tried and tested technique coming through for him once again.

"JL51 has just landed!" Sakura squealed, pointing to the screen above them. Slipping his hands into his pockets, Boyan watched as she skipped towards the arrivals gate.

Moving to the front of the crowd, Boyan followed Sakura to where chauffeurs stood holding signs with passengers' names. He was confident they wouldn't need a sign; Sakura would find them first.

Spotting the face of the woman who had raised her, Sakura ran with arms outstretched. "*Okaasan!*" she said, tears flowing down her face. Dropping her bags immediately at the sight of her daughter, Sensei Sato embraced Sakura. Boyan stared at Sensei Sato, who looked as graceful and youthful as ever. *She hasn't changed one bit.*

With her arms still wrapped around her mother, Sakura looked towards her father. Leaving the warm embrace, Sakura composed herself, reigning in her emotions as expected in a traditional Japanese family reunion in a public place. "*Otousama,*" she said politely, bowing. Dropping his bags on the floor too, *Shihan* Sato grabbed his daughter in his arms. No words were needed. This break from tradition and formality expressed tenfold the love her father had for her and how much she had been missed. At that moment, no one else mattered to *Shihan* and Sensei Sato.

Leading her parents towards Boyan, Sakura said, "Boyan has probably grown since you last saw him?" Placing her bags on the floor, Sensei Sato bowed to Boyan then wrapped her arms around him. Other than Matthew, Sensei Sato was the only other connection Boyan had to his mother. He felt her love for his mother flow through her arms as she said affectionately, "Boyan-*san*, look at how tall you are!" Placing her palm against his cheek, she continued, "You have her blue eyes today."

Turning slightly towards the right, Sakura bowed less deeply to a tall, strong-looking Japanese man standing guard metres behind the Satos. Boyan was surprised he hadn't noticed him before, especially since Sakura had reminded him in the car that *Shihan* Sato always travelled with a senior student, even with his family. *I don't recognise him*, Boyan thought as he inspected the man from afar.

Without confirming with Sakura, Boyan announced, "*Shihan* and Sensei, Sakura will lead you to the exit while I get the car. That way, you won't have to walk so far with your bags." All three Sato family members bowed in response, making Boyan realise Sakura would be far more formal during her parent's visit.

Pulling up in front of the group standing perfectly still and composed at the arrivals pick-up spot, Boyan quickly got out. "Please, *Shihan* and Sensei," Boyan said, opening the back passenger door and gesturing for them to hop inside. Once they were seated and buckled in, Sakura joined her mother in the back. Boyan then opened the front passenger door but noticed the strong Japanese man was not moving. *Okay, clearly you're not getting in just yet*, he thought.

Looking at the array of beautifully coordinated luggage, Boyan reached for the largest suitcase but was immediately stopped by the Satos travelling companion. Boyan stepped back, allowing him access to the luggage and the back of the car. The man picked up even the heaviest items of luggage with no sign of effort and loaded the car with precision. *Bet you're good at Tetris.*

Having lived amongst Japanese culture his whole life, Boyan understood the man's actions. To many Westerners, the man's behaviour may have been perceived as abrupt or even hostile, but Boyan knew better. The man's job and honour as a senior student was to serve the Satos on this trip. Failing to not do so would bring dishonour to himself, his *dojo*, and his family. Without knowing the man, Boyan knew he served not for the money or duty but out of honour, respect, and love.

The drive back to Wollondilly had a far different atmosphere than the drive towards the airport. Boyan checked the rear vision mirror to ensure the Sato family was comfortable. Speaking quietly in Japanese, Sakura updated her parents, on her Australian adventure. Boyan could only make out every second or third word due to the speed of their conversation. Hearing the Japanese word for 'bottle' made him momentarily freeze, but he quickly reasoned that there would be no way Sakura would share their silly game with her parents. He checked their expressions in the mirror again, just to be sure. Taking a deep breath, Boyan began his number visualisation again, knowing it would be a long drive home.

"Boyan my parents want to know about the smoke. Can you explain the situation for them?" Sakura asked.

"Yes, of course," Boyan cleared his throat and sat up. "A few weeks ago, a bush fire started to the west of Wollondilly," he began, watching in the mirror as Sakura translated for her father. While Asami spoke fluent English, her husband occasionally needed help, especially when tired, like after a long-haul flight.

"The fire front is still a long way from the *dojo* and our home," Boyan continued, "but there is only thick bush land between us and the fire, making it hard for the fire fighters to control it." Boyan saw *Shihan*'s concerned facial expression. "We are following all the advice given to the community."

Shihan spoke quickly in Japanese, and Sakura translated. "My father wants to know if there is a plan if the fire comes closer?"

Boyan was about to share the preparations when he noticed Sensei looking out the front car window, relaxed and smiling, unlike her husband who sat forward with a grimace. "Please don't worry. My father has multiple contingency plans in place," Boyan assured.

"Of course he does, Boyan-*san*," Sensei laughed. "He always said, if plan B fails, there are twenty-four other letters in the alphabet."

Boyan smiled at Sensei in the mirror. "He still says that all the time."

"I have no doubt he has thought of every possible threat, challenge and obstacle and has numerous solutions for every risk," Sensei said, placing her hand on her husband's knee. "We are in the best of hands."

Chapter 24
Shihan

Peeking around the door, Olive was greeted by an unusually large gathering inside the *dojo*. Bowing as was now her routine before entering, she announced "*Osu*", albeit softer than usual. Glancing at her watch, Olive wondered, why so many people had already arrived. She noticed Boyan and Sebastian chatting with a male brown belt she hadn't seen before. By her estimation, he was a similar age to them. *Why are there so many students I've never seen before?*

Olive spotted Aednat stretching at the front of the mats but couldn't find Sakura. She hadn't been at school Monday, Tuesday or yesterday and she wasn't at training yesterday either. With her commitment to training three times a week, Olive had grown remarkably at ease within the *dojo*. She held a special fondness for Wednesday and Thursday afternoons and Saturday mornings, as these were her cherished training days. Today, being Thursday, was no exception.

Olive gently set her bags in the corner of the room, then pulled her *dogi* and her *obi* out of her bag, placing them on the seat in front of her. She slipped her pants over her shorts then put on her top, tying it tightly with her belt.

Remaining inconspicuous, Olive stretched her right arm across her body, intending to observe the unfamiliar students while feigning interest in the floor.

"Heya." Olive jerked her head up at the friendly voice.

"Why are there so many people here?" Olive asked Joy.

"Probably because *Shihan* Sato is visiting from Japan," Joy shrugged.

"Who is *Shihan* Sato?"

"Sakura's father. Apparently he's ranked higher than Sensei", Joy explained while stretching her arms above her head. An eerie silence fell over the room. Olive's eyes darted around until she found Sensei and his important guests emerge from his office.

Sensei Sato's resemblance to her daughter, and to the woman in Sensei's photograph was obvious. *She looks more like Sakura's older sister*, Olive thought, in awe of the woman's ageless beauty. "Alright everyone, line up!" Sensei boomed. Stepping onto the mats for the first time since arriving, Olive stood closer to Joy than usual. Looking around the room, Sensei bowed his head with a subtle nod of appreciation. "It is good to see many have taken the opportunity to train under *Shihan* Sato's expertise. We are extremely fortunate to have both *Shihan* Sato and Sensei Sato here in Wollondilly in the lead up to our National Camp. Make the most of it by attending every class you can." Nodding to *Shihan* and Sensei Sato, Sensei commanded, "*Seiza.*"

Olive briefly raised her gaze from her seated position and noticed Sensei Matthew in the traditional Japanese kneeling posture, facing the front. He sat between *Shihan* and Sensei Sato, a hierarchy she pondered for a moment. He seemed to be outranked by *Shihan* but not by Sensei Sato.

Upon Sensei's command of "*Mokuso*," Olive closed her eyes. Inhaling deeply, she envisioned a soothing, golden light flowing into her body through her crown, eyes, heart, and solar plexus. With each exhale, she visualised stress dissipating, leaving her body. This mental exercise that Sensei shared last week, was quickly becoming her way of centring herself and preparing for the training session ahead.

"*Mokuso yame.*" Olive stood in *fudo dachi*, along with about forty-five other students. Space was limited today, with two additional students in each line. "Given we have less space in the *dojo* today, we will need to adjust and be even more aware of each other as we train."

"*Osu*," the students replied.

"I trust you have all warmed up today as I'm going to hand over to *Shihan*." Olive's fists clenched more tightly at her side in *fudo dachi*.

"*Kumite dachi*," *Shihan*'s voice made Olive jump a little. *For a man so much smaller than* Sensei, *he has a loud voice*, she thought. Standing in fighting stance, Olive peered around those in front of her to see *Shihan*. He began speaking almost entirely in Japanese, which she had gotten used to, and was aided by *Shihan*'s demonstration of his instructions.

"*Ichi*," Olive stepped forward with her right foot, punching with her right hand, then her left, then kicking with her right knee. *"Ni,"* Olive repeated the combination. *"San,"* by the third count, she had lost all the concerns she had walking into the *dojo* today. Her back was straight, shoulders relaxed and eyes focused on the imaginary target before her. *"Mawate,"* Olive smoothly shifted her direction with the rest of the group, now facing the back of the hall. She repeated the combination three more times, the familiar movements ingrained in her muscle memory. *"Mawate."* They turned once more to face the front, where *Shihan* paused to explain and demonstrate a modification.

Olive grasped the essence of the technique, an excitement growing within her. She loved *ushiro mawashi geri*. Memories of her victorious tournament fight brought a contented smile to her face.

"Ichi." Olive punched twice with sharpness and power, then thrust her knee into her imaginary opponent's solar plexus. She felt as if she'd done this combination for years. As Olive brought her kicking leg back, she spun with grace, speed and confidence, her momentum transferred into her kicking leg, now coming around from behind. Flying through the air with dangerous purpose, Olive's heel connected with her imaginary opponent's right temple.

"Yame," *Shihan* conceded, after several more repetitions. He nodded at Sensei, who then took charge of the class.

"Osu, Shihan," Sensei began, his eyes scanning his students. "As we approach our final sessions before the camp and grading, it's vital to reflect on why you want to grade," he challenged. "Is it just for the next belt?".

Holding one end of his belt, Sensei continued, "this belt, as nice as it looks, is just material. I know many of you are eager to earn one but," Olive's eyes were fixed on his belt. "But," he interjected, "it's the personal growth that truly matters."

Seeing puzzled expressions, he simplified, "Why do you *really* want a black belt?" Silence fell over the room, the students exchanging hesitant looks, until one brave hand went up. "Yes, Aednat, why did you want the black belt you now wear?"

"Because training for the black belt would make me stronger," she responded.

"Exactly. The journey is the accomplishment. What we learn along the way is the real prize. Keep that focus as you prepare for camp and your upcoming grading."

"Sensei, who can grade at camp?" Olive turned to look at Joy, astonished at her bravery. She had the same question, but was too shy to ask.

"Good question. Camp grading is not just for those going for black belts. All belts will have the opportunity to grade." Anticipating Joy's raised hand again, he continued, "I will advise who is ready to grade in the coming days. There are information sheets about the camp and grading for everyone to take home, just by the door. Have a read and, if you have any questions, come and see me."

After bowing to signal the end of the class, Olive quickly approached Sakura, who had arrived late. "Hey, I've missed seeing you at school and here in the *dojo*. Have you been sick or something?"

"No, I've just been spending time with my parents now they're here, and my exchange year has wrapped up," Sakura replied.

"Wrapped up?" Olive asked, dreading what she was about to hear.

"Yeah, it's been a year since I started living with Sensei," Sakura explained.

"I thought you'd be at school until the end of the year?" She felt her voice waver.

"Since my exchange wasn't set up through an official program, I came to Australia this time last year."

"So you're leaving?" Olive's throat constricted painfully.

"Not right away. I'm here until after the camp ends, so we've still got a few weeks left."

As she looked at Sakura, she tried to convince her eyes not to well up. She was grateful when Sakura changed the topic.

"You going to camp?"

"If my parents allow it, which I'm sure they will. I'm mega keen. When is it?"

"In just over two weeks' time. It's held in this beautiful location – I forget the name of it. It is quite a drive, though."

Olive's excitement about camp held her tears at bay. "What's camp like?" She wanted to know everything.

"I've only been to one here in Australia, when I first arrived, but it was brilliant. *Dojos* from all over Australia were there. Students of all ages."

"Lots our age?"

"Yes, it's like one big *dojo*, everyone training and having fun together. I made so many new friends."

Sebastian interrupted to hand Olive an information sheet. "Are you coming to camp?"

"Sakura just asked me the same question," Olive laughed.

"And your answer?"

Taking the information sheet, she replied, "Yeah, I'm really keen. I hope I can grade."

"You hope?" Sebastian laughed. "You're a shoe-in."

Overhearing the statement, Aednat butted in. "This is a grading, not a tournament. Being an Ass-Kicker won't necessarily get her invited to grade." Olive swallowed at Aednat's remonstration. "She will not only have to demonstrate her fighting ability but all the techniques and *kata* for the belt she is going for."

Olive rubbed her face in contemplation. *Do I know my kata well enough?* Determined to be invited, she vowed to double down on her training at home.

Chapter 25
Argument

"But you look absolutely stunning!" Joy said as she twirled the final section of Olive's hair between her fingers before securing it at the crown of Olive's head. Olive shifted in her chair, her gaze flitting back and forth as she examined herself in the mirror.

"I'm not entirely convinced this colour suits me," she murmured.

"What? Are you kidding? That eyeshadow brings out the colour of your eyes so beautifully!"

Olive leaned in closer to her bedroom mirror, gently running her fingers over her hair. "It's just a lot of makeup," she observed. Joy leaned in even closer to Olive, ensuring her own reflection was visible in the mirror.

"Not only does the blue shade accentuate your eyes, this blush adds a lovely definition to your cheeks, and the foundation blends flawlessly with your skin tone," she insisted. Olive traced her right index finger over her furrowed brow, inspecting it afterward. "Did you really need to use so much foundation? It's caked on," she remarked. Joy took a step back from the mirror, straightening up.

"Sure, this look isn't right for a day at school or picking up groceries, but it's *perfecto* for another party!" she reassured Olive.

Returning her attention to her hair, Olive touched it firmly. "These curls make me feel like I stepped out of a dollhouse."

Joy's nose twitched slightly. "I'm sorry you're not loving it. Personally, I think you look gorgeous."

Olive caught Joy's reflection in the mirror. "I appreciate you playing with my hair, it was really relaxing but I can't shake the feeling I look more like a clown than a party-goer," she admitted.

Joy crossed her arms defensively. "Everyone knows that when you follow a compliment with a 'but', it cancels it out," Joy said, drawing her arms closer to her chest. "This sleepover is turning into a bit of a bummer," she muttered

"I invited you to sleep over so we'd have yesterday and today to practice our *kata* before next weekend's camp grading!" Olive said, spinning in her seat to face Joy.

"And we did!" Joy shot back. "We spent all day yesterday practicing, not just the *katas*, but all the techniques you wanted to work on!"

"*I* wanted to work on?" Olive sprung to her feet. "We're both aiming for our first belt, so everything we practiced yesterday was for both of us!"

"I'm already happy with my *kata* and techniques. I thought it'd be nice to mix things up today and do something different," Joy explained, taking a step back.

"How can you be satisfied?" Olive exclaimed, throwing her hands up. "Your turns in the first two *katas* are off, your thumbs stick out in your punches and your stances need to be longer."

"Who made you Sensei?" Joy asked, tears welling in her eyes. "Not everyone can be as flawless as you, Olive!"

"Flawless?"

"Everything comes easy for you! You stroll into the *dojo* with your natural talent and incredible strength while others have to work tirelessly for it!"

"I work hard!" Olive rebutted, her voice louder than she intended. "Sure, for some strange reason, fighting comes a bit more easily to me, but *kata* is a whole different story." She gestured wildly with her hands, frustration evident in her movements. "I constantly mix up my right and left, which is why I want to practice more. But it seems like you couldn't care less about your grading!"

"How would you know?" Joy threw her arms out from her body. "You're so wrapped up in yourself, Olive!"

"What?"

"Do you even consider anyone else's feelings? Because it certainly doesn't seem like it!"

Olive took a breath. "Look, I'm sorry for the comments about my hair and makeup," she conceded, her tone softening slightly.

"You just don't get it, do you?" Joy locked eyes with her. "I'm not surprised you think this is all about the makeup and karate practice! It just proves that you only think about yourself and have no idea how lucky you are!"

"What the hell are you talking about?" Olive retorted, her expression taking on a mocking tone.

Stepping forward, Joy pointed a finger at Olive. "You show up out of nowhere, with your gorgeous blue eyes, stunning long blonde hair and insane sporting abilities. And you're completely oblivious to everything around you!" Her voice trembled with emotion. "Since you arrived in Wollondilly, it's been 'The Olive Show' with you getting everything you want without a care for anyone else!"

Abruptly, Joy turned her back to Olive and bent down to pick up her overnight bag. Flipping her bag over her shoulder, she strode forward, pushing past her with contempt.

"Where are you going?" Olive demanded.

Opening the bedroom door, Joy responded curtly, "Home."

Olive stared after her, mouth hanging open in disbelief. "Who does she think she is?" she said aloud.

"Everything alright?" Olive's mum appeared at the door, concern etched on her face. "I heard yelling and saw Joy leaving?"

"Joy was yelling, too!"

"What was the argument about?"

A low growl escaping her lips, "Apparently, I'm as clueless as you are," Olive said.

Chapter 26
Camp

The same gentle rocking that soothed Olive to sleep on the tournament bus trip could not distract Olive from the papers commanding her full attention for 14 days. Studying her *katas* and the Japanese language for the techniques had proven much harder than she'd imagined.

I'm getting better and better at kata, she thought to herself, willing herself to believe it. She continued to study the pages, which detailed the instructions of each *kata*. *Lucky there's diagrams.*

There'd been so much driving since her family moved to Wollondilly. Gazing out the window for signs of their current location was fruitless. Sitting up to stretch her arms above her head, Olive looked around the bus. Aednat and most of the others were asleep, while a few were reading or scrolling through their phones. Joy appeared to be listening to music with her headphones on, bobbing her head rhythmically. Olive's stomach turned with a mixture of anger and sadness as she watched her, feeling a pang of annoyance at Joy's apparent ease amidst the tension that was still between them.

Turning her attention away to the front of the bus, Olive could appreciate Sebastian's choice to keep Boyan company as he drove. She'd been disappointed when Sebastian jumped in the front seat, but now she understood Sebastian's reasoning. It was going to be a long drive south and Boyan would need company to ensure he didn't take a nap, too. Watching the friends chat quietly, Olive was grateful Sebastian wasn't someone who forgot his friendships once in a relationship. A quality to be admired, especially given her own friendship debacle.

Stretching her arms once more, Olive sensed an unusual discomfort in her right deltoid muscle. She figured it was from the week's training. With *Shihan* Sato present at every training class in the last fortnight, the atmosphere of the *dojo* had shifted. Not only during the classes, but before and after as well. It was remarkable how a man who rarely spoke could have such a profound impact on those around him. His mere presence commanded respect and discipline. *I'm glad Sensei drove the Satos in his car*, she thought.

Olive sighed as she lowered her hands towards her lap. Turning her head to the right, she noticed Sakura had curled her legs up under her body on the seat, sleeping soundly in a tight little ball. Olive was equally glad Sakura was allowed to ride on the bus, grateful to spend more time with her before she left, and to be given respite from Joy's cold shoulder.

A loud thud sounded from the front right side of the bus. "Sorry, I couldn't miss that one," Boyan announced.

"What was that?" Sakura asked as she awoke, rubbing the back of her neck.

"Just a pothole."

"Wollondilly has terrible roads."

"Yeah, but we aren't in Wollondilly anymore."

Sakura sat up and looked out the window. "Where are we?"

"No idea. We've been travelling for hours so hopefully not long to go."

Noticing that Olive still had the papers in her hands, Sakura gestured towards them. "How's it going?"

"Better than 14 days ago."

"Maybe it's time for a break?" Sakura suggested, her grin widening.

Returning Sakura's grin, Olive nodded in agreement, "Definitely." She folded the well-worn pages and placed them in her backpack. "I'm glad you talked your parents into allowing you on the bus."

"They were cool about it. They understand I want to spend as much time as I can with everyone before I leave."

"It's wild seeing your mum here. I keep having to double-take – you look so alike!"

"Boyan said the same thing to me when I arrived. He's really looked after me this past year, like a brother. I suppose it came naturally to him, seeing as he's so close to my mother, that he told me I looked like her."

Olive turned her body even further around towards Sakura. "Boyan and your mum are close?"

"Yes, he's shared with me that she's the closest to a mother he has. She writes him letters and FaceTime's him regularly. She's always checking in with him."

"Wow." Olive scratched her head in contemplation. "What was Boyan's mum like?"

The bus jolted again as another loud thud was heard. "Sorry," Boyan said again.

"Where are we?" Aednat called sleepily from the middle of the bus.

"Not far now," Boyan said, keeping his eyes on the road ahead. "Everyone awake back there?"

"Oh crap, I've spilt orange juice all over myself!" Joy announced jumping up from her seat.

Turning around in his seat, Sebastian asked, "Do you want us to pull over?"

Looking down at the orange stain spreading over her jumper, Joy replied, "*Si, nescitio lavar mis monos.*"

Sebastian's facial expression transformed from one of surprise to amusement, and he began to laugh.

"What's so funny?" Joy asked, embarrassed.

It took a few minutes for Sebastian to compose himself. "One vowel can change the meaning completely." Joy shook her head, confused.

"I assume you wanted to say that you need to wash your hands?" She nodded. "You said the words beautifully and everything was perfect, except for one tiny vowel." He took in a shuddering breath, trying not to break into fits of laughter again. "*Manos* means hands but *monos* means monkeys. You said you needed to wash your monkeys."

Laughter erupted from almost every seat on the bus, and no one was laughing more than Joy. Olive was the only one not joining in. *Joy was trying to learn Spanish?* She looked at Joy then at Sebastian, realisation hitting her painfully in the chest. *She likes him, too.* Olive rubbed the left side of her chest where her heart was as she looked at Joy again, then wiped a tear from her eyes. *You were right, I was clueless,* she thought.

"Mum said she was amazing." Olive looked back at Sakura, in surprise. Amidst the commotion and her realisation about Joy, she'd completely forgotten her question to Sakura.

"Amazing? You mean, as a martial artist?"

"More than that. She could barely read or write yet she achieved so much."

"That makes sense, if English was her second language," Olive said, feeling a little defensive.

"Oh no, she struggled in her native language, too. Mum said she was almost certain she was dyslexic, and potentially something else too. She couldn't tell her left from her right."

"I know how that feels." Olive pulled her arms around her waist.

"If she was ashamed of it, she never let on, but Mum believes it was why she seemed so aloof. At least, for those who didn't know her well."

Olive thought back to her own diagnosis, feeling deeply for the woman she'd never met. "It must have been very hard for her. I can't imagine they knew much about dyslexia in those days, or at least it wouldn't have been spoken about very openly." *And I still can't.*

"She was fiercely independent, and pretty secretive, which Mum thinks is partly due to not being supported with her learning when she was younger. Her parents died when she was a teenager, and with no other family, she took care of herself from fifteen. Many would have crumbled under the pressure."

"Oh man," Olive shook her head sadly. "That's terrible. At least she found her peace before she passed."

Sakura looked at her questioningly, but the rumble of the bus over the cattle grid made her look out the window excitedly. "We're here!"

Chapter 27
Sensei Chris

An old sign advertising the campsite announced their arrival, and they were welcomed by a two-kilometre winding driveway surrounded by lush vegetation. "Beautiful," Olive remarked as she took in the grounds.

Upon reaching the camp's car park, they found it was already starting to fill with cars and buses, including Sensei's car. With no clear direction of where to go next, everyone began to disembark, stretching and yawning listlessly.

"*Osu*, everyone, how was the trip?" Sensei greeted in a happy tone as he approached the bus. "Alright gang, grab your luggage and head towards the dormitories. Boys are to the left," Sensei pointed, "and girls are in the newer dormitories over to the right. Each *dojo* is roomed together so look for the Wollondilly Karate sign on the door."

As everyone started to move, Sensei waved his hands, "Find your room, get changed into your *dogis* and get to the campsite's great hall, pronto." Olive followed Aednat's lead to their room, then dressed and walked to the hall with her, catching up with Boyan and Sebastian on the way. They seemed to know everyone. Warmth and respect were bestowed to both young men from those around them as they moved to the side of the hall. The warmth changed to what felt like trepidation when Aednat followed, awe tinged with fear.

Attendees continued to flow into the hall as Sakura joined Olive and the others. The hall was so massive it was hard to estimate numbers, but Olive guessed there were more than 300 people in the room. A loud, authoritarian voice cut through the din.

A man Olive had never seen before introduced himself as Sensei Chris, and she wondered why her Sensei wasn't the one leading the group. After a brief introduction, Sensei Chris commanded, "Line up."

The advanced and intermediate belts moved swiftly, leaving Olive and Joy (who was still keeping her distance) and the other beginner belts to hang back with uncertainty. The front six rows were filled with black belts, with twenty people in each row. It was strange for Olive not to see Boyan or any of the Wollondilly black belts in the front row. Boyan stood in the fourth row while Aednat, Sebastian and Sakura were in the fifth.

A strong, still silence emanated from every single student as they stood in *fudo dachi*. Olive felt the intensity of the energy deep in her gut, powerful and moving. Peering past the numerous rows in front of her, Olive spotted Sensei Matthew in the second position in the front line. Why was he lining up with everyone else? He wasn't even in the first position. Thinking of where he'd stood in her own *dojo* when *Shihan*

Sato arrived, it finally dawned on her other teachers could also outrank her Sensei. It still felt weird, though.

Sensei Chris and *Shihan* stood in front of the group, but it was Sensei Chris who addressed them. "*Seiken chudan tuski*," he bellowed. It took a moment, but Olive was relieved to realise she understood the technique, despite his pronunciation of the Japanese words. She wondered if it was Sensei Matthew or Sensei Chris who had the better grasp of the language.

"*Kumite.*" The room moved as one into fighting position, with both fists clenched and stationed close to the face. "*Ichi.*" Everyone began punching and yelling together, continuing as the counting progressed. While the collective power of silence was impressive, the electrifying energy of the united *kia* scream was beyond anything Olive could articulate. She knew she was experiencing greatness few had ever witnessed and, at that moment, she believed anything was possible. Now she understood Sakura's words to her in the bush, which felt like a lifetime ago: "It's hard to explain to those outside the *dojo*, the bond and respect you share with those you train with."

In her peripheral vision, Olive kept an eye on Sensei Sato as she walked around. She looked exactly as she did in the photograph in Sensei Matthew's office. *She can't be wearing the same dogi, can she?* Olive found it difficult to compute that this woman was the same lady Sakura called *okaasan*, who had, until this moment, projected a gentle energy.

When Sensei Sato had first stepped into the *dojo*, Olive had immediately sensed her kindness, compassion and intuition, and perhaps a touch of submissiveness. There was nothing submissive about her now. The change in her demeanour was dramatic, but Olive was in awe that Sensei Sato could be both gentle and strong.

"*Yame, yame, yame,*" Sensei Chris boomed, demanding the immediate halt of training. "Punch with your left hand first," he yelled while demonstrating again.

He was clearly becoming annoyed that some of the students were not preforming the combination of techniques exactly as he wanted. The difference in teaching styles between Sensei Matthew and Sensei Chris made Olive uncomfortable. Sensei Chris was a stern man, but Olive knew it was possible he had a gentler side, though she saw no sign of it now. There was an uneasy energy in the hall, especially amongst those who were going to be grading. Saturday was to be a long day. Olive clenched her back teeth together.

"Come on!" Sensei Chris yelled to the group while looking at Kell. "This is your last chance to practice this combination drill before your grading officially starts." Olive noticed Sensei Matthew's attention was almost entirely on Kell, his only student grading for black belt this weekend. *I'm glad I'm only going for my first belt*, she thought while lowering her head to avoid Sensei Chris's attention. Olive now knew the meaning of what Sensei Matthew had said many times in the weeks leading up to this weekend: "A black belt grading will push you past your comfort zone in ways you will never expect." Olive glanced at Kell. *She's being pushed, alright.*

Olive turned her attention back to her own training, knowing there was nothing she could do to support Kell right now. Feeling the freedom of being a white belt while the brown belts received most of the attention, Olive worked on the combination of techniques that Sensei Chris was teaching.

Remembering to punch with her left hand first, she continued with the proceeding kicks and punches in the combination drill.

With each attempt, she became more confident, and her speed and accuracy increased with each effort. Olive created a bubble around her, blocking out the room's intense energy. Focusing only on becoming sharper and stronger now that she had a firm grasp of the drill. Eventually, a movement in the corner of her eye distracted her, and she realised it was Sensei Sato. *Is she watching me?* She didn't dare turn her head to confirm.

Wrapping up the pre-grading training, Sensei Chris announcing it was time for lunch. It was a chance for everyone getting ready for grading, to fuel up before the real deal. As people started leaving the hall, Olive scanned the crowd for Kell. It was obvious from her body language that Kell wasn't in a good place – you didn't need to be an empath to pick up on her feelings.

Kell moved to the side of the hall then slumped to the floor, head buried in her hands as she sobbed. Not sure how she could help, Olive approached her anyway. Walking past Sensei Chris, Olive noticed his apparent indifference to Kell's breakdown. She wondered if he really didn't care, or if this was just all part of the 'journey'. Either way, she kept her head low to avoid attracting his attention.

Kneeling beside the girl that she didn't really know well, Olive was grateful when Aednat joined them. Raising her head from her tears-soaked hands, Kell took one look at Aednat and started sobbing uncontrollably. Having a fearless warrior before you, after what must have felt like a defeat wouldn't have been easy for Olive either.

"I don't think I'm ready," Kell wept. "I don't think I can do this." Aednat said nothing. A reaction in direct opposition to Olive's desire to put her arms around Kell, to tell her she was amazing and that she could do it.

"I'm not like you. I'm not as strong as you," Kell said, staring gloomily at the floor.

Taking a long breath, Aednat was slow to respond. "Anger doesn't make you strong, just as tears don't make you weak." Kell raised her head to meet Aednat's eyes. "Sometimes, just voicing your fears, saying the words your heart tries to hold back, is all it takes to pave the way to greatness."

Olive thought upon the truth of Aednat's last sentence. Olive often found that after a good cry, the reason for her tears had diminished, and life in general didn't feel as bad.

"Trust your training. You're ready," Aednat encouraged. Standing up from the floor, Aednat stretched her arms behind her back and said, "Let's get lunch."

Chapter 28
Reconciliation

"Ah crap, look at the line!" Aednat said, pointing to the people outside the food hall. "Of course Team Wollondilly Karate are the last ones," Aednat joked, spotting their crew at the end of the line.

Olive's stomach tightened as she saw Joy up ahead, then shuffled up to her. "Hey Joy, can we chat?" she said, gesturing to the right with her head. Joy stepped out of the line without uttering a single word.

Fiddling with her fingers while faced with Joy's cold demeanour, Olive took a deep breath before plunging into the conversation.

"I just wanted to say I'm really sorry," she began, her voice tentative. "You were right, I was clueless." She paused but noted no visible change to Joy's tense body language. "I only worked it out on the bus coming here." Joy's eyebrows narrowed, and Olive wasn't sure if she was confused or just getting angrier. "You've been learning Spanish because you like Sebastian. I feel dreadful that I didn't realise you had feelings for him, too, and probably had feelings for him long before I came along."

Tears welled up in Olive's eyes as she looked into Joy's gaze. She saw the pain and distance reflected there, and it broke her heart. "I'm so sorry I was so insensitive," she wept gently. "I miss us, Joy," she admitted softly, her voice trembling with emotion. "I miss how close we have become. You were my first friend here, and you looked out for me from day one. Can you forgive me?"

"I used to learn Spanish," Joy said finally, catching Olive off guard.

"Used to learn Spanish?"

"All the girls at school, and probably the whole of Wollondilly, like Sebastian," Joy confessed. "I mean, what's not to like?! I thought if I learned Spanish, he might like me." Olive was quiet and still. "But he never showed interest in any girl, not that I saw anyway," Joy gave a small smile, "until you arrived. Sure, I was hurt at first but I wasn't angry at you. You were my friend. I couldn't believe someone as wonderful as you wanted to be my friend." Joy's confession made Olive's tears flow faster. "I was only mad you didn't seem to care that I liked him, too."

Olive shook her head. "It wasn't that I didn't care, just that I didn't know." She grabbed Joy's hands. "I'm really sorry I was so unaware. I'm sorry I hurt you." She squeezed Joy's hands harder. "Can you forgive me?"

Joy wrapped her arms around Olive's neck and pulled her in for a tight hug. "Absolutely," she breathed. "This whole thing has sucked. I miss you!"

Holding the embrace a little longer, Olive said, "I was impressed with your Spanish by the way. You should keep it up!"

"Yeah, nah. I quit learning once I realised he was keen on you. Besides," Joy laughed, "I don't want to risk mixing up *manos* and *monos* again!"

Laughter erupted as the girls relinquished their embrace and turned together to head back to the food hall. "Anyway," Joy added, "I'm kinda keen on Jake."

"Jake, the blue belt?"

"Yeah, he kissed me when we were playing spin the bottle. It happened when you got up to go to the bathroom."

"What? I can't believe I missed that!" Olive shrieked. "How exciting! I'll have to get Sebastian to give me the lowdown on him." She wiggled her eyebrows at Joy and rubbed her hands together.

"Alright, alright," Joy laughed. "Let's eat!"

The large 1970's-era dining hall was crammed with hungry athletes devouring their lunch. Sitting away from everyone else, Olive noticed *Shihan* Sato and Sensei Chris discussing what she assumed was the matter of grading after lunch. *Won't be sitting at their table.* Given that Sensei Matthew and Sensei Sato were both very senior, Olive was surprised they weren't also at the table. *Lucky for them*, she smirked to herself.

Finally finding where their team was seated, Olive and Joy sat down to join them, then grabbed some food from the platters in the middle of the table. While inhaling a chicken and salad wrap, Olive spotted Sakura's mother and Sensei at the far end of the dining room. From watching Sensei Sato's expressions, Olive could tell she was upset as she listened to Sensei talk. Shaking her head with emotion, Sensei Sato then laid her hand over the top of his. This public display of affection towards a man other than her spouse was most unusual for the Japanese way.

"What do you think they're talking about?" Sakura whispered, following Olive's gaze.

"No idea. Your mum looks really upset," Olive replied.

As if feeling their eyes on her, Sensei Sato turned in their direction. Sakura and Olive looked away, facing each other.

"They've both been acting weird," Sakura confessed, "especially my mum."

"Weird?" Olive moving in closer.

"Yeah, ever since she came to the *dojo*, she's been acting strange." Olive slowly turned her eyes back to the scene as Sakura added, "I don't know what's going on, but I think it predates us."

"Huh?"

"I get the sense their emotions are much older than us. This is something to do with their history."

Chapter 29
Grading

Walking in silent solidarity alongside Joy, Olive rubbed her stomach in an attempt to quell her nerves. *Okay, here we go. I've got this*. Olive turned to Joy who was biting a nail rather savagely.

"You okay?" Olive asked, aware of how redundant her question was. Joy looked at her, her lips trembling as she tried to smile. "We can do this," Olive whispered, as much for her own benefit as Joy's.

As Olive walked through the hall's doors, there were no warm greetings between students. Where before the space was electrifying, now it was claustrophobic. At the front of the hall, Sensei Chris, *Shihan* and the Sensei that had lined up in first position earlier, sat at a large table, deep in conversation.

Scattered around the room, students of all levels kept to themselves, stretching and warming their bodies. Rubbing her stomach a little firmer than before, Olive regretted having seconds at lunch.

"As of now, grading has commenced," Sensei Chris announced.

"Let's do this," Olive mouthed to Joy, who had moved onto a new fingernail.

"Only those grading are to line up." Olive caught the glimpse of Boyan and Sebastian standing together, looking straight at her. Boyan nodded his head while Sebastian gave her a thumb's up while smiling encouragingly.

She turned to the front of the hall, holding her head high, then moved towards her position in the line with a steady and fluid gait.

"A karate grading is an evaluation process to determine a student's progress and proficiency. It serves to assess a student's technical skills, knowledge, physical fitness and understanding of karate principles," Sensei Chris said, stopping in front of Kell. "For the next few hours, you will demonstrate not only your skills but your spirit."

Kell looked dramatically different from the emotional teenager she had seen only a couple of hours ago. She stood perfectly still and strong, her two fists clinched at her waist, unfazed by Sensei Chris's presence.

"*Seiza,*" Sensei Chris ordered, "*Mokuso.*" Olive immediately felt the difference of the hard wood floorboards on her knees, compared to the soft padded mats in the *dojo*. Despite her urge, Olive refused to squirm into a more comfortable position. Closing her eyes and drawing air towards her diaphragm, she imagined the breath inside her filling every crevice of her insides with golden, warm, pure energy. Her vision continued as she exhaled, seeing black air leaving her body in her mind's eye, taking her self-doubt, fear and anxiety with it.

"*Mokuso yame.*" Olive opened her eyes and stood. "*Kumite dachi*," Sensei Chris ordered. *Yes!* Olive internally celebrated. *Fighting stance is my stance.*

As Sensei Chris took the grading students through the punches, kicks and blocks Olive had learned when she first joined the *dojo*, the rest of the hall fell away. She remained completely calm and focused, grounded in her body.

"I will get all the white belts to sit down, except for..." Sensei Chris paused as he confirmed with the two men seated behind the table. "You and you," he pointed at Olive and a boy of a similar age from another *dojo*. "

A few of the intermediate belts turned to see what was unfolding. Olive desperately wanted to look to Boyan and Sebastian for some hint of what was happening, but she denied herself, locking her head and body in place.

Standing directly in front of her, Olive wondered why Sensei Chris was focused on the seated white belts, rather than her and the other teenager.

"From the moment you walked into the hall until the moment you walk out, every aspect of how you conduct yourself is being watched and tested," Sensei Chris explained, "even when asked to sit down."

Olive's breath trapped in her chest as she realised his purpose. *He's seeing if they sit in seiza*. She wanted so badly to turn to see if Joy had passed, but knew she needed to stay still. Judging by the Sensei's frown, the majority were not sitting correctly, and she heard them scramble into *seiza*.

Turning his attention to the two remaining white belts, Sensei Chris said, "You will continue for now." As he increased the complexity of the techniques, Olive remained transfixed in her task, yet aware of the increased scrutiny upon her.

"Thank you, Jacob, you can now sit down, too." Surprised to find herself still standing with the higher belts, Olive fought a smile. "Now add in ***ushiro mawashi geri*** at the end of that combination," Sensei Chris called out.

Upon the command, Olive thrust her left arm forward to punch the invisible target before her, followed by her right arm, then her left knee hurtled forward. Olive's balance and posture were aligned to spin round quickly once her left leg returned. Out from behind her spin, her left leg emerged, bringing her heel to head height, where it struck her imaginary opponent's temple forcefully.

"Only green belts and above now. Everyone else take a seat." Olive turned towards Joy only to discover there wasn't room beside her. Sitting in *seiza* further away, she was relieved to have a break from the training and to have the chance to watch Kell.

"*Kata* will be next." Olive gulped. "You guys warm yourselves up, especially the white belts who have been sitting the longest." Sensei Chris shot Olive a glance. ***Did he just nod at me?*** She was unsure. "Everyone grab a quick drink if you need one."

Olive turned to find her water bottle placed behind, knowing it wasn't where she left it. She looked up to see Sebastian and

Boyan still watching her, and Sebastian mimicked the motion of taking a drink.

"Thank you," she mouthed to him.

"*De nada*," he mouthed back, smiling.

"Everyone line up again," Olive moved reluctantly into position. "First *kata*."

Olive tried to recall the first move as Sensei's words came back to her: "It's common to go blank when asked to do your *kata* in front of everyone. If this happens, just breathe and focus on trying to remember even the first technique. You'll find that you remember the rest once you start moving."

She was grateful for Sensei's advice, as well as Sebastian's reminder that, as a white belt, she'd be doing the *kata* with the others, so she wouldn't be watched the entire time.

"*Haijme*." The first technique came back to her, but she kept the movements of those around in her peripheral nonetheless. "Second *kata. Hajime.*" Olive took in a deep breath to counter both her nerves and her increasing heartbeat, which was thumped at the fast pace of the *kata*. She hadn't practiced at this speed before.

"*Osu*, would any white belts like to do either the first or second *kata* by themselves in front of everyone?"

Olive's eyes darted up towards Sensei Chris who was looking in her direction. *Wait, what?* She squeezed her nails into her palms before turning to Joy whose face had turned pale. "Here's your chance to shine white belts." Thankfully, he was no longer looking at her. *No way. I've shone enough already.*

"Okay then. White belts, your grading is now over. You can go and relax for now while we continue with the higher belt *katas*."

"*Osu*." Olive bowed with the other white belts before turning to collapse on the ground beside her water bottle.

"You were amazing!" Olive looked up to feast upon Sebastian's face. "I could see Sensei Chris and *Shihan* were impressed with you."

"Really?" Olive was stunned.

"Yeah, *Shihan* was watching you a lot. The fact that Sensei Chris offered the white belts the opportunity to do a *kata* on their own was most definitely because of you." He sat down beside her and leaned in. "Girl, you just blew the grading away!" Sebastian looked around the hall. "I think everyone will be talking about the white belt with serious skills."

"That concludes the first part of today's grading. We are going to take a twenty-minute break for everyone to hydrate, use the bathrooms and put on their sparring gear." Olive wished she could spar, and wondered why it wasn't included for white belts.

"Every brown belt will have twenty continuous, one-minute, full contact fights, mainly with black belts," Sensei Chris explained. "For those grading but not going for black today, you will mostly be fighting against each other, but you may be asked to spar against a brown belt." Pointing towards her teacher, Sensei Chris continued, "Sensei Matthew is in charge of appointing the fighters today, so follow his instructions."

Olive turned to Sebastian. "You're not fighting?"

"No, Sensei said there were enough black belts to fight and I was happy to sit out, but Boyan and Aednat are fighting." Olive looked around the room and noticed both were in *dogis*, ready to fight.

"*Osu*, Sensei." Olive looked up at Sebastian's words and saw her teacher standing in front of them.

"*Osu*. Olive would you like to fight in the grading today?"

"*Osu*! Yes!" She rose quickly from the floor.

"Great. Get your sparring equipment on and get warmed up!"

Now leading the formalities, Sensei Matthew directed all those who now faced each other to bow, saying "*Otagai ni rei*." Comprised of one black belt and one brown belt, each pair bowed with respect and anticipation. "*Hajime*" shattered the stillness.

As Olive readied herself for sparring, she watched the first rounds, hearing the punches hitting their opponent's chest and kicks upon their leg. It was clear the black belts were not holding much back. As Sensei Matthew had explained before arriving to camp, sparring bouts in a grading were different to tournaments. In a tournament, the aim is to win, preferably in the least amount of time, while sparring in a grading is about showing you were deserving of the belt you seek. That no matter what is given to you, you can continue. Continue to defend, continue to fight. Giving up would most certainly be an automatic fail.

"You'll fight next, Olive," Sensei advised pointing to her partner.

She bounced on the balls of her feet, telling herself *I am excited, I am excited*, while scanning her opponent. They seemed to be roughly the same age, but the blue-belted girl before her was much taller and looked to weigh more, too. Unlike the general obsession with being slim, karate girls had a healthier focus, looking holistically at their bodies, mind and self-esteem. They focused on putting on muscle, by eating right through their training. Being healthy, fit, flexible and strong within your own body type was the goal for every karate student.

With rapid overhead punches to her chest, Olive felt the pounding on her shoulders and pecks. Being a female, her opponent knew exactly where Olive's breast guard stopped thus inflicting the greatest impact. Taking a step to the right to avoid another blow to her shoulder, Olive inadvertently changed the intended destination of her opponent's fist, copping a foul punch to her throat. She screamed in shock causing the referee to stop their fight instantly.

Fear and panic overtook her as she struggled to hold back tears.

"Was that to your neck?" the referee inquired, moving closer to her.

"She punched me in the throat!" Olive answered tearfully, clutching the site of impact.

The referee took a moment to observe Olive's breathing. "Are you hurt?"

Yes, her composure was hurt, as was her mental armour, and probably her ego, too, but Olive couldn't honestly say she was injured. She shook her head. She saw no sympathy in the referee's face and read the implication: she had to suck it up.

The inference stung. Anger flowed quickly within her, pushing aside her fear and panic. It was the injection Olive most needed at that point. It wasn't a conscious refusal to leave the tears on her face, only that she no longer noticed them. She focused totally on the young woman still standing in front of her.

"Hajime" was her cue and Olive responded instantly. She changed her fighting stance, bringing her stronger, more powerful right leg within striking distance. She brought it forward from behind, using the forward momentum of her body. Not only did the movement mask the kick from her opponent but greatly increased its force, too.

She landed the kick in her opponent's solar plexus, the home of a network of nerves. A direct blow can cause spasms, breathlessness and a lot of pain. Still moving in a forward direction, Olive grounded her right leg near the side of her opponent. Changing roles, it was now the right leg hiding the intention of her left. Thrusting her left knee forward and upwards to the solar plexus again, Olive's opponent instantly put her hands in front of her body, waving her arms to signal she needed to stop. Gasping for air, she was in no condition to continue.

Olive moved into *seiza*, resting her left leg a little marginally to the side of her body while her opponent received medical attention. She could feel the pain of injury in her left leg but, as she knelt on the hardwood floors, she felt composed, focused and in total control. Perhaps even dangerous.

Chapter 30
Shower

"Your life is not about you," *Shihan* paused while gazing around the room at the weary athletes before him. Parting from the role of silent adjudicator, he continued, "a life that is exclusively dedicated to the pursuit of one's own needs and wants is a life unfulfilled."

Oh, come on! Olive's silent denial was fuelled by her exhaustion and discomfort.

"Your life is about those you can touch, help and inspire," *Shihan* explained.

Transferring her weight to her right leg, Olive wasn't absorbing the inspired revelations. "With what you have learned about yourself, not only from this weekend's grading but the journey that has brought you to this point, use it to be better family members, better friends, and better humans. Use who you become to make a positive difference in this world." He waited a long moment, allowing his words to sink in. "Grading is now over."

"*Osu!*" the students yelled triumphantly. Olive felt she was the loudest, the word suffused with relief.

As she went to get up, Joy came over to help her up, then wound Olive's arm around her shoulder. As she limped towards the doors, she knew what Aednat meant when she said, "no one really walks out of a black belt grading." *It seems that no one walks out of a white belt grading either.*

Sebastian came over, rubbing his hands supportively on the girls' arms. "What did you think of that?"

"Glad it's over!" Olive muttered.

"Oath. Can we eat now?" Joy pleaded while transferring Olive's weight to Sebastian.

Tightening his arm around Olive's waist for further support, Sebastian said, "*Señoritas*, please allow me the pleasure of escorting you both to tonight's campfire barbeque."

Olive was quick to respond. "Yes, please! I'm starving, too."

"You might want to have a shower and get changed into something warmer, first."

"Nice try, Sebastian," a strong female voice called from behind them. "I'll take them back to the *girl's* room." Aednat appeared in front of them, staring Sebastian down.

"I was just helping, I promise!" Sebastian shot back.

"Yes, and now you can help by saving us a seat by the campfire."

With one arm now around Olive's shoulder, Aednat twisted the doorknob as Joy pushed the door open to their dormitory. Inside they found Sakura, who was seated next to Kell.

"You're injured, too?" Sakura inquired as she watched Olive hobble towards the bed.

"I think I copped an elbow to the thigh when I did a knee kick."

"Probably just a corked leg, but sit down and I'll take a look," Aednat said.

Once seated, Olive looked towards Kell. "You okay?"

"Nothing broken, but I doubt I'll be able to sit in *seiza* for a while."

"Are we all having a great time or what?" Aednat laughed. Pulling Olive's *dogi* pants up to reveal her thigh, Aednat pressed her fingers firmly on the skin. "I think you'll live. Unlike others present, you'll be back in *seiza* in no time."

Looking up at Olive from her crouched position, Aednat asked, "Did you want help getting into-" She stopped, looking into her face intensely.

"Getting into...?" Olive asked.

"Your eyes are normally blue, aren't they?"

"Yeah? Uh, Aednat, what's up?"

"It's just, they're grey now."

Olive went to get up quickly, wondering what Aednat was talking about. "Aarrgghhhh!"

"Hang on, you're injured, remember? Here, use this," she said, handing over a small make up mirror.

"Weeeiiiiird. I didn't know my eyes did that, too." Lowering the mirror, she muttered, "The eyes are the window."

"What did you say?"

Under Aednat's intense gaze, Olive stumbled. "Um, it was just something I read...about empaths."

Aednat leaned in closer and lowered her voice. "You know about empaths?"

"A bit. Ever since Boyan told me about his empathic ability, I've been keen to learn."

"You really are full of surprises. What've you learned?" Aednat moved from the floor to sit beside Olive.

"Boyan mentioned he's an emotional empath, but I'm thinking the fact that his eyes change colour might mean he has multiple empathic abilities."

Aednat nodded. "Like an animal empath?"

"Yes!" Olive whispered eagerly. "From what I've read, animal empaths have a strong connection with fauna and instinctively know an animal's needs. Some think they can even communicate with them somehow."

"He's certainly a horse whisperer," Aednat agreed with a smile on her face.

"This isn't news to you, is it?" Olive asked.

Ignoring the question, Aednat inquired, "What else do you know?"

"Well, after my research on geomantic empaths, I reckon I might be one."

"Interesting." She continued staring at Olive's face in silent consideration before whispering, "I wonder if your eyes are a clue to another window, too."

As Olive wondered what she meant, Aednat got to her feet. "We'll talk more later, but now we need to get you showered, changed and fed! Do you reckon you can manage the shower on your own? I want to meditate for a bit before we head to dinner."

"You meditate? I don't know much about it but have been interested since starting karate." Olive looked up at Aednat, aware she was cutting into her personal time but keen to know more. "What do you do when you meditate?"

Olive watched as Aednat closed her eyes and inhaled, appearing to savour the warm late sunlight on her skin.

"Meditation is my way of connecting with God," Aednat said.

Olive was taken aback by Aednat's revelation, not expecting her to be religious.

Sensing Olive's surprise, Aednat elaborated, "I was brought up Catholic, taught to embrace God's love. I don't often talk about it because it tends to pigeonhole me through other people's beliefs; their filters, experiences and fears. Dealing with some people's expectations can be tough. Maybe they're onto something. Perhaps I am more spiritual than religious."

Though Olive couldn't place who "they" were, she sensed Aednat's vulnerability, realising she was divulging something profound and wrestling with concepts beyond Olive's immediate grasp.

"To me, meditation seems like prayer. Maybe we're all tapping into the same God-like energy?" Aednat posed the question delicately, not knowing Olive's personal beliefs. "God, light, the universe, the source, perhaps it's all the same power, just expressed differently."

Olive was taken aback by Aednat's openness and depth, aware her mouth was ajar. Pausing to stretch her legs, Aednat continued, "My meditation practice connects me to God, or the source of power, if you like. By calming myself, I sense pure love all around me, physically and emotionally."

"Physically?" Olive didn't understand.

"How does it feel when Sebastian hugs you? It's warm and gentle yet firm, right? You can feel him touching your skin as his arms surround, protect and support you." Olive felt herself blush but forced her mind not to wander. "This physical feeling of warmth and love is often what I can feel throughout my body when I am meditating. It is pure, peaceful, and it only wants the very best for me. It totally has my back."

The young woman in front of Olive was so very different from the person she assumed. Not hard, but strong and knowledgeable. Not ruthless, but focused and compassionate. She realised her original evaluation of Aednat was unfair.

"Can you teach me to meditate?" As if a ray of warm sunlight entered an opening in her crown, Aednat beamed with delight.

"Absolutely. But, for now, shower!" Aednat commanded, her formidable voice returning.

After the healing warmth of a long shower, Olive fixated on her next most pressing issue.

"Let's go, I'm starrrrrvvvinnng!" she called to Joy, who was swiping her lips with gloss.

"Yes, finally!" Joy agreed.

"You don't have to ask me twice!" Aednat responded, giving Sakura and Kell a fist pump as they all left the room.

The five Wollondilly Karate teens walked towards the campfire, slowed by Olive. "Hey, put your arm over my shoulder Hoppy, or we'll never get to eat!" Aednat said.

Olive smiled in relief, "Thanks."

"Can I ask you a question?" she asked Aednat as she watched Kell, aided by Sakura and Joy, walk ahead. "You're the only Aednat I know. Where is your name from?"

"It's my middle name, which was my Grandmother's name, which I chose to use."

"Why? Don't you like your first name?"

"Hate it!" Aednat spat. "My drunk and violent dad chose my first name. As soon as I could, I changed it to my middle name, then later I took my mother's maiden name, too."

"Do you still–" Olive went to ask if he was still around, worried for her friend's safety.

"He's dead now, so it's not an issue anymore." Aednat's voice was harsh and direct.

"I'm sorry, you don't have to tell me."

"Nah, good riddance! For years my mum, older brother and I moved, trying to get away from his cruel and controlling ways, but he kept finding us."

"Oh Aednat. I–"

She cut her off, seemingly keen to get the whole horrible story out as quickly as possible. "That's why I love my grandfather so much. Police couldn't keep us safe, so my Pa did till my father died, just over three years ago, just before we moved to Wollondilly."

"Far out, Aednat. No wonder you're a warrior. You've had to be." Olive turned to look at her in wonder.

"Yeah. That's what Boyan says, too." Then she smiled and said, "Right now, this warrior just wants a big fat steak and lots of roasted potatoes!"

Chapter 31
Camp Fire

Boyan sat on the log beside Sebastian, close to the campfire. Looking around those already seated, he laughed.

"All the single ladies are looking at you, man!"

Shaking his head with a smile, Sebastian said, "Doesn't matter. I found my Aednat!"

Boyan gave his friend a faux frown.

"Oh wait, no, that came out wrong!"

"I know, mate," Boyan laughed. "You've only got eyes for Olive."

"You boys talking about us?" Aednat said, holding Olive up on her left side with Joy on her right. Sebastian standing quickly to help.

"What about me?" Sakura rebuked as she tried to lower Kell to her seat. Boyan quickly moving to her aid.

"Food is ready," one of the camp assistant's announced.

"I could eat the hind leg off a donkey," Olive said, then blushed at her outburst.

Boyan watched as Sebastian again jumped from his log like a frog from a lily pad.

"Please, *Señorita*, allow me to be your waiter tonight. I shall bring you back a little of everything."

Olive flushed a deeper shade of red as she responded, "*Gracias.*" Her response stopping Sebastian in his tracks, and Boyan knew why.

"You spoke in Spanish!" Sebastian almost crooned the words.

As Sebastian skipped towards the banquet of food, Boyan sat by Olive. "Now you've witnessed a black belt grading, what're your thoughts?"

Zipping up her jacket to ward off the cool night air, Olive contemplated. "Sometimes I feel like I'm a child wearing my mother's clothes."

The analogy was lost on Boyan, and he was sure it showed on his face.

"I'm totally comfortable fighting but I'm aware of everything I've still to learn." She placed her hands in her jacket pockets. "Like *kata*. It's just not fitting me right now. I need to grow into it."

Boyan smiled encouragingly, finding the explanation both wise and refreshing.

"Two of my favourite people sitting together," Sebastian beamed while holding three plates of food and a paper napkin neatly folded over his arm. He handed one to Olive, then another to Boyan.

"Oh, you beautiful man, thank you," Aednat teased, reaching for Boyan's plate. "I'm positively famished."

"My dear, I did not forget you," Sebastian said, handing the third plate to her. "I'll be back with sustenance for Sakura, Joy, Kell and then myself!"

"Kell, Olive, Joy, how are you feeling after today?" Aednat eventually asked, leaning over to them.

Before anyone had a chance to respond, Sebastian had returned with hands full. "So, what are you beautiful *Señoritas* talking about? I assume you were talking about me?"

Aednat rolled her eyes. "Contrary to popular belief, we karate girls rarely discuss our male counterparts...unless we're discussing how best to kick you in the head!"

Boyan laughed at his girlfriend's wit. While it took a while for her to warm-up to others, her heart, her strength and her humour never failed to amaze him. She was like no one he'd ever met. If she told him she was a time-travelling pirate queen from 16th Century Ireland like Grace O'Malley, he'd probably believe her.

"You think you can touch this beautiful face and my gorgeous Latin hair?" Sebastian teased.

"You're just lucky they don't allow women to fight men in tournaments," Aednat jousted back.

Boyan loved watching these two and their performances. It didn't take a psychologist to see their repartee came from a place of affection and deep respect for each other. Looking around at his *dojo* mates laughing together around the campfire, Boyan savoured the banter. *These are the special people*, he thought. *I'm lucky to call them friends.*

"*Osu*, Everyone," Boyan turned around to notice Sensei Chris and *Shihan* were standing behind them. "After much discussion, we have good news to share," Sensei Chris continued.

Boyan yanked on Sebastian's jumper sleeve to quiet his antics. "I can announce that everyone has passed their grading!" Elated cheers and spontaneous applause erupted. Boyan was filled with happiness as he witnessed Joy and Olive hugging.

"And," Sensei Chris paused, waiting for silence as his eyes scanned the group, resting on Olive. "I can also announce that one student has double-graded, which is most unusual."

Shihan cleared his throat. "Olive Ullman, congratulations on not only achieving your first ever karate belt but your second belt, too!"

"What?" Olive said, spinning around to face *Shihan*.

"You were most impressive, Olive." *Shihan* nodded his approval.

"Enjoy the campfire, everyone, but don't stay up too late!" Sensei Chris called. "You don't want to be tired for tomorrow!"

As a chorus of "*Osu*" rang out, Boyan watched Sensei Chris and *Shihan* retire for the night before returning his focus to the group.

"I didn't know double-grading was even a thing!" Olive said breathlessly, as her hands massaged her temples.

"Oh, it's a thing!" Sebastian celebrated by pumping both his fists in the air. "And only one other student in our *dojo* has ever done it!"

"Who?"

"Boyan," Sebastian said, slapping him on the back.

"In fact, he has double-graded twice!" Aednat corrected.

"*Twice?*" Olive exclaimed.

"Yeah. Like you, I went from White to Orange Senior, jumping over Orange belt, and later I went from Green to Brown…It's not that big of a deal," he said, shifting his gaze to the campfire.

"Stop being so friggen modest!" Aednat said. "It's huge!"

He frowned at her before concentrating on Olive. "You know what? She's right. It is a big accomplishment, and you should be proud of yourself."

"I am…I think." Olive stumbled. "Or I will be, when it sinks in."

"Well I'm proud of us both!" Joy squealed.

"You should be proud of yourself, Joy! I'm sorry, I didn't mean to steal the spotlight." Olive said, and Boyan saw her face start to crumple.

"Nah, man! My best friend absolutely smashed it, and I passed my grading, which I seriously wasn't expecting. I'm stoked!"

"Best friend, huh?" Olive's smile widened even further.

"Yep. The best friend I've ever had."

Chapter 32
Waterfall

When choosing beds in the Wollondilly female dormitory, Olive had been surprised to find no one else wanted the only double bed in the room. Before her room mates had a chance to change their mind, she'd placed her bags on the bed to claim it.

Sleeping deeply after the massive grading day at camp yesterday, Olive stretched her arms and legs out wide as she roused herself from slumber. Wiping the night's residue from her eyes, Olive froze at the sound of heavy nostril breathing close behind her. There was someone else in the bed. Sensing that the presence was asleep, she slowly and carefully turned around to face her uninvited guest. Her annoyance softened to amusement when she saw the brightly spotted pink pyjamas and colourful beanie of the interloper.

It appeared Joy was even more lively while sleeping than awake, dressed in vibrant night clothes and face radiating a comical energy as she slept. Her nose twitched with every inhale and her nostrils vibrated on the exhale and Olive had to cover her mouth to stop from laughing out loud. She didn't want to be responsible for waking this sleeping beauty.

She needn't have worried as a heavy pounding began outside, sure to wake everyone. The throbbing sound permeated the walls of the dormitory, and she could feel it banging inside her own body, a rhythm louder and faster than her own heartbeat. Joy shot up instantly and looked accusingly at Olive.

"Don't look at me like that. If anyone has something to answer to, it's you and your choice of sleeping arrangements last night," Olive said, then started giggling at Joy's adorably confused expression.

"What is that noise?!" Joy demanded.

Aednat stepped out of the bathroom the steam swirling around her like stage smoke, transforming her into a runway model emerging from the mist. "*Taiko.*"

Joy turned to Olive for further explanation, but she was still staring at Aednat. Wearing a fresh *dogi*, Aednat looked radiant. No makeup, accessories or fancy fashion needed. Aednat's natural beauty wasn't just the result of her glowing skin and flowing red hair; it was her character that shone brightest.

"You're stunning, Aednat," Olive said in wonder, then immediately flushed with regret. *Why do I always have to say what comes to mind?*

If Aednat heard the remark, she didn't acknowledge it, much to Olive's relief.

"Come on, get up," Aednat said. "No one's allowed to miss waterfall training."

Olive's feelings were mirrored on Joy's face, apprehension of what this could possibly entail clear in her wide eyes.

"*Osu*, I'm ready!" Tossing her bed covers aside, Sakura jumped up into a fighting stance, fully dressed in her unusually crumpled *dogi*. Olive was aware Sakura ironed her uniform after washing, which made absolutely no sense to her. She assumed it was related to her Japanese culture.

"Did you sleep in your *dogi*?" Aednat asked incredulously.

Sakura answered with a cheeky, almost rebellious giggle. Clearly sleeping in one's karate uniform was *not* a Japanese thing, but a Sakura thing. Yet another quirky part of her personality Olive loved.

As the girls exited their dormitory, they found Kell outside attempting to stretch while looking noticeably rigid in her movements. Each of them greeted her with a nod and a quick "*Osu*" then the five of them walked down to the camp. As she walked with her friends, Olive thought how much the other students from her *dojo* who hadn't come to camp were missing out. But then, she was glad it was just her and her girl gang. Oh, and the guys too, of course.

The friends joined a rapidly growing number of campers gathering around the source of the thumping noise that so abruptly awoke the camp. Amongst the sea of white uniforms, a woman stood triumphantly in black attire. Looking fierce and focused, Olive was shocked to see Sensei Sato standing in what looked like a fighting stance, holding two drumsticks above her head in absolute stillness. No one dared to speak or move.

"Of all the Japanese *taiko* drums, *odaiko* is the largest," she announced while looking at the tall percussion instrument. "With these wooden *bachi* drumsticks, it can be possible to hit the *odaiko* hard enough to produce sound at 130 decibels – matching the noise of jet engines. In ancient Japan, *taiko* drumming was used to signal soldiers on the battlefield."

As if driven by an internal clock, Sensei Sato exhaled while moving her right hand slowly towards the large Japanese drum. It was right on the dot of 6am and clearly the time for rest was over.

The drumming rhythm increased both in noise and speed, wild and free like a horse moving into a gallop. Tears gathered in Olive's eyes, refusing to obey her shut eyelids. She had never heard or felt anything like it. It was almost spiritual. Surrendering to the hypnotic pulse twirling within her, all of Olive's senses were attuned to the sound. She did not want it to stop.

Sensei Sato's voice joined the performance in a series of short loud shouts, like a *bachi*. Watching the verbal and percussive display, Olive knew that maintaining such speed playing needed great stamina, yet she showed no sign of tiring. *She's a warrior in drumming as well as karate*, she thought, awestruck.

After the last drum strike an eerie silence descended, yet Olive could still feel the beat inside her. Holding the power of the drumming within her, she sensed that those around her were still, as moved by the performance as she was.

Finally, Sensei Chris broke the hush. "*Osu*," he called, turning to walk towards the bush. The students began to follow, alone or in small groups, heading in a direction that Olive was not familiar with but was already apprehensive about.

Walking silently with her friends, Olive noticed they were heading downhill, the bush turning to rainforest as they descended. Under the thick canopy of rainforest trees, little light reached the floor, making the area not only darker but several degrees cooler, too. At the bottom of the gully, the dry bushland of the camp was nowhere to be seen, replaced with a variety of palms and Lilly Pillys trimmed with lush green moss. She was reminded of a survival tip she'd learned in a nature magazine; that you could tell which way was north by looking at which side of the tree the moss is growing. As moss needs cool, dark places to grow, it grows on the south side of the tree, in Australia. Olive hoped she wouldn't need to use this knowledge on this particular trip today.

In the distance, Olive saw a clearing in the canopy. The light flooding in alerted her to their destination and the noise confirmed her suspicions. Stepping into the light-filled area first, she closed her eyes and paused, allowing her other senses the chance to feast on the delights now surrounding her. She could imagine the sunlight flowing through her crown, heart and gut. Filling every being of her body. Filling her with warmth, love, and calm.

Eventually, she opened her eyes and she was floored. It was amazing. How had no one told her about this place. Joining Olive in the clearing, the friends nodded their heads in appreciation.

"The waterfall," Aednat exclaimed, like she was introducing an old friend.

Following Aednat's lead, the friends walked towards the edge of the large circular pool. Olive looked up to the water source but was quickly distracted by the sound of splashing water. Without a *dogi* top, *Shihan* Sato was wading to the middle of the pool, where all could see him. He was absolutely ripped. With not an inch of body fat, every muscle in his arms, shoulders, chest and stomach was clearly defined. *He's a machine*, Olive thought. *Not many guys in their fifties look like that!*

The other Senseis followed closely behind, though most kept their *dogi* tops on. Surrounded by strong, determined and accomplished teachers, *Shihan* gazed upon the numerous *karateka* standing in *fudo dachi* before him. "Living with my fears was always worse than the experience of those fears. Fear is not the problem but the resistance to it." Olive's ears and mind were open. She knew that *Shihan*'s words were wisdom few would ever benefit from hearing. She was determined to listen, learn, and hopefully understand. If not today, then one day in the future.

"Your Sensei*s* have taught you that feelings of fear, pain and even being uncomfortable are your friends. These emotions can bring about strong behavioural changes, when one is brave enough to face and learn from them. They are not the enemy." *Shihan* stopped, allowing time for contemplation and self-reflection.

Sensei Chris broke the silence with one firm command. "*Hajime!*" Holding back to survey the group for clues on what was expected, Olive watched as some of the young men took off their *dogi* tops. Looking towards Sebastian, she was pleased to note he too was part of the topless segment, and she kept her eyes on him as he waded into the water.

"*Otagi*, everyone!" Sensei Chris yelled, as if a direct rebuke to Olive and the other stragglers yet to be immersed.

When Olive's right foot first touched the icy water, shock filled her body instantly and she began to panic.

"*Otagi* everyone!" Olive raised her eyes to Sensei Chris then began walking further into the pool, her fear of being the only one out of the water greater than her fear of being in it. Moving carefully over the large, smooth pebbles, she became breathless, the cold overcoming not only her senses but her respiratory system.

"For many, yesterday was gruelling. Bodies will be weary and some even injured." Olive wondered how Sensei Chris was able to speak in such cold water. "For newbies, the cold may feel overwhelming, but it brings healing. Welcome the discomfort you feel. These waters will start the process of healing your injuries, while helping your vascular system and uplifting your spirit."

Olive was not sure what he meant by the vascular system but she knew from her first aid lesson at school that ice was recommended for sprains and strains but not broken bones. Had anyone fractured a bone at the grading?

"Push-up position!"

Wait, what? Olive watched in horror as the black belts lowered their bodies into the water. *Surely he couldn't expect beginners to do this?* She watched the coloured belts submerge their hands, leaving the white belts to exchange concerned glances with each other. However, as soon as one white belt made the decision to lower their body towards the water, Olive knew she would need to as well. She was not going to wait for Sensei Chris's command again.

If the icy water wasn't uncomfortable enough, kneeling on the large pebbles only added to the unpleasant experience. Grateful to be wearing sneakers, she extended both legs so they were partly submerged while she placed her hands on the rocks. Olive's legs, hands and arms were now also feeling the effects of the icy water. She soon realised her feet were less painful than before and she wondered if that was because they were becoming used to the temperature or if her nervous system was simply overwhelmed with the messages from her other limbs.

"*Hajime!*" Sensei Chris commanded.

"*Osu!*" the group yelled in chorus, though Olive's own response was more muted. She hoped they'd stay in this position, hoping to keep her chest and stomach out of the water. If that meant staying in high plank indefinitely, so be it. Her hopes were shattered with Sensei Chris's next word.

"*Ichi!*"

Refusing to obey her own mind let alone Sensei Chris's instructions, Olive's body shook in dissonance. Willing herself to lower her whole body into the water would be to go against thousands of years of evolutionary survival instincts. Her brain was screaming for caution as her own mother's words filled her mind: "Just because you can, Olive, doesn't mean you should". Olive always found it hard to walk the line between what she should and shouldn't do. Should she push on, push her limits? Or was this the moment where she should pause to watch and learn for a better time to proceed?

The decision weighed heavy on Olive. Though her eyes were fixed on her blue-tinged hands, she could feel Sensei Chris's gaze, checking the group were completing the push-ups.

"*Ni, san, shi,*" he continued, his count slow and measured. Determined to make her own decision, Olive shut out the count, his voice and everyone around her. It was just her and the large pebbles in the wintry water. Through the stillness, as calm and peace settled over her, one clear thought emerged. A thought appearing to come out of nowhere yet immediately rang true. *We don't discover ourselves in victories or triumphs,* it said. *It's in our defeats, pain, suffering and fears that we find wisdom.*

Olive was not certain if the words were a recollection, spoken in a time now forgotten, nor did she care. She was only interested in how they made her feel, which was totally devoid of fear. On the count of "*hachi*", she bent her arms and lowered her body into the water.

Olive expected instant discomfort but the lack of it was in itself shocking. While pushing her body back up with arms extended, Olive wondered if this is what *Shihan* had meant about the experience of his fears. The counting now seemed far away as she paid attention only to its rhythm. Her breathing synced up with her movements, inhaling as she lowered her body into the water and exhaling as she pressed up again. Aware that her senses were dulled, Olive was fully focused on her task, completing stronger and more numerous push-ups than she ever had completed before.

"*Yame.*"

Olive was disappointed to hear Sensei Chris' instruction and didn't want to obey. She felt like she could keep doing this forever.

Chapter 33
Goodbye

Hot water now cascaded down Olive's body, bringing feeling back to her limbs. Closing her eyes, she leaned forward to let the water run over the back of her head and neck. "Ah yes," she purred aloud. Three-minute showers were mandatory at the campsite to conserve water, but Olive was determined to savour every one of the 180 seconds of soothing warmth.

"Breakfast is on," Aednat called, and the announcement hurried Olive into warm clothes and out of the dormitory for the last time. Breakfast was markedly different from yesterday's lunch and dinner, the sit-down, cooked feast replaced with individual takeaway packs. The small box brought home the sad realisation that they were going home.

New and old friends embraced while luggage was packed and moved towards cars and buses. Spontaneous group photos transpired everywhere in an array of poses, though fighting stance was the most common. Joy was ablaze with energy, jumping into numerous group photographs, even those she wasn't invited to. Olive knew Joy wasn't intentionally photobombing, just genuinely felt she belonged. She giggled thinking of the campers looking at the images later and wondering who the random dark-haired girl was.

"Time to get goin'," Boyan said, his voice conveying that he too didn't want to leave.

Olive turned to walk to the bus, but a hand on her arm stopped her. Sensei Matthew looked sombre as he handed Olive an envelope addressed to her mum and dad.

"I need to see your parents before the Satos return to Japan next week."

"Is everything okay?"

"You aren't in any trouble, Olive. I just need to ask them some questions."

Olive watched as Sensei walked towards his car, a small tendril of unease curling around her stomach. What could he possibly want to speak to her parents about?

With the envelope held firmly in her right hand, Olive climbed into the bus. Looking around, she found Sebastian at the back and walked to him.

"Why aren't you sitting in the front with Boyan?"

"You don't want to sit with your boyfriend?" Sebastian smiled wider as he gestured Olive towards the spare seat next to him.

"Boyfriend?" Olive raised an eyebrow, but felt her cheeks warm.

"Too soon?" Concern broke through his usual confidence. She sat down and turned towards him.

"No, it's not that, it's just..."

"It's just what?" Sebastian coached softly.

"It's just that it's the first time you've said boyfriend."

Sebastian stroked her face then leaned in to place a gentle kiss on Olive's forehead, creating a rush of warmth throughout her body. It was a simple gesture, but it spoke volumes to Olive, echoing a connection she hadn't quite put into words yet. *I'm his girlfriend.* The thought mixed with Sebastian's lingering touch created a cascade of emotions. A flutter of excitement mingled with a hint of vulnerability. It was as if each of Sebastian's caresses unravelled a thread of her defences, inviting her to embrace this newfound closeness.

"What's the envelope?" Sebastian asked.

"Huh?" Olive was still tipsy from the feeling his touch and words provoked.

"The envelope in your hand?" he repeated, pointing to the stationary.

"Oh yeah, hah." Olive had forgotten all about both the envelope and Sensei's words.

"Sensei handed it to me, just before getting on the bus." Olive's fingers carefully checked the seal for a possible entry point. "He said he wanted to see my parents before the Satos returned to Japan and I was to give this to them."

"Do you know why he wants to see your parents?"

"Not a clue," Olive replied without taking her eyes from the paper. "Maybe it's about the double-grading?"

Sebastian shook his head. "Why wouldn't he just say that?" He paused, mulling something over. "Boyan was right."

Her eyes shot up to meet his. "Right about what?"

"Boyan told me last night that Sensei Matthew and Sensei Sato have been acting weird and he believed you were the reason."

"Why me?" Olive said, feeling hurt Boyan had singled her out as the cause.

"I don't know but I think Boyan knows why. He started to tell me after you girls left the campfire but Sensei interrupted. Why don't you just open the envelope and find out?" Sebastian suggested.

She turned the envelope over, showing him the firm seal. "Can't do that without my parents knowing."

"Hmmmm... oh well, won't be long before you find out!"

Chapter 34
Awareness

Olive had been awake for several minutes but she refused to vacate her cozy refuge. *Monday again*, she moaned internally, pulling the bed covers up over her face. *No one should be expected to go to school after such a brilliant weekend!*

A smile encroached upon her forlorn mood as she lay reminiscing, memories soothing her melancholy. Noticing a multitude of dust particles dancing in the sunlight coming through the window, she moved her arm out from under the bed covers. She watched in fascination as the dust moved around the room faster as she waved her arm about, then stopped and watched it settle on her hands.

This vision triggered a memory of Aednat's meditation story. *It can't be that simple*, she thought but closed her eyes nonetheless. Laying perfectly still, Olive began just as she had in her previous, tentative attempts at meditation. Inhaling deeply through her nose, she imagined warm, golden light coming in with her breath. Wonderous light filling every cell of her body with love, healing, and warmth. She breathed out slowly and completely while imagining her breath was removing pain, stress, and illness from her body.

Noticing she felt sleepier than before, she thought it might be better to sit up while meditating. She pushed herself up and wiped sleep from her eyes before inspecting the tip of her index finger. *Yuck!* Olive rubbed the grey-tinted between her fingers, freaked out by the colour and consistency of the substance. Throwing her legs over the bed, she walked over to her mirror and peered into it, prising her left eye open further for a closer inspection. *What the hell?*

Olive's eyes were mapped with the red lines of blood vessels. Moving a little further back, she looked over her face. *I look like I've been crying all night!*

She jumped onto her unmade bed to look out the bedroom window, all thoughts of meditation now completely forgotten. Peering out through the window, Olive was greeted with a grey haze that felt foreboding and sinister. She could barely see the next-door neighbour's flag. Olive's breath stopped as she registered that it was waving to the east, flapping like a drowning swimmer.

She raced out of her room and down the stairs, calling out for her mum as she ran.

"It's okay, Olive, we're here!" her parents called out in unison from the living room.

She found them surrounded by an assortment of luggage. "What are you doing?"

"They've changed the fire rating to Watch and Act. We're just preparing in case we have to leave quickly, that's all" her dad said calmly. "The fire's coming now?" Olive heard the panic on her voice and her mum stopped packing to face her.

"The conditions have changed, yes, but we don't have to go anywhere right now. We're just making sure we're ready."

"School has been called off today, Ollie."

Her happiness at her father's news was only momentary. "But we're supposed to be meeting with Sensei this afternoon!"

"We still can meet him. I'll give him a ring to see if we can do it this morning instead."

Olive caught the look her mother gave him. Not wanting to be present for an argument, Olive turned to go back to her room.

An hour later, Olive and her mum stood outside the *dojo*, her mum holding a plastic binder filled with paperwork.

"Are you sure my birth certificate is in there?" Olive asked, feeling tense.

"Yes, I checked before we left." Her mum looked back to where her dad was parking the car, then turned back to Olive. "Are you sure you have no idea why Sensei Matthew wants to see us and see your birth certificate?"

Olive gave her a look of frustration in reply. Her mum let out a long breath then reached over to stroke her hair, like she did when Olive was little. "I can only imagine what you've been feeling since Sensei gave you the letter."

Without removing her eyes from the ground, Olive squeezed her arms tighter around her waist, attempting to ease the tension in her stomach. Pressure in her chest made her take shallow breaths, pressure which only increased with her restricted inhalation and further fuelled the churn in her stomach. The perfect cycle of anxiety.

Olive closed her eyes, forcing herself to focus on what Aednat had told her to do when they were by the campfire. If there was any time for meditation, this surely had to be it. In her mind, Olive counted back from 50, slowly imagining each number's appearance in her mind. By 35, she felt a little less stressed, but her mind started to wonder off.

"Just bring your thoughts back to the last number you reached and continue," Aednat had said. "Be kind to yourself, just as you should be when learning any new skill. Being angry, frustrated or discouraged is not only unfair on yourself but also unhelpful when meditating."

Taking a deeper breath, Olive continued again from 35, dimly aware of her pulse beginning to slow a little. Upon reaching zero, Olive followed the next, slightly stranger, instruction Aednat had given, and imagined she was floating about 300 metres above the *dojo*. Past the dark smoke to where the sun was still shining, uninhibited by the clouds. Here surrounded by warmth, Olive imagined the light was pure love, and was entering her body, gloriously flooding through every inch of her body. Filling her with goodness and healing, both physical and emotional.

"We going in?" Her dad's voice broke her concentration.

Olive opened her eyes to a look of concern and bewilderment from her parents.

"Yep, let's go." Olive said, feeling infinitely lighter than she had five minutes before. *Man, I need to meditate more often*, she thought.

The smell of vinegar greeted the Ullmans as they entered. Boyan was on his hands and knees on the *tatami* beside a large bucket, scrubbing the mats in a circular motion.

"Surely there must be an easier way to clean those mats," Olive's mum whispered, wrinkling her nose.

"*Osu*," Olive said. Boyan turned around and nodded, but didn't get up to stand. She felt his reluctance and noticed his strange expression as he gestured towards the office.

"Sensei is out the back," he said, then turned back to his cleaning.

Olive's dad put his arms around her and her mum. "Okay, ladies, let's get this done."

Olive looked at her father, his chest out and head held high. Olive knew that whatever lay waiting for them, he was ready to protect and defend his family if need be. He may not be a black belt, but he wasn't a man to mess with, when it came to the females in his life.

As they entered the office, Olive saw Sensei was speaking to Sensei Sato, while *Shihan* Sato sat quietly in the corner of the room. Olive was surprised *Shihan* was not a part of the conversation. *Whatever this meeting is about, it doesn't involve him*, she realised. *It's not about karate.*

"Welcome, please take a seat." Sensei gestured towards the chairs next to him.

"Why do you need to see Olive's birth certificate?" Olive's mum blurted out.

Nodding his head slowly and calmly in recognition of her angst, Sensei gesturing again to the chairs. "This will be easier to explain if we are all seated."

Sitting between her father and mother, Olive looked towards her Sensei. His eyes were tired and showed signs of his own anxiety, but she also saw his compassion. Her mum was perched on the front of her chair, trying to appear relaxed and comfortable though neither was true.

"I mean no disrespect, but please can we get to why this meeting has been called?" Moving further forward in her seat, she added, "the timing isn't great with the Watch and Act warning." Olive's dad reached for her hand, trying to soothe the tension that had driven the blunt demand.

Clearing his throat, Sensei nodded his agreement. "Would it be okay if I saw Olive's birth certificate?"

Olive's mum reached into the clear plastic pouch and pulled out the document. However, as Sensei reached for the paper, she didn't release her grip, creating a brief, awkward moment where both teacher and mother held onto the certificate simultaneously, their eyes meeting.

Her mum's ferocious protectiveness dominated the moment, her body language speaking volumes. This was a woman not to be trifled with, especially not when it came to Olive. Despite the tension, Sensei responded with gentle, reassuring eyes which seemed to say, "I understand, and I care."

Releasing her grip reluctantly, Sensei moved the document closer to his face. Nervously, he turned the paper over and studied it with brief yet fierce scrutiny. After carefully placing the document on the coffee table in front of him next to another equally-sized document, Sensei raised his hands to his head to massage his temples.

"This somewhat confirms what I have suspected from the beginning." Without moving his eyes from the paper now on the table, he whispered, "What are the odds that you found your way to my *dojo*?"

Not able to contain her respectful demeanour anymore, Sensei Sato reached for the document. Tears began welling in her eyes, unnerving Olive. Speaking rapidly in Japanese, Sensei Sato appeared elated, and perhaps a little unhinged.

"Please," Olive's dad pleaded, "my family are in anguish. What does all this have to do with Olive?"

Sensei Sato stopped instantly and sat back down, and Sensei placed his hand on her knee. An action which seemed to ask for her silence. Turning around in his seat, Sensei pointed to the photograph that Olive had admired the last time she was in his office.

"That photograph is of three very dear and lifelong friends," he said, looking at Olive. "Sensei Sato, myself and Izabela Antov."

"What does Boyan's mother have to do with all this?" Olive said abruptly.

"When Izabela died, she stated in her will that she wished for Boyan to live with me." He leaned over to pick up the other document on the table. "This is Boyan's birth certificate."

Olive looked at it, taking in the name printed near the top. "Boyan Creed? But Izabela's last name is Antov and Boyan uses Antov as his last name?"

She saw her mum's eyes narrow. "Olive told me Boyan was adopted. Why would you adopt your own son?"

Responding first to Olive, Sensei attempted to clarify. "That really is a question for Boyan, but Antov is what he prefers." Turning his attention to her mother, he said, "I believe if I took a paternity test it would clearly show Boyan is, in fact, my son."

With this admission, Sensei Sato again sprung to her feet, angrily firing questions to Matthew in Japanese. He held his hand up to ask for permission to speak without turning to face his friend.

"No, Asami, it is not possible that he is my son–" Another round of vibrant Japanese words interrupted him. "I'm just saying the test would show he is my son."

Turning to face the Ullman's confused expressions, Sensei continued. "Sensei Sato didn't know Boyan's surname was listed as Creed on his birth certificate." Still facing a wall of bewildered faces, he continued, "I now believe the explanation for Creed being recorded as his surname, wasn't because Izabela and I were close friends, but because Boyan's real father was my brother."

"David Creed?" Olive's father asked.

"Yes," Sensei said. Sensei Sato sat down and lowered her head into her hands. "David and I were identical twins."

"I did wonder...I noticed how alike you were when I first met you."

"My understanding is that not all DNA is compared when doing a paternity test," he said, turning to his long-time friend. "Results are given with percentage accuracy according to the number of matches between two sets of DNA. As David and I would have the same markers, if he was the father, it would likely show that I was the father, too."

Clearing his throat and sitting further up in his seat, Olive's father stared at Sensei. "I dread to ask the question, but what does this have to do with Olive's birth certificate?"

"I already knew Olive's date of birth from the karate trial form you completed when she started." Sensei looked at Olive, "And from the very first time you entered the *dojo*, I saw you are the spitting image of Izabela." Olive opened her mouth to speak but quickly closed it again. "Not only does your freakish natural karate ability match hers, but Sensei Sato and I have both noticed the smaller mannerisms you share with her."

Olive pointed to the name of her biological mother on her birth certificate. "Isabella Creed is Izabela Antov?" Sensei was about to speak but she put both palms up towards him. "You are saying Boyan's mother Izabela Antov is actually Isabella Creed, the woman listed as my biological mother on my birth certificate?"

"Yes, I am saying that Izabela Antov placed her name as Isabella Creed on your birth certificate."

Shocked silence fell heavily on the room as Olive's mum reached out to grip Olive's hand. "That makes no sense!" Olive exclaimed. "Why would she list her last name as Antov on one birth certificate and Creed on another?"

"That I can only speculate, but your date of birth matches, and the hospital recorded on your birth certificate lists Bowral Hospital as your birth location. That was the hospital that Izabela-" Matthew stopped. "Bowral hospital is such a small hospital, Olive. There was very likely only one child born that day, at most a handful. And you look just like her."

"I don't understand," Olive exclaimed, her voice trembling with a mix of confusion and anger. "If that's true, why would she do that?" She looked accusingly at her parents, her heart pounding in her chest. "Did you know?"

"No, no, no, Honey. This is all new information, and I'm not even sure it's true!" Olive's mum replied, squeezing Olive's hand harder.

"Why would she change her name on my birth certificate?" Olive eyes darted towards the documents on the table. "Even the spelling of her first name has been changed!" She shook her head, feeling a wave of frustration and betrayal wash over her. Memories of years ago flooded back—hours spent poring over records and databases, chasing leads, following dead ends, when she was first told she was adopted. "All my research trying to discover who Isabella Creed was, it was all fruitless. I never had a chance of finding any information about my birth mother!"

Looking between Sensei and Sensei Sato, Olive pleaded, "Why would she do that?"

Sensei leaned forward to place his hand on Olive's shoulder, and seemed to search for the right words. "Truthfully Olive

I don't know. It seems your birth certificate provokes more questions than it answers." Rubbing her shoulder gently, he continued, "If your parents are open and willing, I am prepared to get a DNA test and Boyan has already confirmed he will, too. Would you be prepared to consider that?"

Olive stared at the ground in deep contemplation. She thought back to the conversation she'd had with her father after Sebastian's party. As they'd sat at the kitchen table, when he'd told her about his old colleague David Creed, and she'd thought what an odd coincidence it was, that he and Sensei had the same last name as her birth mother. She'd dismissed it, assuming it was a common last name. As she'd laid in bed that night, reliving the dreamy dance she'd had with Sebastian, she'd idly googled the number of Creeds in Australia – 85, and that was only those listed on the White Pages.

In the midst of Sensei's revelation, she looked at that action in a new light. Why had she felt compelled to find out how many Creeds were in the country? To prove a point to herself? To quash the small seedling of hope that she might finally have an answer to the question she had long ago deemed unanswerable?

"Then, if what I believe to be true is confirmed, maybe we can work together to uncover the reasons behind Izabela's name change, and why Boyan, Sensei Sato and I were led to believe both Izabela and her child both died in childbirth all those years ago?"

Olive's dad looked searchingly at his wife, as if hoping for approval of his next words. He cleared his throat. "Maybe we'll also finally find out why Olive was given to us for adoption after only being on the waiting list for a year." He looked out the window, shaking his head in wonder. "Crazy to think it's possible that Olive's biological father could be a man I worked with years ago, before she was even born."

"Boyan!" Olive's head shot up, and she turned to look at the office door, in the direction of the *dojo* where he'd been cleaning. "Boyan is my brother?" Though her words were more of a proclamation than a question, it was only dawning on her that she could have a sibling. One that she already knew.

"If this turns out to be true, the probability of you finding each other like this would be ridiculously low," her dad muttered.

"It's just so unbelievable. And, if I am to believe it, then it is also just so unbearably tragic. It's almost Shakespearean. All those lost years..." Olive's mum sniffed and looked to Matthew, her face softening for the first time since she entered the room.

Olive didn't have time for this. All this talk about probability and Shakespeare, as if this wasn't her life that had just been blown apart. Olive stood abruptly, her chair screaming over the polished wood floors, and walked out of the room. Entering the main training hall of the *dojo*, she found Boyan stretching on the mats, his cleaning finished. Upon seeing Olive, he stood quickly.

"How long have you known?" Olive accused. "Was this all just some plot? Get close to the new girl, warm her up, make her feel like she belongs, to soften the blow when you finally tell her that everything she thought she knew was a lie? Were the others in on it, too?"

Boyan opened his mouth to answer but she didn't wait for his reply. She ran to the barn exit doors, bumping into Sakura as she entered the *dojo*. Without turning to apologise, Olive was gone.

Chapter 35
Escape

Her feet pounded against the dry cracked earth in time with her rapidly beating heart, while the choking haze of grey smoke further confused Olive's mind. She ran aimlessly, driven only by a primal urge to be elsewhere.

She soon felt the ground beneath her feet begin to slope downwards. As the descent steepened she slowed her pace, knowing what awaited her at the bottom of the gulley. As the topography flattened out again, Olive squinted her eyes against the grey foe hindering her sight and bearings. "Where is it?" she said in frustration.

She stomped her foot against the bone-dry creek bed. "It's all gone! There's nothing left!!" The drought had caused the creek to completely dry up. The promise of being calmed by the soothing, refreshing creek was snatched away from her, just like what she had believed about her past. She was overwhelmed by the harsh reality of the once vibrant creek now barren, a victim of the relentless dry spell ravaging the land. Her heart sank as she gazed upon the cracked earth and parched rocks that had once been embraced by the gentle flow of water. Her knees buckled under the weight of this final blow to her last shred of hope.

With no concern for her clothes, Olive sat in the dirt of the dry creek bed. She pulled her knees to her chest and laid her heavy head on them. Her long blonde hair fell around her face, a prelude to the tears building. Olive felt the smudge of dirt across her face as she tucked her hair behind her ear and began to cry.

As her sobs intensified, Olive felt a tightness in her chest, the tight grasp on her knees and the pressure from her heaving cries hindering her breath's access to her lungs. She rolled onto her side, laying her body on what only months ago was a free-flowing creek.

As she lay in the foetal position, Olive released her internal torment, the sound of her cries echoing off the rock of the gully. The feeling of betrayal was swift and brutal. *Why would she do that to me?*

She'd come to terms with her birth mother's death years ago and had moved past the misguided but tenacious belief that it had been her fault, or her mother's. But this new information unleashed a well of anger inside her, pulling her to her knees. "All those years searching for her," Olive howled aloud. "For what? It wasn't even your name!" Rage and a deep, smothering sadness crushed her chest, limiting her ability to breathe. She channelled the vehemence of her emotions into screaming louder, "Did you not care for me at all?"

She collapsed, exhausted, onto her side again and rolled her head over the silt-covered ground, the rocking motion providing momentary distraction from the pounding tension in her head. She continued the movement again and again, searching for relief.

Eventually, discomfort from the hard ground beneath her, forced her to a seated position. As she sat, she became aware of the surreal silence now accompanying her. Not a creature crawled, nor a bird sang. Olive rubbed her upper arms, seeing the long streaks of dirt covering her new white t-shirt. Right now, she couldn't care less.

She noticed the darkening light around her, unsure if it was the result of increasing smoke or the setting sun. *How long have I been here?* Though she had no wish to return to the situation she had run from, she knew she couldn't stay here forever. She stood, then looked for the best way out, turning around on the spot. All she could see was grey and dark brown, the land around her an undecipherable smudge. Which way was the *dojo*? Charred air hit her nostrils as she tried to take a deep breath to quell the fear beginning to rise within her. It wasn't nightfall, it was smoke. She had to get out of here now.

She stepped cautiously with her right leg, attempting to gauge the land directly in front of her. Was it going up? Uncertain, Olive turned her body 180 degrees before stretching her left leg outwards, tapping the ground now in front of her. *Where the hell am I?*

Olive got down on all fours, wildly feeling the earth with both hands as she crawled forward, her heart beating harder within her chest. The rocks grazed the palms of her hands and ground hard against her knees, forcing her back into a squatting position. She began waddling forward like a baby duck, relieved to find the ground was going up. Unable to see more than half a metre in front of her, Olive continued upwards in a variety of animal-inspired movements, from a duck walk to a frog jump and then a monkey crawl, all while continuing to feel the terrain in front of her.

Just as she began to feel a little hopeful, a sharp pointed object snagged her cheek. A spike from a low-lying shrub had hooked her skin like a fish. The searing pain and shock made her scream, halting her ascent. Her hands flew to her face and the branch that was caught on her skin. Using her left hand to keep her skin taut, she carefully dislodged it and felt the warmth of blood running down her face. Olive wiped the warm viscous liquid across her jaw and mouth, the taste of blood scaring her more than the pain. She pulled the sleeve of her t-shirt to the wound.

"You're okay," she said to herself in a trembling voice. "Don't panic, you're okay." She rubbed the side of her face, noting the blood soaking into the white fabric. "Keep going, don't give up."

Placing both hands back on the ground, Olive jumped forward from her crouching position, and immediately hit her head against something solid. Olive reached forward through the choking darkness, feeling a cold, metal structure in front of her. *The fence!* She pulled herself up to a standing position with the aid of the structure in front of her. At last, she knew where she was!

Keeping both hands on the fence, Olive sidestepped to the left until she got to the junction between the back fence of Sensei's house and the side driveway of the *dojo*. Moving around the corner, she tried to remember what was between her current location and the back gate fence that led into the *dojo* grounds. Was there a garden somewhere or just a driveway? She couldn't recall.

Like a sea crab coming out of its shell, Olive continued her cautious side-stepping manoeuvre along the fence. She knew she needed to cross the driveway at some point. Reluctant to leave the structure bringing her comfort, she crouched down to the ground and turned her body in what she believed to be a 45-degree angle from the fence line, up towards the *dojo*. *If I can find the dojo fence, then I can just walk along until I find the back gate,* she thought, cheering herself on.

A siren sounded from close by, and Olive assumed it was a fire truck pulling out of the Fire Station. She felt a rush of chills against the back of her neck and spine. She froze as she listened for the direction the truck was heading, and realised it was coming her way. As the truck passed the *dojo*, Olive saw the flashing lights piece through the smoke. *If I can see that, then I must be in the middle of the dojo driveway!* From her crouched position, she continued forward, optimism increasing her speed. *Keep going, just keep going.*

This time it was Olive's hands that found the metal fence in front of her. Unlike the solid corrugated metal of Sensei's boundary, the *dojo* fence was made with metal bars. Now she needed to work out where exactly on the fence line she was. Searching the ground around her, Olive found a long stick to assist her. At each step along the fence, she pushed the stick through the bars and trashed it around, hoping to hit something indicating where she was.

Eventually the stick scraped against something to her left and her heart leapt in response to the sound.

"That's the toilet block for sure!" she yelled triumphantly. She followed in the direction of where the stick had hit, while keeping her hands on the fence until she felt the different shape of the metal beneath her hands. *The gate!* She dropped the stick and searched the top of the gate for the latch, hoping it would be unlocked. *Found it!* Her heart skipped a beat when the latch pulled up without resistance. *It's open!*

Though these surroundings were much more familiar to Olive, the diminished visibility didn't make it easy. She walked slowly with both hands out in front of her until she felt the texture of old paint fragments crumbling off the wood before her. Running her fingers carefully over the outside of the building, she realised she was at a door when she felt the padlock. *It's unlocked also, yes!*

She unhooked the lock from the latch and heard the creaking sound of the doors swinging open. Instinctively, she pulled her hands to her head. While she was able to stop the left barn door's impact, the right door smashed into her head. A deep, throbbing pain at her temple caused Olive to cry out, the sensation mingling with her frustration and exhaustion. She didn't need to see her face to know blood was once again coursing down it. She tasted its bitterness on her tongue, matching the flavour of her feelings. She screamed again, this time in response to the unfair hand she'd been dealt.

With her arms wrapped around her head, she walked through the doors with trepidation. Triggered by the motion sensor inside, the lights came on allowing Olive to see her surroundings for what felt like the first time in hours. With her vision blurred from the smoke, her pounding head and her tears, she moved towards the stack of old karate mats to sit down, whimpering.

The smell of smoke mingled with the scent of turpentine, paint and mildew as she crumped to the mats, feeling the creep of cold in her limbs. Seeing what looked like a pile of old drop sheets beside her, she reached down and tossed one over her shoulders. With great effort, she balled up another sheet in a dismal attempt to make a pillow then laid down on her side.

Her legs began to throb, so she pulled them to her chest and rubbed them with her hands. Yielding to the feelings of abandonment and conceding to her physical injuries, Olive shut her eyes completely. Overcome with exhaustion, she collapsed. Sleep descended with dangerous swiftness.

Chapter 36
Siblings

"She hasn't come back yet?" Boyan stood quickly upon hearing the news, pressing his phone firmer against his ear. "Why would she be here at our house?"

He opened the back sliding glass door to the verandah, peering into the back yard, "I can't see anything with this smoke!" He went back inside quickly, retreating from the thick black air. "Have they checked their house?" Boyan paused, "Yep, dumb question. Alright, I'm coming now."

Boyan grabbed a jumper from the back of the loungeroom chair and tied it around his waist then snatched a water bottle. As he paused at the front door to slip on his shoes, he had a thought, *Sebastian*. He pulled out his phone again to call his friend.

His right foot tapped rapidly against the tiles beneath him while he waited for Sebastian to answer.

"What's up?" Sebastian's familiar greeting, though delivered in his usual cheerful tone, did little to quell the frantic tapping.

"I need your help. Olive is missing."

"What?" The change in Sebastian's tone was immediate.

"She bolted into the bush earlier today and she hasn't come back yet."

"Into the bush? Why?"

"Ah mate, I don't know where to start," Boyan confessed, as he pressed his fingers into his forehead. "Can you get to the *dojo*? I'll fill you in later. We need to track her down."

"I'm already on my way!"

Locking the house door behind him, Boyan ran to the *dojo*, faster than he ever had before. He raced through the hall towards Matthew's office, not bothering to take his shoes off nor close the door behind him.

"What are you looking for?" Boyan asked, surprised to find Matthew leaning into the back storeroom cupboard.

"There's a torch in here somewhere," Matthew replied, without turning around. "I thought it might help."

Before Boyan could help him find it, Sebastian walked through the door.

"Has Olive been found?" Sebastian asked hopefully.

"Not yet," Matthew said, turning from the cupboard with the torch in his hand.

"Boyan said she ran into the bush. What happened?" Matthew shot Boyan a look. "What?" Sebastian asked, feeling the tension in the room.

Breathing out deeply, Matthew hesitated before explaining. "Olive found out today Boyan might be her brother."

"What?!"

"Boyan will fill you in, but I need you both out looking for her," Matthew said, handing the torch to Boyan. "She can't be too far from the *dojo*. You boys look to the west and north of the *dojo*, I'll focus on the bushland to the south." He handed them both a walkie talkie. "Leave them on the channel that they're set to." He picked up another large metal torch from his desk. "Keep talking so I know you both are okay. Keep your shirts over your mouths and flash the light so hopefully Olive can see it. It's going to be hard to call out in this smoke, so listen carefully to see if you can hear her."

Boyan and Sebastian walked quickly out of the *dojo* office. "You okay?" Boyan asked his friend.

"How can I be dating your sister?"

"Yeah, it's messed up. But that's the least of it."

Turning his head to face Boyan, Sebastian's facial expression pleaded for an explanation.

"Olive is Izabela's daughter, her birth certificate proves she didn't die at birth," Boyan explained.

"What the hell?" Sebastian shook his head.

"I know, it's crazy, but there's more. Matthew just confessed he thinks our father is David."

"Who?"

"Matthew's twin brother!"

Sebastian stopped walking "What? That's seriously messed up, mate!"

"Agreed, but it all makes sense now. Why I can feel her emotions more deeply than anyone else. And why I feel so weirdly protective towards her." Boyan paused momentarily to reflect. "But I didn't see the whole David thing coming!"

"You know, I always believed you had to be Sensei's son. I've always said you look like his younger brother!"

"We look similar from the back but other than that I don't really see the resemblance."

"*And* Creed is your last name according to your birth certificate," Sebastian probed.

"Yeah, but Matthew thought Izabela did that because they were so close." Boyan handed Sebastian the torch. "You take this one, I'll grab the one we have at home."

"Yeah but who does that?" Sebastian said, tossing the torch between his hands. "Who changes their son's surname to honour a friend? I know you don't want to hear this but you've been wrapped up in Sensei's denial your whole life!"

Boyan slowly nodded his head, seeing frustration warring with fear on his friend's face. "I know, mate," he soothed. "I have a lot to work out. But for now, let's go find your girlfriend." Sebastian nodded eagerly. "You head straight down towards the creek bed and then go north in a zigzag pattern. After I grab my torch, I'll go west of the creek and work my way up through the bushland towards Olive's house. Stay on the walkie talkie."

Sebastian nodded and ran from the *dojo*.

Boyan reached for the torch positioned on the top kitchen shelf, then turned when he heard a noise. *What was that?* Suddenly, an intense pain hit him, and he fell to his knees, clutching his head. Fear, grief, and agony flooded through him, like he had never experienced before. *Olive.* He grabbed the torch and rushed out the back doors and into the garden, then jumped over the side fence. Boyan switched the torch on but the light reflected off the smoke and into his eyes, making it even harder to see. "Useless thing," he muttered.

He reached for his mobile phone, and turned the small torchlight light on, waving the beam towards the grey smoke, but it did little to penetrate the dense air. Amongst the acrid smell of burning vegetation and the ominous atmosphere, Boyan closed his eyes and whispered the number three, three times. With eyes still shut he completed his meditation mantra until he felt calm and clear. *I might not be able to see her, but I can feel my way.* Boyan opened his eyes and turned confidently to the left.

He put his phone back into his pocket, freeing his hands to reach forward as he took careful steps. He soon found the *dojo* fence and followed it until he found the gate. It was wide open – proof she'd come this way. With both arms outstretched before him, Boyan searched for the side of the *dojo*. His left hand brushed up against one of the *dojo*'s storeroom doors and found it open too.

Taking a step into the storeroom, Boyan's eyes squinted against the light. Blinking, he allowed his eyes to adjust to the sudden brightness before cautiously moving forward. His heart raced with anticipation as he strained his eyes to scan the room, searching for any sign of her.

"Olive!" Her limp, still body against the mats made him gasp. Moving closer, he saw reddish-brown blood against her white cold skin, causing his breaths to come faster and shallower. He placed his hands on her shoulders and squeezed harder than he meant to.

"Olive!" He moved his face closer to hers, tilting his head to the side to try to feel her breath on his cheek. His heart stopped as he waited for confirmation. Finally, he felt the faint whisper of air upon his face and it was like a defibrillator restarting his heart.

"Please, Olive, you need to wake up," he said, louder, as he squeezed up and down her arms. As he tried to bring life back to her limbs, his sickening dread ebbed away, replaced by a warm, loving feeling. Slowly, Olive's eyes fluttered open.

"Boyan, you're crying? What's wrong?" Olive asked, struggling to sit up. He looped an arm under her back and helped her up.

"I thought you had..."

"I had what?" Olive asked, looking at him in confusion.

"You looked dead," Boyan took a deep breath, trying to calm the shaking in his hands. "I thought I had lost you." Olive looked down at his trembling hands and he clasped them together for support.

"I'm sorry I scared you," she whispered.

"I only just found you, Olive." He squeezed his hands together harder.

She searched his face. "You already believe we're siblings, don't you?"

"If I'm honest with myself, I think I've known for a while." He shifted closer to her. "Even though I was just three, I've got memories of our mum. I can still feel how safe I was in her arms, and her pure, unconditional love she had for me. It's something I'll never forget."

She looked down, and Boyan could feel the grief deep in her heart, so strong tears formed in his eyes. He placed his hands over Olive's. "I feel those same feelings of safety and love when you are around me, like she is with me." He held her hands tighter. "Like she's with both of us."

Tears spilled from Olive's eyes, raw emotion expressed in soul-wracking sobs. Her body shook with the ferocity of her sadness. He wrapped her in his arms, desperate to take the pain from her.

"She loved you, she wanted you, but," Olive's body shook harder against Boyan's embrace, "she didn't want me!"

Rubbing her back was all Boyan could think to do while he waited for her emotional intensity to ease. "Olive, I think your name proves otherwise." Her sobbing eased to whimpers as she breathed in shuddering gasps.

She pulled back and looked into his face. "How?"

"Peace, love and balance – that's what 'Olive' means," Boyan said, looking deep into her eyes. "We were joking not that long ago about what Izabela would've called me if she'd found balance before I was born. She called you Olive. I now know she found peace in the end, and I have no doubt that she loved us both very much."

Olive placed her hand over her lips as she took in his words. "Then why did she change her surname and the spelling of her first name on my birth certificate?"

"I don't know, but I'm certain her decision had absolutely nothing to do with her lack of love for her children. In fact, I feel it has to do with just how much she loved us."

"That makes no sense!" Olive rebutted.

"You're right," he said, nodding. "Just like it makes no sense I've ignored the fact that Creed was listed on my birth certificate as my surname."

"Is that why you don't use Creed as your surname?"

"Maybe," Boyan admitted, "but mostly because using Antov connects me to my mum." Boyan smiled. "Our mum." Silence joined the conversation momentarily while Boyan dwelled on the situation of Olive's birth. "She chose your first name, Olive, and she made the decision to change her surname before she died. Either she secretly married David Creed between when you and I were born, or there is something more to all of this. Regardless, I know she loved and wanted us both with every cell of her being." Moving the tears-soaked hair gently away from her face, he smiled at Olive. "I wouldn't be surprised if she was somehow responsible for us finding each other."

"Boyan!" Sebastian's voice sliced through the smoke.

"Olive's in the storeroom!" Boyan yelled back. Within seconds Sebastian's mobile phone light was illuminating both their faces.

"Olive, are you okay?"

Boyan raising his hands to shield his eyes from the light. "She's injured but she's okay."

As Sebastian raced to her side, Boyan moved away to give him space. He watched his best friend gently caress the uninjured side of her head with one hand while placing his other arm around her body for support and warmth. "We've all been so worried!"

She looked up away from the two of them, shame colouring her cheeks. "You probably think I'm an idiot."

"Not at all, I once did something similar."

"You did?" Olive asked, resting her head on his shoulder.

"Before I met Boyan or joined the *dojo*, there was a time I didn't come home after school, after a really bad beating." Olive placed her hand on Sebastian's chest as she listened quietly. "Mum found me late that night, curled up, twisted in pain, and weeping in the darkness. I can only imagine the hell I put my parents through. That was the day my mum instantly changed her pacifist position and immediately started searching for local self-defence classes." Stroking Olive's hair gently he continued, "When Boyan first came round to our house, she said it was a sign."

Olive nodded then took a deep breath. "Can you both help me back into the *dojo*? I've caused my parents enough stress."

Sebastian took off his jacket and draped it over Olive's shoulders, then he and Boyan hoisted her up gently, and slowly walked outside.

With the predicted wind change arriving earlier than expected, the visibility had improved, making the journey to the dojo much easier. Stepping into the hall, Sebastian lowered Olive into a chair.

"Olive!" Her mother and father yelled, then rushed to her side.

As they hugged her, Boyan saw the relief change to frustration, as their fear found a way to escape.

"Where were you?" Olive's mum yelled. "Do you have any idea how stupid it was to run off into the bush with a bush fire coming?"

"We've been sick with worry!" Her dad scolded, his face pale.

"Look at you!" her mum exclaimed, moving her hands gently across her daughter's face. "You could've been killed!"

Olive threw her arms around her mother's neck. "I'm sorry I scared you, I'm sorry I ran off." She started crying. "I'm so, so sorry."

Olive's dad dropped to his knees to hug them both.

"Let me take a look at your face," Matthew suggested, approaching with the *dojo*'s first aid kit. He took out an antiseptic wipe. "This is going to sting." Olive scrunched her face as the wipe touched her skin, and Boyan winced in empathy.

"Sorry, Olive," Matthew said, carefully inspecting her face. "The cut looks worse than what it is. I doubt you'll need stitches."

"But it looks so bad," Olive's mum said, worry suffusing her voice. "Her eyes look unfocused. Could she be concussed?"

"I think she could be," Matthew said, turning to look at the concerned parents. "I think you should take her to get checked out."

"Right then, Olive," her dad laughed shakily, "time for another trip to the hospital!"

Chapter 37
Enough

"What now?" Olive's dad grumbled as he reached for his phone at the same time Olive reached for hers.

"Did you get the same message?" Olive said, looking down at her screen. Her dad looked up from his phone to reach for Olive's.

"Yep, it looks like the RFS have downgraded the fire threat."

"Finally some good news!" Her mum announced, walking into the room and waving her phone in the air.

"Does that mean I can go for a jog?" Olive asked.

"Are you serious?" Olive's mum squawked. "Are you so concussed that you don't remember what the doctor said? They ordered you to rest for the next 48 hours – at least!"

"Just kidding," Olive smirked.

Her mum's phone rang, cutting off her cry of frustration at Olive's little prank. "I mustn't have put it back on silent after the search," she admitted with annoyance, then answered in a clipped tone. After a minute of listening to the caller, she shot Olive a look.

"Would you like visitors?" she asked, pulling the phone away from her face.

"Yes! Who's coming?"

"Okay, we'll see you then," Olive's mum confirmed into the phone then hung up. "That was your Sensei," she said, and Olive heard the reluctance in her tone. "He and Boyan are coming around to see how you are."

The time before the doorbell rang throughout the Ullman's house felt like an eternity, and Olive's constant checking out the front window did nothing to speed up the clock. After ten or so laps between the window and kitchen, her guests finally arrived.

"There she is," Sensei said, his smile wide as he came through the front door. "How are you feeling?"

Olive touched her head gently. "I'm okay. My head hurts a bit."

"What did the docs say?" Boyan asked, taking a seat in the lounge room chair next to Olive.

"Sensei was right – I have a mild concussion but everything else is okay."

"That's great news," Sensei said, and Olive saw him and Boyan sigh in relief.

The doorbell rang again, and Olive's mum jumped to her feet. "Who could that be?"

"Goodness!" she heard her mum exclaim. "Well, I guess you all better come in too."

Olive turned around to see Joy coming through the door, followed by Sakura, and Aednat, who turned to look out the door she had just walked through.

"You coming in or not?" Aednat asked.

Sebastian entered, holding a large crockpot. "Sorry, I was taking my shoes off."

"We've all taken our shoes off!" Aednat remarked, while pointing at the group's feet.

"Yeah, but no one else is holding a huge kitchen pot full of hot food!" Sebastian said, then handed the crockpot to Olive's mum. "My mum thought you could use some homemade Chilean food."

"That is so nice of her," she said, taking off the lid and inhaling deeply. "Oh wow! Please thank her from me!"

Joy squatted down next to Olive and looked over her face. "Oh, you poor thing," she said. "Are you in a lot of pain?"

Olive shook her head while looking around the room at everyone who had gathered to see her. Her eyes started to well with tears as her bottom lip wriggled about under her teeth's grip. She looked down at her hands and began pulling at a cuticle.

From behind the group, Aednat stepped closer to Olive. "You okay?"

Olive looked up briefly, catching Aednat's concerned expression then dropped her head again. How could she possibly voice words to the storm inside her? Would they even understand? She closed her eyes, her breath shuddering in her chest.

"I don't know who I am," she whispered finally, sharing the fear growing inside her heart since yesterday. "I'm not like Izabela, I don't have superhuman strength, nor am I brave like you, Aednat, or focused like Sakura."

She exhaled in a huff, allowing a small release of her frustration. "I can't make people laugh like Sebastian, and I'm only just starting to learn how to be warm and friendly like Joy. Though I could never hope to be as bright and bubbly as you are," Olive said, glancing at her best friend before lowering her head into her hands. A sense of surrender washed over her. "I'm just... nothing special," she murmured softly.

She heard the room gasp in surprise, all except Boyan.

He leaned over to her, and gently pulled Olive's hands away from her face, making her face him. "Olive, remember that day I got on your case for not paying attention in the bush?"

Olive nodded while frowning at the reminder. "I regretted it instantly. It was like I felt your frustration as if it were my own." Kneeling beside Olive's chair, he continued, "I couldn't explain it then, but I realised our connection runs deeper than I thought. Like we're linked."

He leaned in closer. "I get where you're coming from," he whispered, just loud enough for her to hear. "I've struggled too, trying to find my place alongside Izabela's legacy and abilities. Your feelings? They're valid."

Olive's eyes began to sting as tears started to form. "You are enough," he said, loud enough for her friends to hear. He smiled softly, and she saw the love radiating. "As you are – right here, right now – Olive Sapphire Ullman, you are enough."

Even in her turmoil, she understood why he said her full name. In doing so, Boyan was acknowledging Olive's adopted parents and their sacred role in raising Olive.

While part of her heard his words "you are enough" to mean "you will do", like she was a second prize, the other part knew this was not what he meant.

Aednat stepped forward and placed her hand on Olive's shoulder. "You are enough, just as you are. You are beautiful, broken and all." Olive was touched by Aednat's solidarity and knew she was sharing her own learned wisdom.

Sakura came up to her next. "Despite what you believe about yourself, Olive, and despite your pain, you keep showing up in life, every day. You are already doing what many in this world avoid. Without changing, you are already enough."

Joy clasped her hands together and brought them to her chest. "Olive, I can't even begin to understand how you are feeling," she said, her voice husky with emotion. "I'm just grateful you are my friend. You don't want me to change or be anything other than who I am, even though you are so freaking awesome. Olive, you are more than enough!"

A lifetime of believing the wrong things couldn't be undone in a moment, but Olive was beginning to see things differently. Inside, a small voice began to call out in affirmation of her friends' words.

From the back of the room, Sebastian finally stepped forward. "There is no mistake that you are enough and you belong here, right now." He looked deeply into her eyes, and she read the love and deep acceptance within them. "You were born with a purpose, Olive, just like all of us. No one in this world is a no one." He pulled a clean tissue from his pocket and handed it to her.

As she took the tissue, she saw his concern melt away, an inspired look coming into his wide eyes. "Do you have a pen and paper?" he said, rising suddenly.

"Should be in the top drawer of the TV unit," Olive said, confused. Walking to the draw, Sebastian pulled out an exercise pad and a black permanent marker. Taking the lid off the marker, he began to write Olive's full name in large capital letters.

"From the very first day you told me your name Olive, I knew you belonged. Your name announces to all that you are destined to be here, and, you are special just as you are."

Bewildered expressions descended on the room. Olive saw her friends look between each other and the page.

"Check out the mother of all *dojo* acronyms!" Sebastian said, pointing to the paper. Only Boyan showed a glimmer of understanding on his face.

Sebastian circled the first letter of Olive's first, middle and last names then turned the exercise book around for all to see. Without waiting to see if they'd caught on, he wrote those letters in big, bold handwriting: an 'O' for Olive, 'S' for Sapphire and 'U' for Ullman.

Together, those letters made a new word, a word everyone in the room knew. Even Olive's mum and dad had become accustomed to hearing it spoken.

"*Osu*, Olive. With the first name that Izabela gave you and the middle and surname from your parents, your acronym is literally *Osu*." Sebastian smiled encouragingly. "You don't need to understand why this has all occurred to know, there is serendipity at play here. Something, or someone, greater than all of us has had a hand in your life to bring you to this point."

The confused silence now turned to awe-filled quiet. Everyone knew he spoke truth. "My mother often says the universe conspires to give to us that which we most deeply want."

Olive knew Sebastian was right. She could not recall a time when she had not wished to know the secret of her biology. A small smile grew as she realised she had received what she had most wanted. Looking at Boyan, her smile widened in acknowledgement of the gift she was given, far greater than she had ever dreamed. A brother.

Epilogue

Olive leaned closer to the mirror to apply her eye liner, drawing a subtle wing shape. This close to the mirror, she could not help but read the message she had placed there. Three months ago, Olive had written in red lipstick, "I AM ENOUGH". Words to serve as a constant reminder of the day she wrote them; the day after she discovered her biological family. The day she started to believe she was worthy of the fortunate life she had.

From her driveway, a car horn sounded, hurrying her. Racing out of the bedroom, she ran to her parents and hugged them tightly, now a common practice.

"Love you both," she said, then grabbed her purse.

"Have fun," her parents called out in unison.

Stepping onto the recently renovated front verandah, Olive laughed when she spied the vehicle. Sticking out of the sunroof and holding a large black and white umbrella, Sebastian called, "Señorita, your chariot awaits."

Olive's heart burst with love for his antics. He was certainly a clown, but he was her clown and she loved him for it. His ability to make her laugh and take life less seriously was a gift, one beginning to rub off on her.

"Wait there, I'll come get you," Sebastian yelled as he folded the umbrella down. As if he was in an elevator, he slowly descended through the sunroof then closed it.

The falling rain was getting heavier but Olive refused to complain. Turning to the right, she smiled at the flag which for months had hung limp and soaked. The rain responsible for finally putting out the Yellow Valley Fire continued intermittently for months, allowing Wollondilly's inhabitants a chance to rest, free from the fear of fire.

"Señorita," Sebastian's words and outstretched hand stole Olive's attention away from the neighbour's drenched, motionless flag. With one hand around his back, they walked towards the white limousine. The door slid open to reveal the spacious interior filled with cheers and laughter. Sebastian helped her inside then climbed in.

"Okay, okay, calm down everyone," Sebastian hushed the gathering. "Now the birthday girl is here, it's time to get this party started." He placed his arm lovingly around Olive's shoulders before continuing.

Uncharacteristically, Boyan joined in the excitable cheers. Discovering they were siblings had not only had a profoundly positive effect on Olive; she'd seen the change in him, too. He seemed more connected to his friends, and to himself. They were healing together.

Though he'd told her he hadn't felt the need for the DNA test, he'd taken it regardless, as had Olive. Neither of them were surprised to learn they were truly siblings. Boyan had even laughed about the close match between them and Sensei, which proved David was their father. "You really are my dad," he'd joked. They'd not only found each other, but discovered who their biological father was and gained an uncle. Now was the time for celebration.

Boyan raised his hands to speak. "To the coolest sister a brother could have – Happy Birthday, Olive!"

"Happyyyyy," Sebastian began, prolonging the last syllable to allow everyone to join in.

Olive snuggled closer to Sebastian as he led a round of 'Happy Birthday'. She loved listening to him sing. As the song continued, she looked around the inside of the limousine, filled with her best friends. *This is the first time I've celebrated my birthday since I discovered I was adopted*, she thought as happy tears fell onto her cheeks.

Fully immersed in the moment, Olive looked at the faces before her. Each person was unique yet bound together by a shared love for life and for each other. As she did so often these days, Olive smiled, finally and wholeheartedly believing in her own worth.

The once seemingly contradictory concepts were now harmoniously aligned in Olive's mind. She understood now, achieving remarkable feats didn't require extraordinary qualities; rather, it involved a unique approach to life. Olive realised her beliefs about herself, held the key to unlocking what was possible. With newfound conviction, she embraced believing greatness was within reach, both for herself and others.

Olive had embarked on a journey of self-discovery, a journey which encompassed both her mind and body. She recognised the importance of surrounding herself with positive influences, nurturing empowering beliefs, and cultivating daily habits conducive to growth—like her ongoing dedication to karate training.

As the limousine drove towards Sydney for a night of birthday celebrations, Olive's heart was filled with abundance. Filled with gratitude knowing tonight was just one of many adventures that she would have with her friends.

She knew that their friendship would be lifelong, just like Matthew, Asami and Izabela.

Japanese Glossary

Bachi   Japanese wooden drumsticks

Dachi   Karate stances

Dogi   Karate uniform

Dojo   The place of the way (the venue you learn *karate)*

Fudo dachi   Karate relaxed yet aware stance

Geri   The word on its own means diarrhea, but next to a directional word like *mae* (front) *geri* means kick.

Hajime   Beginning (in karate, it's a command to begin)

Hachi   Eight

Hiza geri   Knee kick

Ichi, **ni**, **san**   One, two, three

Karate   Empty handed

Karateka   Practitioner of karate

Kata   Form. In karate it is techniques performed in a set routine

Kiai   Unified energy (loud explosive scream)

Kumite   Entangled hands (Karate sparring or fighting)

Mae geri   Front kick

Mawashi geri   Round house kick

Mawate   Turn around

Mokuso   Eyes closed, silent meditation

Mokuso yame   End of closing eyes meditation (eyes open)

Obi   Karate belt

Odaiko   Largest of all the Japanese drums

Okaasan   Less formal way of saying mother

Oi tsuki   Jab or punch with your front hand

Osu   A respectful karate greeting to replace many words and expressions like; yes, I agree, excuse me, hello and goodbye. A philosophy of perseverance, patience, respect, and gratitude. In Japanese culture, *osu* is a strong assertive word that has a 'let's kick butt' spirit. It is not a word you should say carelessly. In Japan, outside of karate, the word *osu* is not spoken by women. Outside of karate the word *osu* is hardly spoken at all in Japan. As *osu* has a silent 'u', sometimes you will see the spelling to be 'oss'.

Otousama   Very polite / formal way of saying father

Otagai ni rei Karate bowing to everyone or to your opponent

Rei Respect

San Suffix meant to show respect, like Mr or Mrs. On its own it means the number three.

Sayonara Goodbye

Seiken chudan tsuki Middle body punch

Seiza Formal and traditional Japanese seated position

Sensei Teacher (one who has come before in life)

Shihan Teacher of teachers

Sosai ni rei Bow to *Sosai* (founder)

Taiko Japanese drums

Tatami Karate training mats or tournament mats

Tobi Jump

Uke To receive (to block a technique)

Ushiro mawashi geri Back spinning kick

Yame Finish or stop

Renowned and highly trusted in the 1990s and 2000s for her striking and distinctive flair as a professional photographer, Sarhn photographed four Australian Prime Ministers, immortalised numerous celebrities, and vividly captured a plethora of sporting legends through her lens.

After retiring her camera, Sarhn followed her passion for martial arts into founding a karate dojo, channelling her desire into making a profound and positive impact on the lives of her students. Imparting invaluable life skills such as strength of character, compassion, respect, self-awareness, focus, courage, determination, discipline, and confidence.

Sarhn.com

Dear Reader,

Thank you for embarking on this adventure with Olive. I would love to stay connected. Join my email newsletters to receive updates on future books, hear about book signing & reading events, and discover special opportunities that you won't find anywhere else.

As a special thank you, you will receive a behind 'Osu' story reveal video. Visit my website sarhn.com to subscribe or scan the QR code below.

Warmly,
Sensei Sarhn

Show your love for 'Osu'

If you found 'Osu' inspiring and or enjoyable, please:

1) Leave a review on Amazon (and or wherever you purchased 'Osu' from). Your words can inspire others to pick up the book!

2) Recommend it to friends on social media. Get creative and have fun. Don't forget to tag Sensei Sarhn.

3) If you are on 'Goodreads' and or 'BookBub', please let everyone know you have read 'Osu' and share a review.

4) Maybe visit your local library and or book store and recommend they stock 'Osu'.

Thank you and Osu!

Acknowledgements

I would like to thank my husband Brett, daughter Willow, and my mother Carol for their love, support and unfailing belief in my ability to finish this novel. Thank you to Shihan Daniel Trifu for your encouragement to "write what you feel you need to write."

Thank you to Ian Parkin, who always makes me laugh and gave me some great advice earlier in the 'Osu' publishing journey. Thank you to Heather Dyer for always listening to my writing ideas with total excitement. Thank you to YuNiOn; Masae Ikegawa and Graham Hilgendorf, for the knowledge regarding Taiko drumming.

Thank you to Nicole Palmer for your excitement for 'Osu' and for pointing me towards my editor, Haylee Kerans (who was just what I needed to whip this novel into shape).

Thank you to 'Osu' Launch Team!

Adam Chambers, Alexis Gilberd, Alison Rourke, Allison Black, Amber Mackay, Amber Moley, Amber Shortus, Anita Valenzisi, Annalise Reid, Anne-Maree Clarke, Annette Kane, Annette Mackay, April Holdsworth, Alex Sommer, Ash McMahon, Ayat Yasser, Azrielle Hornstra, Bec Bradford, Bec Weekes, Bree Edge, Brett Gumbley, Brett Jones, Brett McArthur, Caleb Dyer, Candice Muzevic, Carol Chambers, Carol Nelson, Caterina Pitts, Catherine Ford, Cathryn Louise, Christine Hornstra, Christine Walsh, Cindy Kaye, Cindy Jenart, Clarissa Johnson, Cody Podres, Connor Robinson, Cooper Lenz, Curtis Lewsey, Daniel Fear, David McArthur, Debbie Diplock, Debbie Stephenson, Debby Neich, Deb Shaw, Dekoda Bowes, Dhea Bartlett, Domonic Vella, Eesa Lihu, Eli Pollard, Eliza Mulcair, Emma Clout, Emma Dyer, Emma Simons, Erin Henderson, Felicia Williams, Georgia Turner, Hannah Collins, Hayley Hickman, Heather Andrusiw, Heather Dyer, Helen Facey, Henry Dyer, Hilde Swendgaard, Ian Parkin, Jaime Gardner, Jane Dyer, Jannikke Ercilia Toresen Berger, Jasper Bowes, Jennifer Hill, Jenny Dzidowski, Jen Pritchard, Jen Taylor, Jessica Wright, Jess Savoie, Joanne Heaton, Ibrahim Abuamer, Jodie Bosnjak, Jolyne Allard-Silva, Julieanne Brown, Karen Calandra, Karen Heap, Karen Johnson, Karen Stiles, Katarina Milinkovic, Kate Bentham, Kate Murphy Kontos, Katie Banks, Katie Rose Jabbie, Keean

Webb, Keith Ferrero-Lamelas, Kelly Ware, Kerri Chambers, Kerrie Milne, Kerrie O'Grady, Kerry Murphy, Kristen Collins, Kirsty Hassall, Kristy Dunkling, Kylie Eastham, Kylie Sanderson, Kym Farrell, Laura Cowell, Laura Taylor, Leean Flavell, Leeanne Gray, Leeanne Handley, Leif Usher, Leigh Chambers, Leo Postin, Lexus Benier-Alleaume, Lillian Shephard, Linda Podres, Linda Roberts, Lisa Boland, Lisa Mendham, Lisa Maree, Lisa Parker, Lisa Vella, Louise Schaap, Lucas Postin, Lucja Nowowiejski, Lynne O'Brien, Marbecc Webb, Marcus Aaron, Margaret McAteer, Margherita Marc, Marsha Lake, Meura, Maria Morton, Mark Chambers, Matt Cameron, Meg Cherry, Melissa Murphy, Melissa Owen Doughty, Melissa White, Mel Sheehy, Mia Cooke, Michelle Clark, Michelle Ferguson, Michelle Loriso, Minna Johans, Misty Lee Talbot, Mody Sy, Mohamed Elfiky, Monica Lamelas, Naomi Murrin, Narelle Richardson, Natasha Jones, Nathan Keefe, Nicole Palmer, Nicole Speakman, Olivia Hogarth, Omar Sh, Orla Rose Bulger, Pat Chambers, Paul Gerardis, Penny Ryan, Peter Chifney, Phil Dartnell, Rahma Abdelmaksoud, Rasharne Page, Rebecca Bonanno, Rebecca Coyte, Rebecca Dirickx, Rebecca Hogarth, Ric Ainley, Rick McDonald, Riley Hogarth, Robert Stewart, Rob Jones, Rose King, Samantha Laing, Samantha Sayers, Sarah Roberts, Sarah Sesamee, Sara Osaulenko, Shanon McManus-Reid, Sherree Sparks, Shylah Owen, Silvia, Simon Hornstra, Simon Philpin, Sonny Hoang, Sophie Hogarth, Sophie Ligouras, Sue Nadin, Suz Sewell, Tamha Owen, Tania Niwa, Tanya Buttigieg, Tatia Power, Teressa Simmons, Tiana Podres, Tina Andrejas, Tracey Sanders, Tricia Vass, Valerija Lepore, Velat Sadun, Wayne Vayro, Willow Gumbley, Willow McArthur, Wilton Jones, Whitney Toresson, Xavier Hornstra, Yana Johnson, Yvette Grace, Zack Carlson, Zeta GY